BE COURAGEOUS

BE COURAGEOUS

AN ACTS OF VALOR NOVELLA TRILOGY

ACTS OF VALOR
BOOK SEVEN

REBECCA HARTT

ALSO BY REBECCA HARTT

Rise UP Publications
www.riseUPpublications.com
Phone: 866-846-5123

Released July 2024
ISBN: 978-1-664457-759-2

BE WITH ME

PROLOGUE

 emories of his last birthday flickered through Grayson Saunders' mind as he regarded the thirteen candles on his cake. They hadn't cut the cake last year until 11:00 P.M. because his father had to work late, but Grayson hadn't minded. Dad's job with the state police was important. He'd given Grayson the best birthday gift ever—a brand-new paintball gun and *two* containers of ammunition. Too bad they'd never gotten to use them together. Jerry Saunders had died two months later in a sting operation.

Grief knuckled Grayson, followed by regret. Staring into the flames of his candles this year, he could still hear his father singing the "Happy Birthday" song off-key while his mother and sister held the melody. *What did I wish for last year?*

His gaze rose to take in the people standing around him. Their dining room was in a different house in Suffolk, Virginia. His mother's brown eyes, set in her heart-shaped face, shone with worry, not with happiness. Her voice was as tuneful as ever, though, as she and Olivia, his blonde, freckle-faced little sister, sang to him. This year, a baby nestled in his mother's arms—his father's legacy, supposedly. And the man standing next to his mother, smiling slightly but not singing, wasn't his father.

Grayson had nothing against the baby, three-month-old Mary Mae. Her whimsical smiles and sky-blue eyes made it hard not to love her. She looked a lot like Olivia's baby pictures, which suggested she was just what his mother had said: a parting gift from their father. But that head of auburn curls was the exact same hue as his mom's new boyfriend's hair. Supervisory Special Agent Casey Fitzpatrick worked for the FBI, and from the day he'd swept into Grayson's life, it was obvious his mother loved him.

Whenever people saw them all together, the baby's hair made everyone think they were one big, happy family. But they weren't even a family at all. And Jerry Saunders, the rock on which Grayson had built his life, was gone.

As the song came to an end, his mother frowned at Olivia, who was standing next to him with her lungs expanded and her lips puckered. "Honey, let Grayson blow out his own candles."

Grayson gestured. "Go ahead. I don't even want any stupid cake."

He swiveled on the balls of his tennis shoes and stalked out of the formal dining room, ignoring his mother's protest. Down the hallway and out the front door of the old farmhouse he went, shutting it forcibly behind him.

"I hate this place."

Soon after his father's death, they'd moved to what used to be their grandparents' horse ranch in the middle of nowhere. He hated his new school and the country bumpkins who attended it. He hated the way Fitz had stepped into his father's shoes, canceling out Jerry Saunders like he'd never existed.

Fueled by the feelings roiling in him, Grayson ran in the direction of home—his *old* home, even though it was almost nightfall. He tore up the long driveway toward the country road, rocks crunching under the soles of his shoes. The white gravel seemed to glow in the twilight, keeping him from running into the pine trees pressing in on either side.

By the time he reached the two-lane highway where the sign for his mother's hippotherapy business stood, he was breathing hard and pressing a fist into the stitch in his side. He paused to catch his breath. *What am I doing?*

He couldn't just run all the way to Norfolk, which was several miles away. And as much as he wished he could, he couldn't turn back the hands of time.

"Dad?"

If only he could talk to his father, Dad would tell him what to do. He'd always had such good advice—like the time Grayson was being bullied in school. His father had told him to walk with a buddy, to keep his cool, and not let the bully get to him. *"He's just looking for a victim, so don't become one."* Grayson had done exactly what his father said, and the bullying stopped.

His mom didn't solve problems as well as his dad had. Her idea of helping was to stick Grayson into a room with a counselor who forced him to talk about his *feelings*. He would rather go to the dentist and have every one of his teeth pulled.

Dashing the moisture from his cheeks, Grayson hugged himself against the late-October chill. Isolation wrapped cold fingers around his heart. Only the crickets and the tree frogs in the woods were aware of his presence. Even the moon, which sometimes peered down at him with motherly concern, was hiding her face behind the cloud cover.

All at once, the beams of a car shot through the darkness, startling him with its proximity. A car had been parked just up the street on the shoulder of the road, idling so quietly he hadn't even heard it.

As it started forward, heading toward Grayson, he asked himself if he couldn't catch a ride to Norfolk. The car approached him slowly, the only vehicle in sight. It was a ratty, dark-colored Buick with a dented fender. The driver's window came down, and a middle-aged man with a mane of gray hair stuck his elbow and his face out to regard him.

"Hey, you want to go somewhere?"

Grayson couldn't tell for sure, but in the glow of the man's dash, it looked like his face was tattooed. "No, I'm good." He took a precautionary step toward home, then another.

The man sent him a lopsided smile. "You look just like him."

Goose bumps scrabbled up Grayson's arms. He'd heard that line all his life: He had his mother's coloring but his father's features. "You knew my father?" What were the odds that this man would be waiting right here on the very night Grayson was remembering his dad?

"Sure. I knew him. Great guy. Wanna go for ride? We'll talk about him."

Intuition whispered for Grayson to run. "No thanks. I have to go back now."

Right on cue, he heard his mother's whistle, a shrill sound that could be heard a mile away.

Grayson gestured toward it, whirled, and sprinted back up the driveway, fueled by fright this time. "Coming!"

Casting glances behind him the whole way back, he reached the house in record time, even with the stitch returning. His mother stood in the front yard, a lonely silhouette backdropped by the lights in their big yellow farmhouse. He ran up to her, intending to tell her about the creepy man in the street.

"Grayson." She met him midway, then pulled him into her honeysuckle embrace and held him fiercely. It felt strange being an inch taller than she was, more like he was supposed to be comforting her.

"Gosh, I can feel your heart pounding." Stepping back, she eyed him in the dark while brushing his hair out of his eyes—he wouldn't let her cut it. "Honey, it's okay to be sad and angry. I miss your father, too. Every day. And I've decided we should go to counseling together. That way it won't be so bad."

Hearing the emotion and the worry in her voice, Grayson realized telling her about the weirdo in the car wasn't what she needed to hear. "It's fine, Mom. You don't have to."

"No, I want to. I've wanted to for a while. I've just been busy. Come on inside. Try your cake; it's really good."

Reentering the house with her, Grayson spotted Fitz sitting in his dad's favorite armchair giving the baby a bottle, and his resentment came surging back. Sure, Fitz would leave and go back to his own home soon, but it was only a matter of time before he married Grayson's mom and moved in with them.

Maybe I should have gotten in the car with the stranger.

How much worse could it be to run away than to live here pretending everything was fine, knowing it would never be fine again?

CHAPTER 1

The older male counselor checked his watch, then lifted his bright eyes at Faith's son. "Grayson, would you give me ten minutes to talk with just your mother?"

Even as Faith's anxiety rose, Grayson shrugged, clearly relieved to escape early. "Sure." He flicked his russet bangs out of his eyes, rose to his feet, and started for the door.

What was the counselor going to say to her?

"Have a seat in the waiting room, honey. I'll be right out."

As the door clicked shut behind her son, Faith steeled herself. The fading sunlight visible through the blinds reminded her of how much she still needed to get done to be ready for her clients in the morning—two injured veterans hoping to improve their motor skills through hippotherapy. Thank goodness for Fitz, who was watching Olivia and the baby tonight, or Faith couldn't have joined Grayson's counseling session like she'd promised.

"So." Robert sat forward, bracing his elbows on his knees and talking to her in a low voice, making sure, it seemed, that Grayson couldn't overhear him. "I'm glad you were able to join your son tonight. It's been good for him to hear how much Jerry's death has grieved you."

"Of course." Did he think Jerry's death *didn't* grieve her?

He rubbed his palms together. "Grayson hasn't said as much—you can see how tough it is to get him to talk at all. But from the few comments he has made, I gather he believes you've substituted Jerry with your gentleman friend, Fitz, I believe his name is."

Heat stole up Faith's neck, suffusing her face. "Yes, Fitz. He's been a big help."

Robert nodded his head of silver hair. "I'm sure he has been." He hesitated, then asked. "How long has Jerry been deceased, Faith?"

She hated that word, *deceased.* "Ten months and twenty-one days."

Robert's eyebrows shot up. "You know that right down to the day."

"Of course. I loved him completely. He was my first and only."

He drew a breath, then said hesitantly, "Forgive me if I'm wrong, but you don't still seem to be grieving him as heavily as Grayson is."

The words turned her heart inside out.

"I'm not judging," he added quickly. "It's just an observation."

She considered his observation for a moment, then explained. "When Jerry transitioned to the tactical team about six years ago, I was devastated. It's basically a SWAT team, very dangerous work. I don't know how I knew it, but I knew the job would take his life, so I did everything I could to talk him out of it. But then I gave up because I understood he needed that constant adrenaline, or he would get depressed. I cried every night for months because I sensed what was coming. God put that knowledge into my heart in order to prepare me. And when it happened, I was devastated, but not surprised."

Robert nodded sympathetically. "I see. Yes, that makes sense. But here's the thing: Grayson never saw Jerry's death coming. It's still a shock to him, and it's going to take time to accept that his father is gone. His anger, I believe, stems not just from his father's death but from feeling that you're moving on so quickly."

Dismay pegged Faith to the chair she was sitting in.

"Now, I'm not going to tell you what to do. That's completely up to you, Faith. I'm not living in your shoes, so I don't know what it's like. But if you can postpone your relationship with Fitz and let Grayson mourn his father's death, he will heal faster, and he won't be so angry."

A feeling like shame twisted through her, keeping her from speaking.

Robert shrugged apologetically. "I'm just thinking about it from Grayson's perspective. He said something about his new sister and Fitz both having the same hair. I don't think he's a hundred percent sure whether Mary Mae is his whole sister or his half."

Faith's cheeks turned cold as the blood drained from her head. "Of course, she's his whole sister!" She clutched the arms of her chair, suddenly defensive. "Her red hair comes from my mother!"

The therapist held up both hands. "I didn't mean to upset you, only to explain where Grayson's anger is coming from."

Faith pulled herself to the edge of her seat, battling a mix of self-righteousness, shame, and regret.

"Take a moment," Robert gently advised, "to just sit there and digest what I've said. It's important to Grayson that you remain his steady constant."

Faith nodded and came to terms with what she was feeling. She'd prided herself on being a good mother, but what kind of mother was she, putting her own needs above those of her children? She'd welcomed Fitz into her life within a year of Jerry's death because she'd needed *help* finding her twin sister, who'd disappeared on a mission trip to Venezuela. Then, too, she was overwhelmed with starting up her business while caring for her children, not to mention a new baby, born nearly two months early.

But Grayson's needs were different. He needed to see his mother make it on her own. And now that her business was thriving, she could afford to hire someone to watch the kids.

Dread dragged her heart to her feet. Was she really going to push Fitz away as Robert had advised? Considering what had happened to his own family years ago, it had taken so much courage on Fitz's part to open up in the first place.

Expelling a long, grounding breath, she stood up and briefly met the counselor's eyes. "Thank you."

His smile was both sad and sympathetic. "Call me if you want to set up a future appointment."

"I will." She couldn't think about her busy calendar right then. All she could do was pine over the loss of her burgeoning romance with Fitz and pray she wouldn't lose him forever.

Fitz sat in the comfortable recliner while the baby dozed in the crook of his arm. Little Olivia practiced somersaults on the living room carpet while watching a show on the Disney Channel. It was moments like this that provided a balm to the terrible wound inside him. He would never fully recover from the murder of his wife and three children—retaliation from a mob he had incarcerated—but times like these were healing.

His highly trained ears pricked at the sound of a vehicle crawling up the driveway. Was Faith back already? Unable to check his watch, as it was trapped under the sleeping baby, he grabbed his cell phone off the adjacent lamp table. They hadn't been gone an hour yet. What's more, the engine didn't sound like her mini van's.

Righting the recliner, Fitz unfurled his lean frame, careful not to waken Mary Mae, who slept peacefully along his muscular left arm. He crossed to the large window at the front of the room where he lifted the gauzy white curtain to see outside. The car there braked abruptly.

Backed by the dark trees and positioned beyond the corona of the porchlight, its license plate could not be read. But Fitz was an expert when it came to the make and model of cars, and that one looked to be a Buick Regal, circa 1999. The fact that the driver had caught sight of him and was hanging back suggested evil intent. Fifteen years in the NYPD topped by nearly a decade in the FBI informed Fitz's conclusion.

Sparing a thought for the Glock 19 currently secured in his glove box out in his Lexus, Fitz went to lay the baby in the playpen when the car shot forward and swerved. Rather than back all the way down the driveway, the driver was attempting to turn around.

Fitz hurried to the door to let himself out. By the time he stood on the covered porch, the vehicle was roaring away, and he hadn't even read the license plate.

His heartbeat raced. Did someone intend to break in while Faith was away? Who would drive into rural Suffolk to rob a home? Maybe the driver had gone up the wrong driveway and felt guilty for intruding on the homeowner's evening? No. Whoever it was, they hadn't wanted to be seen. Their motives could not have been good.

After slipping back inside, Fitz locked the door and waited for Faith to return. He would tell her what he saw and offer to sleep in the recliner with his Glock close at hand, just in case.

Not fifteen minutes later, while straightening up in the kitchen, Fitz heard a car door close and then another. Spying the outline of Faith's minivan through the gauzy curtain, he went to open the door for her and Grayson, his heart lifting as it did every time he laid eyes on her.

With her sparkling brown eyes, russet hair that looked red in certain light, and a smile that made demons flee—thirty-three-year-old Faith Saunders was everything a man could ask for. He couldn't get enough of her.

Twenty-two months ago, she'd been the ER nurse who stemmed the blood pouring out of the shrapnel wound in his neck. Who'd have guessed she would become the most important person in the world to him?

But as she closed the distance between them, her gaze met his, and he forgot about his happiness. Given the firm set of her lush lips, Grayson's counseling session must not have gone well.

"Hey." Fitz greeted Grayson as he loped onto the porch. All he got was a curt nod by way of reply.

Faith followed her son with lagging steps. "Is the baby sleeping?"

"Yes." As always, he tried to soften the rasp of his injured vocal cords, his sole memento of the attempt on his life that had sent him to the ER two years ago.

She gestured for him to join her on the porch swing. "Can we talk out here?"

"Sure." Thoughts of the stranger in the car went out of his head as he shut the front door to join her. His stomach tensed with the expectation of bad news. He held the porch swing still for her to sit, then sat smoothly next to her, giving the swing a little push and recalling that magical evening in late July when he'd first envisioned being part of her life.

"How was therapy?" He was almost afraid to ask.

To his relief, she stretched out a hand and coiled her fingers through his. Nothing made him feel more complete than when their hands were linked together. It made him relish the moment he would finally get to lie with her in bed and become partners for life.

She drew a shaky breath, the sound of which notched his concern higher.

"Eye-opening." Her hold on his hand tightened. "The counselor made me realize that I'm moving on from Jerry's death too quickly. It's making Grayson angry that I seem to have forgotten about his father, that I seem to have replaced him with you."

Fitz nodded. This wasn't news to him.

"He might even think that Mary Mae is your baby because of her coloring."

Given Faith's watchful gaze, she thought this news was going to freak him out. Fitz had seen that thought cross Grayson's face at the hospital when he'd first brought out the baby for her siblings to see for the first time. "Yes, I know."

"You do?" Faith shook her head, clearly appalled. "How can I be so blind? All I saw was his anger. I didn't realize it had anything to do with me."

Fitz went to reassure her that she wasn't the cause for Grayson's belligerence, but she cut him off, squeezing his hand harder. "I don't know how to say this, and it's not what I want, but I have to...I have to let you go for a while."

The words caught him utterly off guard. Three months earlier, nothing in the world could have compelled him to get involved with a woman who had three children close to the same age as the children he had buried, along with their mother, nearly eight years earlier. He had carried around a shattered heart ever since, never believing that he might fall in love again. And then, just when he'd found the courage to risk everything, she was setting him aside?

"How long is a while?" His gruff voice, caused by the injury to his vocal cords, failed to mask his incredulity.

"I don't know." She covered her crumpling face with her free hand.

Torn between protecting his feelings and comforting her, Fitz pulled his hand from her grasp and put an arm around her. She turned immediately toward him, making it harder to put up a wall and guard his emotions, especially when she pressed her face against his chest and her shoulders shook with a stifled sob.

Over the lump in his throat, Fitz sought to reassure them both. "It's okay." Yet picturing the flat, lonely evenings ahead of him, he knew it wasn't going to be okay. He would have to do exactly what he did after burying his family: lose himself in his work and cut off his emotions. Whether he could return to the world of the living after this rejection wasn't something he could promise.

He forced himself to think about Faith. "Who's going to help you if not me?" He'd been joining her every evening in grooming the horses and refreshing their water and feed.

She sniffed sharply and lifted her head to look at him. "I'll give the babysitter more hours and hire someone to help me with the horses."

"I guess I'm pretty expendable, huh?" He let himself wallow in self-pity, but only for a moment.

"No." She shook her head fiercely, even as her eyes filled with tears. "Not to me. Please don't leave forever, Fitz." She swallowed hard. "This isn't what I want," she repeated, "but I have to put my children first. Please say you understand."

Pushing aside the selfish feelings that welled in him, he searched himself for the words to give her. His conscience used to speak to him in the voice of his late wife, Mary, often supplying scripture to back up her opinion, but since Faith had become a constant part of his life, Mary ceased to speak to him. All he could come up with was, "Love is patient."

Even so, the relief that relaxed Faith's expression and even teased a wan smile out of her told Fitz those were the right words to say. No doubt Faith interpreted them to mean that he would be patient and wait for her. But given the rising impulse to jump in his car and flee, that really wasn't the promise he was making. He'd put his shattered heart into her hands, and now she was giving it back to him. How was he supposed to feel?

"I should go." The memory of the Buick crossed his thoughts, but he didn't bring it up now. Someone had taken a wrong turn, that was all. Faith had enough on her plate. "Good night."

He pressed a kiss to her lips, savoring their satiny texture in order to remember it forever. Then he tore himself away, standing and patting his pockets to verify he had his keys and wallet.

Without another word, he strode away, off the porch toward his Lexus.

Some mechanism of self-preservation kicked in, blanketing his emotions in an icy layer that kept him from feeling anything.

He shut himself inside his car, starting up the music on his smartphone as soon as he hit the ignition button. With the opera *La bohème* floating out of his speakers, he backed up and pulled away. He didn't so much as glance in his rearview mirror, but his peripheral vision—honed from his years as a street cop—left him with a clear impression of Faith standing on her porch, watching him leave.

Faith looked up at the sound of someone walking toward her office, located at the back of the big new barn and overlooking the riding ring. Her office doubled as a waiting room with several mismatched chairs for caretakers to sit upon while watching Faith work with her patients outside. The ring was already cloaked in darkness, no thanks to daylight savings time, making it dark by 5:00 P.M. Her children were in the house with the babysitter, so who could this be?

Just before the door swung open, Faith knew it was Grace. Being mirror twins, they shared an inexplicable psychic connection.

Grace stepped into the cozy space and grimaced at the sight of Faith sitting behind her laptop. She'd been typing a code into the form that would prompt a payment by one of her patient's health insurance companies.

"You're still working?" Grace's tone betrayed both incredulity and concern.

"This is the last form." Faith pinned her attention on her screen, verified the code was accurate, and clicked ENTER. "There, all done for the night." After exiting the program, she shut her MacBook Pro and pushed her chair back.

Grace had notched her hands above her hips. "You haven't returned any of my texts this week."

"I know. Sorry, I've been really busy." Faith came out from behind her desk, light-headed with hunger. Fitz would have had dinner waiting for her, but the babysitter only fed the kids—food that wasn't particularly good for them.

Grace's astute gaze slid over her as she approached her twin. Anyone looking at them would have a very hard time telling them apart. They both wore their hair long, falling midway down their backs, but where Grace parted hers on the right, Faith's part was on the left. Grace was left-handed; Faith right-handed. She used to be fuller figured, having just given birth to her third baby, but she'd lost most of her baby weight from nursing Mary Mae, and the last five pounds had fallen off her after sending Fitz away.

"You're losing weight." The candid observation was typical of Grace, who rarely minced her words.

"I guess so. I haven't eaten dinner yet. Want to join me?"

"Sure."

Faith led the way out of the office before flipping off the lights. As they crossed through the dark barn, Otis, the old bay gelding they'd grown up with, nickered at them while the three therapy horses dozed in silence. The house's porch light provided the only illumination, shining through the barn's double doors, currently wide open to let in the fresh fall air.

Faith sensed Grace's sidelong glances.

"What's going on with you and Fitz? I thought he would be here."

Sorrow pooled in Faith's chest, slowing her to a stop. "We're on a break for Grayson's sake."

"What?" Grace's voice rose nearly an octave. "Why am I just now hearing about this?"

"Because I didn't want to bother you. You're a busy teacher with two kids at home."

Grace grabbed her arm, stopping her forward progress. "But why? I thought you got along great."

"We did." Faith drew a deep beath. "Grayson's counselor told me my son's anger stems from me moving on too quickly. So, I'm giving him time." Just talking about it made Faith's throat tighten.

Grace, who knew better than anyone what Faith's sacrifice was costing her, pulled her into a familiar and supportive embrace, smelling of nutmeg as she always did. *I'm so lucky*, Faith reminded herself. Because of Grace, she'd never been truly alone in the world. Not even when Jerry had died.

"I'm sure he'll wait for you," Grace murmured in her ear.

Remembering the way Fitz had walked off her porch and driven away without a single backward glance, Faith wasn't so sure. "I don't know." She let her arms fall and stepped back. "I'm afraid he's going to pull away for good. He didn't want me telling you this because he doesn't want anyone pitying him, but he lost his entire family, a wife and three kids, to the mob—retaliation for putting their boss in jail."

"Oh my gosh." Grace gaped at her, horrified.

"It took a lot of courage for him to risk his heart again, and then I trampled it by pushing him away."

"I'll pray for you both," Grace promised. "I'm sure God means for you to be together."

Faith managed a smile. How it gladdened her heart to hear Grace confess to praying at all. Not that long ago, after losing a baby and a husband, she'd been sure God had forgotten her. Discovering love again in the form of Amos McLeod and gaining two adopted sons, she'd realized God had been loving her all along.

"You're right." Shaking off her gloom, Faith continued forward and shut the barn doors with Grace's help.

Thank God Grace had come by tonight, reminding her that He had watched over her all her life. He wouldn't stop now.

CHAPTER 2

TWO WEEKS AFTER CHRISTMAS

Grayson hustled toward the head of the driveway at eight fifteen in the morning with the ham-and-cheese sandwich his mother had made tucked into a brown paper bag inside his backpack. It was the first week in January, misty from the cold snap that swept in suddenly. Grayson shuddered in his sweatshirt, wishing he'd put on a jacket like his mom had told him to. But doing exactly the opposite made him feel independent.

"Hurry," she called off the front porch after him. "You're late!"

He didn't acknowledge her, just walked a little faster. Then, hearing the distinct roar of the bus, he broke into a hobble—not that he was eager to get to school. He hated his new middle school, which was full of kids who treated him like he'd come from another planet. Only Cameron, who lived right down the road, had befriended him.

Grayson was still fifty yards from the road when heard the bus slow down at the head of his driveway. Brakes screeched. Red lights flared, rosy pink in the mist. He picked up his pace, confident the bus driver could see him running toward her with his backpack jiggling. But, apparently, she did not because, instead of coming to a stop, the bus picked up speed again.

"Hey! Wait!" Grayson's shout went unheeded as the bus roared away.

He reached the head of the driveway breathing fast. Seeing nothing in either direction but asphalt, ditches, and trees, he uttered a curse word, which made him feel like a grownup. But then he turned helplessly around and started back home, only to stop in his tracks as he pictured his mother's dismay.

She would have to take him to school, but not until *after* Olivia's bus came and the babysitter showed up. With her first patient arriving at nine o'clock, that didn't leave her enough time to drive to his middle school and back again. That meant the babysitter would have to do it. Grayson cringed at the thought. Grownups did not have babysitters.

If only Dad were here.

Longing swept through Grayson. He used to sit in the front seat of his father's state police cruiser, listening to the chatter on the radio. That joy would never happen again. Loss bored into him, only slightly less painful than it had been a year ago.

The purr of a car motor pulled Grayson from his abstraction. He turned around, wishing his father's silver-and-blue Ford Interceptor with its distinctive grill would materialize from the mist and rescue him. Instead, a ratty purplish Buick rolled toward him. With a spurt of alarm, Grayson recognized it.

As with the last time, the window lowered, and the man's elbow came out. Grayson took a precautionary step backward, but the shaggy-haired man didn't have tattoos on his face. He had a thick brow ridge, days-old bristles, and a scar hatching one corner of his upper lip. Otherwise, he looked normal.

"Hi again. Looks like you missed the bus."

His voice was friendly, his deep-set eyes direct. How could he have known Grayson missed the bus?

"No, that wasn't mine," Grayson lied. "There's another bus coming."

The man's hairy eyebrows quirked. "You don't have to lie to me. I knew your father, remember?"

"Yeah." That's what he'd said the night of Grayson's birthday.

"My name's Brian. Hop in. I'll give you a ride to school." The locks gave a click.

Grayson remembered his fear on their previous encounter, but it had been dark that night, and he'd thought the man had tattoos on his face. This morning, he seemed harmless enough, and the fact that he'd known his dad meant he had to be a good guy. Besides, this way, he wouldn't have to ruin his mother's morning. "All right."

Hearing no cars coming, Grayson approached the door behind the driver's seat and slipped in. The car smelled of cigarettes. He'd scarcely closed his door when it started forward.

"I'm at John F. Kennedy Middle School," he volunteered. "Do you know where that is?"

"Sure, sure. Don't worry. I'll get you where you need to go."

As he fastened his seat belt, Grayson noted the tattoos on Brian's knuckles with a stab of concern. He didn't know any state policemen with letters tattooed onto their hands. What's more, there was trash under his feet and an old rag on the seat next to him.

"How do you know my dad?" Maybe this man used to work with him, though all the state troopers Grayson knew kept their cars clean.

The driver angled his rearview mirror so he could look back at him. "We did a job together once. Nice guy, your dad."

The compliment didn't match the hard edge to the man's voice.

Then again, his father had worked with a tough group of men, not always known for using the right intonation with their words.

They came to an intersection. Without coming to a full stop, Brian rolled past the stop sign and turned right instead of going straight.

Grayson's alarm ticked upward. "Oh, this isn't the way to my school."

"No worries. I know a shortcut."

The words failed to reassure Grayson. It occurred to him that he'd better call Cameron to explain that he'd missed the bus. Unzipping the small pocket on the front of his backpack, he withdrew his cell phone and noticed Cameron had already called *him*, only his phone hadn't rung because it was still on DO NOT DISTURB.

"You got a cell phone?"

The sharp question had Grayson stuffing his phone under his leg. "No."

"What's in the bag?" A thick arm came over the back seat, snatched the backpack out of his hands, and slammed it down on the front seat, where Brian proceeded to paw through it.

This isn't normal. Grayson thought fast. "I was going to eat some of my lunch."

Brian's search turned up his bagged lunch and a notebook with his homework in it. He shoved the bag away from him, clearly relieved not to find a cell phone.

Stunned, Grayson kept quiet. This man wasn't planning to take him to school.

Brian braked abruptly, turning them off the road onto a dirt track Grayson had never noticed before. As they bounced through ruts and brushed past branches pressing in on them, his heart started to pound. This situation had all the earmarks of an abduction, and his father had told him if he got snatched to try to get away in the first few minutes.

Grayson peered around. This road was probably only used by

hunters. But thanks to playing paintball wars with Cameron, Grayson was good at hiding in the woods, even with the mist lifting. He just had to get out of the car.

Moving stealthily, he released his seat belt. It came apart with the barest of clicks, covered up by their sudden lurch in and out of a rut. Keeping the strap pinned under his right arm, he placed his left elbow on the door's armrest. The man's eyes rose to the rearview mirror, and Grayson froze. A cold sweat filmed his upper lip.

I'm seriously being kidnapped. He gripped the phone hidden beneath his leg.

When Brian looked back at the road, Grayson assessed their speed. He would jump first, then call 911 as he was running away. Once he heard a voice on the other end, he wouldn't be so scared. Luckily, Brian was driving slowly, but Grayson would still need to push off to avoid getting run over.

He summoned his courage as Brian drove over a fallen branch.

Now!

Grayson jerked the door handle with his free hand, but the door was locked. Brian heard him and braked hard. Throwing up his hands to keep his face from hitting the seat in front of him, he dropped his cell phone, which tumbled to the floor of the car. He kicked it under the driver's seat as the car stopped moving forward.

His door came unlocked with a loud click, but there was no point in jumping out now because Brian was already there, wrenching Grayson's door open. Grayson dived across the back seat, hoping to escape out the other side, but the man caught the back of his belt and dragged him closer. As his legs came out of the car, Grayson glimpsed his cell phone, hidden deep under Brian's seat.

"I should've known you'd give me a hard time."

Brian pulled him out of the car. He wasn't on his feet one second before the man shoved him facedown over the trunk while pulling his hands behind his back. Grayson kicked and squirmed, but he was no match for the bigger man. In seconds, his wrists were bound together with a zip tie.

Breathing hard, Brian jerked Grayson upright before popping open the trunk with his remote.

"Get in, kid. You brought this on yourself."

Grayson eyed the dank trunk with its stained and trash-littered carpeting. "No. Please, I'll be good. I won't try to escape again."

A heavy hand on the back of his head forced him to bend over. At the same time, Brian hoisted him by the back of his pants, causing him to fall forward. He tucked his chin to protect his face and rolled onto a shoulder, which took the weight off his legs. Brian promptly heaved him the rest of the way in. As Grayson went to kick him, his captor slammed the trunk closed.

Wake up. Wake up. But this was too real to be a dream. He'd been crammed into a cold, dark trunk with his hands trapped uselessly behind his back. Gasping for air Grayson tried to subdue the panic rising up in him.

"Mom!"

Of course, she couldn't hear him. As far as she was concerned, he was at school by now. It would take hours for her to realize he was missing. His only consolation was that his cell phone— providing his captor didn't find it first and toss it somewhere— would tell his mother where to start looking for him.

Faith, bundled up in a long brown coat, wearing gloves and a hat, wondered if her client, a forty-year-old veteran who'd been inside a jeep in Afghanistan when it rolled over a mine, was warm enough, but she didn't want to break his concentration to ask him.

Mark had been riddled with shrapnel during his final tour, and some of it was still in his body. In subsequent months and years, pain had caused him to lose much of his muscle tone. On their first session at Back in the Saddle hippotherapy ranch, it was all he could do to keep his balance. For that reason, Faith had put him on their smallest mare, only fourteen hands high, but today, on Mark's fifth session, he was riding Blossom with so much confidence that Faith had let him hold the reins.

"You're doing great." She smiled up at him, proud of his accomplishment.

As she spoke, the cell phone in her pocket buzzed, drawing Mark's attention and causing him to wobble in the saddle. "Keep your eyes forward," she reminded him while ignoring the call. If the man lost his balance, she would be hard-pressed to catch him.

It was Fitz who'd pointed out that she'd get squished if she had to catch any falling patients. Faith's heart gave an ache at the memory of his teasing. The suspicion that he would never be part of her life again hollowed her out. If he meant to return one day, he would answer her texts, which he did not.

Mark clicked his tongue, prodding Blossom into a faster walk —not quite a trot as Blossom could tell he wasn't ready.

Faith picked up her pace. "Not too fast."

"It's easier at this speed."

Not for Faith, it wasn't. But this was how she got her exercise, walking and sometimes running dozens of times around the riding ring four days a week. As they performed their second circuit, her phone vibrated again in her pocket. A moment later, it chimed, telling her the caller had left a message.

She was out of breath by the time Mark's therapy session ended. In their reflection following his ride, she asked him whether he had noticed his improvement.

"Absolutely." Mark's cheeks were still ruddy from the cold. He rubbed his hands together as he sat across the desk from her. "I used to get fatigued just walking from my bedroom to the kitchen. You have literally brought me back to life, Faith."

His gratitude warmed her. "Well, thank you, but it's really Blossom who's done the work. I'm just there to catch you if you fall." Fitz would have said something like that. How she missed his droll remarks!

Mark laughed, his eyes crinkling at the corners the same way Fitz's eyes did. "I like you."

The artless confession took her aback.

Mark cocked his head. "Any chance I could take you on a date sometime?"

Faith sent him her most professional smile. "I'm afraid I can't do that. It's a violation of my patient policies."

"What if I wasn't your patient anymore?"

Her cell phone, now sitting on the desk between them buzzed a third time, saving her from having to answer him. "I should really get this."

Smiling ruefully, Mark pushed to his feet. "See you next week, same time."

"Great. Bye." Faith waited until he'd reached her door before answering. "Hello."

"Mrs. Saunders?"

"Yes."

"This is Mabel from John F. Kennedy Middle School. Is Grayson out sick today?"

A drop of concern fell into Faith's stomach. "Um, no. He should be in school."

"Nope, he's not here."

"Oh?" Faith's thoughts went to his best friend. Maybe they were skipping school together. "Is Cameron Potts in school?"

"I'm not supposed to tell you that but, yes."

"Huh." Faith shot a worried gaze out of her many windows. "Would you call me, please, if Grayson shows up?"

"Sure." Given Mabel's tone, she was certain Grayson was skipping.

Faith hung up, then remembered the calls she'd received earlier and checked the source. Cameron Potts had called her twice.

Unease twisted her insides as she put her phone to her ear and listened to his message.

"Hey, Mrs. Saunders. I'm just looking for Grayson. He didn't get on the bus this morning, and his phone bumped me over to voice mail. Can you tell him to text me? Thanks."

Faith's mouth went suddenly dry. She could tell by Cameron's tone alone he was telling the truth. Grayson hadn't gotten on the bus. She remembered him leaving the house a minute late. Had he missed his ride and was now walking to school?

She speed-dialed his cell phone, but as it had for Cameron, Grayson's voice mail answered. His phone was probably still on DO NOT DISTURB, a setting she insisted he use at night so his friends wouldn't wake him up.

Faith checked the time on her phone. Her next client wasn't due to arrive for another half hour. She could jump into her van and drive toward the school, hopefully to encounter Grayson along the way. The urge to share her concerns led her nowhere. She couldn't bother her twin sister, who was probably already at the elementary school where she taught. Jerry was dead, and Fitz wasn't talking to her.

Faith left word with the babysitter, grabbed her purse, and slipped into her van. With no time to scrape off the layer of frost on her windshield, she sprayed wiper fluid on it and used her wipers to clear it away. But as she traveled up her long driveway, a fresh layer of frost began to form, obscuring her vision. She cranked on the defroster to combat it.

The country road on which they lived was completely devoid of traffic when she emerged from her driveway. She lowered her windows to look each way, then turned left, peering through the widening bit of clear glass to keep from driving into the ditch on the side of the road. God forbid Grayson had decided to walk to school and been hit by a driver like her, whose windshield wasn't clear.

But she saw nothing to indicate that was the case. She drove all the way to his middle school, twelve minutes away, without seeing him. It was hard to believe he wasn't in the ugly two-story brick building, but Mabel hadn't called her back.

Before turning around in the empty bus lane, Faith tried Grayson's number again. Again, it bumped her over to voice mail. With a heavy weight in the pit of her stomach, she started back home. Maybe on the way back, she would run into Grayson. Maybe he'd stopped into a convenience store somewhere to spend some of the money he'd gotten for Christmas.

But when she didn't see him in or around the little market at the gas station, her thoughts became more frightened. Had Grayson run away? She knew he was still lost without his father, still unhappy about changing schools. Had she driven him to this?

Or could he have been kidnapped? Who would want to abduct a thirteen-year-old boy? *Don't answer that.* Deviants of every kind lurked in this world.

She arrived back at her big farmhouse with a prayer on her lips. "Oh, Father, please let him be here." Perhaps Grayson simply didn't want to go to school today. Yes, that made the most sense. He was hanging out in the woods around the house. She didn't have to be so fearful. Besides, her next client would be showing up any minute.

An hour later, as her second client pulled away, Faith went into the house where the babysitter was sitting in the outdated kitchen feeding Mary Mae squash from a jar. The sixty-something grandmother type lived not five minutes up the road. Sonja glanced over at Faith and did a double take. "Everything okay, dear?"

Faith sighed. "Not really, no. Grayson didn't show up for school this morning. I think he might be hanging around the property. I don't suppose you've seen him?"

"Not me, honey." Sonja slipped a loaded spoon into Mary Mae's mouth. "Has he ever done this before?"

Faith thought back. "No. Never. It's just...he hates his new middle school." She crossed to the nearest window and tried to imagine where Grayson might be. Turning around, she started for the front door in the adjacent living room. "I'm going to take my old horse for a spin around the property. Grayson might be up at the creek."

"Hope you find him."

Their dried-up Christmas tree, which she had planned to drag out of the house over her lunch hour, taunted her as she burst out the front door and returned to the barn to saddle up Otis. The three therapy horses watched her, clearly curious to know why Otis was about to get ridden and not them. She mounted him in the middle of the barn and rode him out the open front doors. The billing and note-taking she ought to be doing would have to wait, as would her lunch, which she still hoped to eat before her next client showed up.

After rounding the house, she urged Otis into a trot. "Grayson!"

Her voice carried in the still forest. But all she heard over the horse's hooves was the distant screech of an osprey.

Otis carried her through the woods along the path leading to the creek. Faith had grown up in this forest of pine, cedar, and dogwood trees playing hide-and-seek with Grace, her only sibling and Grayson's namesake. All her life, Faith had a best friend—first Grace, then Jerry, then most recently Fitz. Isolation wrapped cold fingers around her heart.

"Grayson! You don't have to hide, honey. It's cold out here. Come on home. I won't take you to school today."

But no one answered her. She came upon the creek at last, just a narrow, little estuary comprised of mudflats and marsh grass. Taking in the leaden sky and the naked limbs of the surrounding trees, Faith suffered a sudden certainty that Grayson wasn't here. She was wasting time.

Wheeling Otis sharply about, she headed back toward home. Her heart had begun to thud. Her innards congealed with fear. Where could Grayson be? Should she call the police first? Or Fitz? He would know what to do.

She returned Otis to his stall, rushing to remove his bridle and saddle. With just half an hour left before her next client arrived, she put a call through to Fitz while pacing in her office. The Christmas lights still strung across the wall of windows lent a kaleidoscope of color to her peripheral vision.

Fitz wasn't going to answer. Then again, this was his cell phone number, and he couldn't take it into the office. She hung up and dialed his office number, gratified when he answered on the second ring.

"This is Fitz."

"Hey, it's Faith."

With four ongoing investigations, Fitz didn't have time for a phone call, let alone a call from the woman he was trying to purge from his thoughts, but her tone alone made all thoughts about work vanish. "What's wrong?"

"Grayson is missing."

The news didn't alarm Fitz. He waited for more details.

"He apparently missed his bus this morning. His friend Cameron alerted me first and then the school. I hopped in the van to see if he was walking to school, but he wasn't. Then I came home and took Otis out to the creek, thinking Grayson was just hanging around and avoiding school. But he's not anywhere."

Fitz pictured the way Faith looked right then, her long, straight hair swirling around her shoulders. Her soft brown eyes would be huge with worry, her wide mouth ruddy from the cold.

"Don't worry." He wanted to soothe her fears. At the same time, he wished she hadn't called him at all, stirring up emotions that had settled to the bottom of his soul like sand. "He's probably hanging out at somebody's house. He'll be back when he's hungry—"

"No." She cut him off firmly. "He doesn't have any friends here

38

besides Cameron. Something isn't right. He wouldn't just vanish like this."

Fitz scraped his teeth over his lower lip. "I hear your concern, and I can give you some advice, but it's the local police who need to get involved. The FBI can't touch abductions until twenty-four hours have elapsed."

"Who would abduct him?"

The panicked question made Fitz want to kick himself for even mentioning the possibility. "Look, he's probably fine. Does he have his cell phone on him?"

"Yes, but he's not answering it."

"Did you set up the *Find My Phone* app when he first got his phone?"

Her silence told him the answer was *no*. He could tell her composure was slipping. "That's something Jerry would have done. I didn't do it."

He could hear her self-recrimination. "Faith, it's okay. The police don't need that app to find him. They can still locate him using pings off the cell phone towers. Do you know if his phone is fully charged?"

"It should be. He charges it overnight."

"Good. Good. Then call the local police. They'll find him for you."

She drew a shaky breath. "Okay. Thank you. It was good to hear your voice."

She hung up abruptly, leaving him steeped in feelings of loss, longing, and helplessness. Lowering the receiver back into its cradle, he pushed his emotions away by sheer force of will.

His work was all that mattered now. He couldn't afford to get involved with her again. He'd been so much a part of her life that he'd nearly lost the ability to turn off his feelings, and that gift was the only thing that had kept him alive after losing his family.

Turning his thoughts back to the projects screaming for his attention, Fitz pretended Faith hadn't called him at all. He was opening the shared file on the local merchant with ties to the mob when the memory of the Buick sitting in Faith's driveway the night he was babysitting flashed into his thoughts.

Could a peculiar incident that had happened over two months ago have anything to do with Grayson's disappearance now?

Nah. Shoving the memory aside, he focused on the report in front of him.

CHAPTER 3

I *should have listened to Mom and put on a coat this morning.*

Grayson's thin gray sweatshirt, even with a sleeveless T-shirt underneath, did nothing to insulate him against the wet chill filling the car's dark trunk. Thanks to his long arms, he'd managed to wriggle his entire body between his bound wrists, bringing the zip tie in front of him. Curled into a tight ball, forehead pressed to his knees, he vacillated between pretending he was still asleep in his own bed and trying to determine where they were headed by the roughness of the road and the speed at which they traveled.

He'd lost all track of time. Had he been stuck in this foul-smelling enclosure for an hour or for just a few minutes? Would the driver, Brian—if that was really his name—find him alive when he finally stopped and opened his trunk, or would Grayson die of hypothermia?

I can't believe this is happening.

As reality crept over him, the gravity of his situation made him fight to break the restraints so he could potentially escape, but the plastic zip tie held tight.

"Dad? Help me! Tell me what to do!"

The memory of his father's face was still vivid. Jerry was a big guy, over six feet tall with light-brown hair and blue, blue eyes. Grayson could still feel his father's hands, heavy on his shoulders. He would look deep into Grayson's eyes and say things that stuck with him.

Listen up. Concentrate on staying warm. Pull your hood over your head.

Wow! The voice resonating inside his head and all around him sounded more real than his crazy situation. Grayson hastened to obey the words. Reaching over his shoulder with his bound arms, he clasped his hoodie and worked it over his head. His fingers were stiff and uncooperative. There was no string to tighten the hood around his face, but the cloth around his skull warmed his ears immediately.

"Dad, don't leave me. I'm scared." He spoke the words through teeth that chattered.

I'm right here with you, son. I won't leave.

Grayson burst into ragged sobs. A fog seemed to fill his mind.

He must have fallen asleep, for he came awake as sunlight shone through his eyelids. The realization that the car had stopped speared into his sluggish thoughts. But he couldn't get his lids to lift.

"Kid! Wake up!"

Brian was shaking him roughly, but the concern in his voice penetrated Grayson's awareness. Why would the man care whether he was dead or alive?—unless Brian was planning to ransom him for money. That was better than anything else he might be planning.

Grayson managed to slit his eyes open. His captor was bent over him, framed by hazy sunlight. "You good? Sorry, kid. I didn't realize it was so cold. Can't feel the cold, myself."

With gentler hands than before, he helped Grayson to clamber out of the trunk. His joints ached as he drew himself vertical, peering around. Dismay filled him as he took in nothing but open farmland in every direction, as far as the eye could see. A long dirt driveway had taken them off the main road to a small, dilapidated farmhouse with a sloping roof and a little window over the wide front porch. Its metal roof, the peeling off-white paint, and boarded-up windows gave it a dismal air.

The front porch sagged like the porch at his own house used to before Fitz fixed the pillars under it. The branches of an enormous tree—his mom would know what kind—towered over the house, nearly touching it.

Brian jerked Grayson up the steps, not seeming to notice or at least not commenting on the fact that his hands were now in front of him. His backpack was apparently still in the car.

"Come on in, though it won't be much warmer till I get the woodstove going."

"Where is this place?"

Brian cast him a scowl. "You don't need to know."

To Grayson it looked a lot like the flat farmland he'd stared at every summer on their way to vacation in the Outer Banks of North Carolina. Then again, a quarter of Virginia was comprised of farmland just as flat. He knew that much from a fourth-grade geography lesson.

The tilted porch boards groaned beneath their feet as Brian drew him up to the door. While he worked to unlock it, Grayson's gaze fell on the collection of empty beer cans piled into paper bags. At least Brian was recycling. Actually, he probably turned in the cans for money.

The door swung open with a moaning sound, and Brian pushed Grayson into the house ahead of him, shutting and locking them in. Grayson's first impression of the home was that it hadn't been lived in for many, many years. A staircase divided the dining room from the living room.

Brian shoved him onto a brocade-covered couch that faced a newer television set. Bookcases and little tables were positioned before all three windows, two of which were boarded up. A layer of dust filmed everything, and the ceramic pots on the tables clearly once had plants in them, but now held nothing but dried-up dirt.

"All are from dust, and to dust all return." The passage of Scripture that popped into Grayson's head made him shudder.

"Here." Brian pushed him down on the couch. It was so old Grayson could feel the springs give way beneath him as his captor tossed him a blanket that was moth eaten and stale smelling. "Keep warm with that while I heat up the house. And don't move." He pointed a threatening finger. "I'll shoot you in the back if I have to."

Alarm jangled at the threat, but as Brian knelt before the wood-stove, Grayson saw nothing in his pocket that looked like a pistol. Then again, he might have an old shotgun lying around. Guns were a dime a dozen in America. Cameron's older brother had even offered to sell one of his to Grayson.

Watching Brian scrape the remnants of previous fires into a box, Grayson tried to read the letters tattooed on his hand and couldn't. He lifted his gaze to the man's scowl. Brian seemed preoccupied by what he'd done—or was that just wishful thinking?

Grayson remembered how his father had spoken to him in the trunk of the car. *Dad? Are you still there?*

The voice didn't answer. Grayson swallowed down his disappointment. He'd probably been hallucinating from the cold.

Brian rose with the box, pointed a warning finger at Grayson, then walked into what had to be the kitchen at the rear of the house. A second door opened as Brian stepped outside. He was back in the living room in less than a minute—too soon for Grayson to bolt out the front door, as his joints were still aching.

Brian carried an armload of firewood. He knelt before the stove a second time, fed it some kindling, lit it, then added the larger logs.

Grayson studied the man's profile in the flickering light. The worried grooves on his prominent forehead suggested he was a desperate man. And a desperate man was a dangerous man—how many times had Grayson heard his father say that?

"Do you have any water?" he asked as Brian closed the wood-stove door. Dry heat had begun to radiate from it, chasing off the chill and making him realize he was parched.

His captor regarded him for the longest time. What was he thinking? Grayson wasn't sure he wanted to know. But then Brian stood with a grunt and went back into the kitchen. Grayson heard a refrigerator open, and his captor came back carrying a cold bottle of water.

"Here." He held it out to Grayson. "Can't drink from the faucet. The well water tastes like sea salt."

"Thanks." Grayson seized the information with gratitude. Then they probably *were* near the ocean. He twisted off the cap, then gulped down half the cold contents before he decided he'd better save the rest.

Brian went to peer out the front window as if expecting the police might show up any minute.

Regarding his captor's broad back, Grayson dared to imagine what was next. Brian had a plan, that much was certain. Grayson thought about his phone, lying out in the car and broadcasting his location, but only as long as the battery lasted. From what he knew of his phone, it would last almost forty-eight hours.

Had his mother realized he was missing yet? Had she called the cops?

Grayson gave a thought to Fitz, and bitter irony twisted through him. If his mother were still dating the FBI guy, the Feds would probably already be looking for him. But because of Grayson's attitude, his mom had given Fitz the boot. Now look who might pay the cost.

Brian wheeled suddenly from the window, bearing down on him. "Get up." He grabbed Grayson's arm and hauled him to his feet. So much for the softening Grayson had sensed in him earlier.

Grayson dropped the blanket but hung on to the water bottle. His heart pounded. "Where are we going?" Maybe Brian was going to kill him now.

"Upstairs."

That sounded better than immediate death, but the rickety old steps bowed beneath their combined weight as Brian propelled him up the stairs before him. The landing was lit by weak sunlight shining through the dust-smeared dormer overtop the porch.

Brian shoved him through the door facing the back of the house. "Use the toilet. It's the last chance you'll get for a while."

The door clicked shut behind him, and Grayson found himself alone in a small bathroom that had wooden siding about hip high and a single window over the tub. He stepped into the tub and looked out at the back of the house. If he jumped from here, he would land on concrete steps outside the kitchen.

A banging on the door had him wheeling toward the toilet.

"Don't dawdle."

Quick to obey, Grayson stepped over to the rust-stained toilet bowl, unzipped his pants, and looked around while emptying his bladder. Behind him stood a stained porcelain sink and a speckled mirror that reflected his frightened expression.

Look for a weapon.

His father's voice sounded again in his head. Grayson gasped and quickly zipped up his pants. There were no sharp implements anywhere.

A pounding on the door startled him. "Time's up."

He flushed the toilet. "I have to wash my hands." Twisting on the faucet, he eyed the brackets holding the mirror to the wall. If he got the mirror off he could break it into shards to be used as weapons.

The door opened abruptly. Brian stepped inside, twisted off the faucet, and dragged Grayson back onto the landing. "Germs are your least concern, boy." He drew him toward the door that put them directly over the living room.

As it swung open, Grayson balked to see the only window straight ahead of him was boarded up. The sunlight framing it gave just enough light for him to tell the room was wide with a low, sloped ceiling and a wooden floor. The twin bed and dresser were the only furnishings.

Grayson sensed what was coming. "I don't want to be in here."

"Nobody asked you, kid. Sometimes we get what we don't want in life."

Brian shoved him hard toward the bed. Taking a seat on the lumpy mattress, Grayson discovered it was covered by a faded quilt that smelled no better than the blanket downstairs.

Brian had backed hastily out of the room, then shut the door behind him. It gave a click, locked from the outside.

As soon as his steps sounded on the stairs, Grayson crossed to the door to check the lock. His hands closed around a doorknob that was sturdy and felt brand new. It didn't so much as jiggle. His knees started to jitter as a fresh wave of fear rose inside him. Brian had clearly planned this ahead of time. Backing to the bed, Grayson sat back down, shivering and thinking.

His mother would tell him to pray. He'd grown up believing God really loved him. But why would a loving God do this to him or to his mother?

"Father, please help me." He spoke as much to his heavenly father as to his earthly one.

An answer to his prayer seemed to come about an hour later when the front door slammed and the whole house shuddered.

Brian had stepped outside. When the old Buick started up with a roar, conflicting emotions filled Grayson. On one hand, his cell phone was still under Brian's car seat, meaning nobody was coming *here* to free Grayson. On the other, now was the perfect time to attempt his escape.

～

"You're sure he's not hanging out with a friend?"

Faith drew a steadying breath. The Suffolk County police detective on the other end of the phone wasn't taking the situation seriously.

"I'm positive." She implemented the voice her twin sister used in a classroom full of first graders. "We are new to the area, and my son's only friend called me from school asking where he was. You can track him down using his cell phone. He had that with him."

A skeptical pause followed her request. "Are you divorced, ma'am? Sometimes the father gets tired of only seein' his kid every other weekend and decides to pick him up."

Faith heard a distinct popping sound, almost like someone had clapped their hands right next to her ear. "His father is dead, sir. What's more, I think I'm talking to the wrong people."

Without further explanation, she hung up on the detective and dialed Jerry's old work number still programmed into her phone. Jerry still had dozens of friends in the state police force. *They* would take her seriously.

Brian needed a drink, something stronger than the beer in his fridge. Nor could he just sit around the house all afternoon, thinking, *What now?*

He'd been planning to nab Saunders' kid for so long, he could scarcely wrap his head around the fact that he'd gone and done it. Reality was terrifying. He had to take the edge off his fear.

Where was the rage, the grief, and the bitterness that had motivated him in the first place? Brian wrung the steering wheel beneath his hands as he flew down Route 168 toward the North Carolina border. According to the terms of his parole, he was never supposed to leave the state. But the liquor store in Moyock was closer to his house than the one in Virginia. And no one would ever know, especially since the surveillance camera in the store was all for show, according to its owner.

Besides, crossing the border was nothing compared to kidnapping. If Brian was caught for that, he'd get thirty years for violating his probation, just like he'd gotten ten years for violating his previous probation. It never paid to get in trouble again.

The cycle had started when he was a teen. Selling his ADHD medication to college students had gotten him two misdemeanors and six months in jail. Once your name was in the system, the punishments got longer—hence the ten years he'd served for simply selling a semiautomatic weapon to the wrong person. Heck, Brian would probably get thirty years or more for kidnapping a cop's kid—even if he didn't kill him. Thirty more years in the pen would probably do him in.

Regret tightened a noose around Brian's throat. Every day for ten years he had dreamed about teaching Saunders what it felt like to be betrayed by a friend. To lose everything. He had planned, when he got out of prison, to do to Jerry what that man had done to him.

His plan had started unraveling when he found out Saunders was dead. What was the point of punishing the man if he wasn't alive to fret and suffer? Still, Brian had been nurturing his vengeance for so long, he'd decided to go through with it.

Then there was the kid himself. Grayson didn't cry or whine. He'd been smart enough to move his zip-tied hands to the front of his body. When Brian opened the trunk and saw him curled up in there, blue with cold, he'd been horrified, thinking he'd killed him on accident. Imagine how it was going to feel to kill him on purpose.

Turning into the strip mall where the liquor store was located, Brian bought cigarettes and the biggest bottle of cheap whisky he could find, intending to watch TV and drink until his doubts went away. Back in his car, he set the bottle on the seat next to him and tore the cellophane off the box of cigarettes. He shook out a cig and put it to his lips. Taking the lighter from his pocket, he flicked it and sent it tumbling by accident between his seat and the console.

Cursing, Brian dug a hand into the crevice, but the lighter had fallen out of reach. With a growl of frustration, he climbed out of his car and hauled open the door behind his. As he bent down to feel under his seat for the lighter, his hand curled around an unfamiliar object.

Surprise, then shock, reverberated down his spine as he stared at what was obviously a cell phone, turned on with plenty of battery left. The unlit cigarette fell from his lips as his jaw went slack. The kid had lied to him! What's more, he'd cleverly hidden his phone beneath Brian's seat.

Brian turned hot, then cold. He jerked his head up, half-expecting the police to swarm toward him right here in the parking lot. The phone would lead them straight to him.

He had to get rid of it, along with the backpack that was still on his front seat. First things first, though. After powering down the phone, Brian dropped it onto the cement slab and stomped it with his heel. The gratifying crack made him smash it again, then grind it with the heel of his boot while glancing nervously at the camera inside the liquor store.

The owner better not have fixed it without telling him. Just to be safe, he'd better not toss the phone into the bin close to the building. Picking up the battered device, careful not to get glass in his skin, he got back into his car, then cursed as he realized he had yet to recover his lighter. All in good time. He had to ditch the evidence first.

A short distance up the highway, Brian slowed his speed and dropped two tires onto the shoulder while lowering his passenger window. Then he hurled the cell phone into a thicket, followed by the lightweight backpack, which fell just short of the bushes.

Should he get out of the car and toss it farther in? A car was coming up the road behind him. Nah, nobody was gonna notice it peeking out of the tall stalks of dead grass.

Punching the accelerator, Brian spun up gravel as he fishtailed back into the slow lane. Anger burned in him over the kid's sneakiness. Young Grayson had deceived him. Like father like son.

Jerry Saunders had come into Brian's secondhand gun shop, declaring he was new to the area. They'd bonded over their common interest in firearms. Brian hadn't had any idea his new friend was an undercover state police officer checking to see if the gun store owner abided by state laws and did his due diligence running background checks.

A decade-long bitterness gnawed at Brian anew. So maybe Saunders wasn't alive to suffer the way he had suffered. But the only way to be free of the canker eating away at him was to go through with his original plan.

One bullet to the back of his head. The kid would never feel it. But the score would be even—a life for a life.

CHAPTER 4

Faith hadn't visited the State Police Field Office since Jerry's death. Two stories high, its brick façade and large tinted windows, not to mention the enormous antenna looming over it, gave the building an intimidating demeanor. Stepping through the door, the institutional smell brought back memories of visiting Jerry at work, only Jerry wasn't here anymore. The familiar, round face bearing down on her and wearing an encouraging smile belonged to Seth Malloy, Jerry's senior special agent.

Seth pulled her into a bear hug. "I need your signature before we can track Grayson's phone."

She stiffened. "Seriously? I thought you were doing that already."

"Sorry, Faith." He stepped away from him. "Gotta jump through the appropriate hoops, but you're here now, and the process won't take too long."

It was four o'clock in the afternoon. Grayson ought to have gotten off the bus an hour ago, only he hadn't. Nor had Faith waited for Olivia's bus to drop her off. Leaving the baby and Olivia both in Sonja's care and promising to pay her babysitter overtime, Faith had driven out here to assist the state police in finding her son.

In Seth's office, she signed a document giving him consent to monitor Grayson's cell phone. Seth promptly sent the request to their cell phone provider.

Then they waited. Seth filled the tense moment with chitchat. His wife was expecting their second child in February. He asked about Mary Mae and Olivia, then gently asked how Grayson was coping with his father's passing.

"It's been hardest on him than on anyone," Faith admitted.

Seth nodded, his expression sympathetic. "Any chance he may have run away?"

"I...I really don't know." It was galling to admit she had so little insight into her own son's thought processes.

"Well, that'd be a whole lot better than him being abducted, you know what I'm saying? Running away is a lot less glamorous than it seems. He might soon realize that and call you to come pick him up."

Faith shook her head. "I just don't think he would do that to me." Especially since she'd given up Fitz for him. "Plus, he would have told his friend, Cameron, and Cameron was the first person to tell me Grayson wasn't at school."

"Hmm." Seth sat back in his seat. "Well, if he's not found within twenty-four hours, the presumption is he was taken across state lines, at which point the FBI takes over."

Faith's stomach somersaulted at the mention of the FBI. Of course, Fitz would never get involved as he was a supervisor now.

Seth's cell phone rang, spiking Faith's blood pressure.

He snatched it up. "Chief Agent Malloy."

The frown that creased his forehead told Faith the news wasn't good. Her stomach knotted.

"Yes, please do that," he finally said, "as soon as possible." He hung up and sent Faith a pained look.

"That was my cell phone provider?"

"It was. Grayson's phone isn't online anymore, which means either he turned it off, it's lost its charge, or it was destroyed."

Faith felt the blood in her head drain toward her thumping heart.

Seth stretched out a hand and touched her arm. "Don't be discouraged. I've requested a trail. If the phone was on at any time, we'll know where. Hang tight, mama. We're going to find your boy."

Just calm down and use your head.

His father's voice was back. Grayson stopped ramming his shoulder into the door and stilled his racing thoughts. The first thing he needed to do if he was going to escape was to free his wrists. Hadn't his father taught him how to snap the plastic zip tie?

Thinking back, Grayson discovered the memory was still crisp. He dropped to the floor to untie both of his tennis shoes. Taking the inner lace on his right shoe, he painstakingly fed the tip through the cuff around his wrist. That was tricky part. Next, he tied that lace to the inner lace of his left shoe. A nice, sturdy knot was required. Rolling onto his back, he peddled his feet in the air which caused the laces to saw against the plastic restraint. Within seconds it snapped. *Yes!*

It took longer to undo the knot he'd made than to break the zip tie. He had to hurry. Brian could be home at any moment. Plus the seam of light framing the window had faded since the man's departure, telling Grayson it was getting late. He needed to escape now.

Clearly the door, a solid piece of wood, wasn't going to be his way out. That left the window. Crossing to inspect it, Grayson saw where the original pane of glass was broken, leaving ragged shards still sticking out of the frame. The plywood boarding up the window wasn't as sturdy as the door. He could tell by the air seeping in between the board and the frame that the nails keeping the board in place were spaced more than a foot apart.

Watch the glass. Get up on the edge of the bed and kick with your sole.

Grayson dragged the bed closer, then stood on the side railing for extra height while gripping the headboard for balance. He brought his right knee to his chest, then struck the board with his heel. The squeak of nails coming out encouraged him. He kicked again, this time breaking off a bit of the remaining glass.

The third kick resulted in a three-inch opening. Mellow sunlight filled the bedroom along with damp, chilly air that smelled of freedom. The distance to the ground made his stomach lurch. But his subsequent kicks brought the branches of the big tree into view. If he could grab hold of that thick branch there, he wouldn't have to jump.

Many kicks later, the board came off the window and sailed to the ground. Using his shoe, Grayson broke off the remaining glass before sticking his feet outside until he was sitting on the windowsill. He ducked his head under the frame and nearly pitched to the ground before catching himself.

You're okay, buddy. Get your bearings.

With shallow breaths, he took in his surroundings. This side of the house clearly faced south because the sun was to his right, shooting beams of gold through the distant trees and turning the western sky pink. On a main road to his left, he could see cars driving with their headlights already on. If he could make it to the road, he could flag someone down who might help him.

But first he had to get to the ground, and no way was he jumping. That left using the tree branch about three feet away. The tree itself offered plenty of limbs to climb down. Magnolia. The name of the tree came to him suddenly, as did a recent story of how Aunt Grace had jumped from the second-story window of a warehouse in Venezuela last summer. If she could do it, so could he.

Ready? Grayson inched his butt to the edge of the sill. *Set.* He pressed his heels against the side of the house. *Go!*

He launched himself, stretching out his arms and striking the knobby limb so hard, he nearly lost his grip. Hanging on for dear life, he managed to wrap his legs around it, making him instantly more secure. Then he began to slide and clamber toward the trunk. The sun had dropped out of view, making it harder to see the branches he encountered.

He was moving down the trunk, stepping from limb to limb, when the sound of Brian's car reached his ears. The corner of the house blocked his view, but its headlights burnished the dead, lumpy grass in the huge front yard. Fear prodded Grayson to move faster. The engine died, the lights went out, and the car door slammed.

Don't check on me. Don't check on me.

As Brian entered the house, Grayson reached the lowest branch and jumped. All at once, the light from the landing shone in the window he'd just escaped from. Grayson started running.

"Hey!" Brian shouted down at him through the open window.

Grayson bolted. Taking the quickest way to the road, he cut straight across a front field that hadn't been mowed for years. Even though the grass was dead, it had left a thick, irregular layer on the ground, hampering Grayson's speed. The toe of his tennis shoe caught on a section of stiff grass. He pitched to his knees before he clambered up again.

He used to be pretty fast. Back at his old school, he could beat all the other sixth-grade boys when they raced. But throughout seventh grade, he'd been playing tons of video games instead of getting exercise, and now running hurt.

The road was still half a football field away when he heard Brian gaining on him. A fearful glance back showed his heavy-footed silhouette steadily overtaking him.

"Stop!"

Fear hindered Grayson's coordination. He stepped into a low area, spilled to his knees, and had trouble getting up again.

When Brian tackled him from behind, it was almost a relief not to have to run anymore. But now he was right back where he'd been earlier that day. Despair crashed over him as they lay on the damp grass, both of them panting. Brian kept a burly arm around Grayson's thighs, keeping him from moving.

The grass smelled like the hay his mother fed to the horses. Nostalgia rolled through Grayson. He never thought he would miss the barn she'd enlarged for her business—the reason they'd moved in the first place. But, right then, he would give anything to return to the life he'd hated.

Brian muttered a string of curses. Grayson could feel the man's heart pounding against his thigh before Brian lifted his weight off him.

"Come on, kid." He grabbed Grayson's arm and pulled him upright as he stood. "We're going back."

While the man's tone was gruff, his words full of resolve, he didn't sound like a homicidal maniac.

Grayson took heart from that as Brian towed him back into the house, through the front door. He flicked on a light switch, then locked the door behind them like before.

As they entered the warm living room, Grayson realized how cold he was. Brian shoved him toward the couch. Grayson immediately drew the blanket around himself, shivering.

His captor vanished into the kitchen. When he marched back into view, he was holding a length of rope. Grayson's heart stopped beating, then took off at a trot. "You don't have to tie me. I won't run again, I promise."

"Hah. Think I'd take your word for it? Your father was a liar. Bet you are, too."

Offended, Grayson stiffened. "My father was a good man!"

"See? Now that's a lie. Put your hands together and hold them out."

Too furious to be scared, Grayson did as he was asked. "That's too tight," he protested, as Brian wound the rope around both wrists. To his surprise, the man added more slack, but he wasn't content with just tying Grayson's hands. He went down on one knee and tied the remaining rope around both ankles.

Grayson frowned down at him, surprised that Brian's burly hands could be so nimble as he fashioned an intricate knot. "I won't be able to stand up."

"That's the idea, kid."

The man stood with a grunt and went back into the kitchen. When he came back holding a shotgun, Grayson's eyes fixed on the weapon, and his cheeks turned cold.

"You try to escape again"—Brian held up the shotgun but didn't aim it—"and I'll kill you before you even make it to the road." He crossed to the stairs where he snatched up the brown paper sack sitting on one of the lower steps. Grayson could tell at once there was liquor in it.

Numb with shock, he stared at his bindings while considering the awful likelihood that Brian would get drunk, turn ugly, and then shoot him. All Grayson could hope for was that his phone, still out in the car, would bring the police—or, better yet, the FBI—swarming in to save him.

Regret nipped at him for rebuffing Fitz, who probably would've found him by now. Why had he done that? It wasn't going to bring his father back to life. Even Grayson could see how much of a help Fitz was to his mother.

Brian propped the shotgun next to his armchair and placed the liquor on the little table next to it. Then he knelt before the wood-stove, where he stoked the embers and fed the stove two more logs. The shiny scar at the corner of his lips reflected the fire as he grimaced. When the stove emitted a humming sound, Brian closed it tight, then shot Grayson an inscrutable glance.

"I found the phone you hid beneath my seat. Thought you were being sneaky, didn't you?"

The words incinerated Grayson's final hope. His mouth went dry. "What did you do with it?"

"Destroyed it and threw it away."

Grayson could only stare at Brian, devastated. That phone had been his only link to the outside world. Now nobody was going to be able to find him.

Grayson jerked awake, finding himself lying across the musty-smelling couch, his wrists still bound by the rough length of rope that kept him from stretching out across the couch's full length. But at least Brian hadn't stuck him upstairs in the second bedroom. It had to be the middle of the night. The woodstove's heat was practically oppressive.

Rising to his elbow, Grayson spotted Brian in the armchair, eyes open, staring sightlessly at the stove. The bottle of liquor he'd bought rested between his thighs. From what Grayson could see, it looked empty.

He's drunk. Don't talk to him.

Grayson figured his father knew best, but then he noticed Brian had draped the blanket over him. Why would he do a thing like that if he meant to harm him? Perhaps he intended to ransom Grayson for money. He was burning up under the blanket. He had to pull it off.

At his movements, Brian looked over at him, glassy eyed.

"Why did you take me?" Grayson asked the question without meaning to.

Brian's vague smile made him realize the man hadn't understood the question. "Go back to sleep, Tommy," he crooned in a gentle voice.

Grayson glanced at the hand fisting the liquor bottle. That was it! The letters on Brian's knuckles spelled TOMMY. He'd tattooed the name there as a constant reminder. Encouraged by the man's gentler tone, Grayson dared to ask, "Who was Tommy?"

Brian blinked in confusion, banishing the glassiness from his eyes. He visibly shook himself, muttered a string of oaths, then took a swig from his bottle.

More than half the bottle was still left, relieving Grayson. When Brian didn't answer him, he dropped his head back down on the couch and closed his eyes, trying to sleep again, though the rope chafed his wrists and he longed to straighten his bent legs.

"Tommy was my son. My world. And it's your dad's fault that he's dead."

The words brought Grayson's eyes back open. Brian hadn't moved, but he was fingering the shotgun's barrel, which was propped on the arms of his chair, across his lap like a tray.

Grayson came up on his elbow. "What do you mean? My father never would've hurt a kid."

"Hah. Shows how much you know."

Anger stole a portion of Grayson's fear. "My father was a good man! Don't you talk bad about him."

Brian's face whipped in his direction. Slamming his bottle onto the table next to him, he picked up the rifle and stood, weaving. Grayson flinched against the cushions as Brian tucked the barrel under his arm and pointed the rifle at him. His ragged breaths sounded over the crackling woodstove.

Grayson turned hot, then cold. "Please, don't…"

Brian stepped in his direction.

This is it. I'm going to die now.

But then Brian brushed past the couch and went into the kitchen, where he thumped around, muttering to himself.

The adrenaline in Grayson's veins subsided slowly. A ray of hope shot through his bleak doom. Maybe Brian wasn't going to kill him. Maybe he would get to go home soon.

Oh, please let me go home, God.

The ranch wasn't so bad. He could fish in the creek whenever he felt like it. He had a forest right there for having paintball wars with Cameron. And he could get a hug from his mother whenever he needed one.

I won't ever complain again. I promise.

The slamming of a cupboard broke into his silent pleas. He kept his eyes shut, pretending to sleep as Brian came back into the room, still holding the shotgun. A peek through his lashes showed his captor back in his chair. This time the rifle was propped against his seat instead of over his lap. As he snatched his bottle back up, Grayson relaxed, but not completely.

For some reason, Brian blamed Dad for Tommy's death. He had to be wrong about the way Tommy died. Dad would never kill a kid. But if Brian's plan was to avenge Tommy's death, the only way to do that was to kill Grayson.

Grayson gulped as the hope he was clinging to vanished. *Am I ever going home?*

CHAPTER 5

*F*itz set his morning coffee next to his keyboard, then sank into his office chair to begin his Friday. The first thing he did every morning was log on to the Trilogy platform used by the Bureau and monitor the cases being run by his special agents. He skimmed the latest updates.

Well, well. That businessman with ties to the mob had realized he was under investigation and wanted to turn informant on his fellow mobsters. Fitz's lips curled with disdain. So much for honor among thieves.

At precisely eight thirty, his phone rang, as it did every weekday when Peter Gray, the senior agent in charge in the Norfolk field office, touched base to hand down new orders.

"Good morning, sir." As much as possible, he smoothed the grating sound made by his injured vocal cords.

"Is it, though?"

No day was a good day for Peter. Fitz's biggest fear was ending up just as cynical as his SAC.

"I'm putting you in charge of a kidnapping case. Kid by the

name of Grayson Saunders has vanished from his home in Suffolk…"

The humming in Fitz's ears kept him from hearing what Peter said next. *Faith's Grayson Saunders?* Who else would it be?

"…cell phone, before it stopped working, pinged several towers in southeast Virginia and just over the border in North Carolina. State police have launched an AMBER Alert and sent over their report. I'll forward it to you now. Keep me apprised."

The phone clicked in Fitz's ear. What a nightmare. His past rushed back to him. Rory, his son, had been Grayson's age when he'd been killed. *Please, God, not again.*

Guilt clamped down on Fitz for ignoring Faith's frantic call the previous day. In his defense, he'd thought Grayson had been skipping school like most teens did at least once. But his failure to return after twenty-four hours without a word suggested there was more to his disappearance than first met the eye.

Needing to pull a team together, Fitz tapped out his favorite subordinate's extension, gratified when Charlotte answered right away.

"Patterson-Strong."

Fitz had hand-picked her when she was just Charlotte Patterson. She'd married Navy SEAL Lucas Strong six months after the couple helped Fitz round up a group of extremists entrenched in the government and the military. The six-foot tall beauty with short auburn hair had been heading to CIA training when Fitz lured her to the Bureau instead—though her husband probably had more to do with her decision than Fitz did.

"It's me. Grab Lowe and meet me up in the command center. We've got an abduction case."

"Uh, slight problem. Lowe just called in to say he's too sick to come to work."

Fitz blinked several times as destiny interfered with his plans, leaving him just two choices: He could either find another pair of special agents, or he could step in for Lowe, roll his sleeves up, and get thoroughly involved. His battered heart quailed. Faith's vulnerability was going to suck him right back into having feelings for her.

"No worries," he heard himself say. "I'll stand in for Lowe."

"Yes!"

Fitz could picture Charlotte's grin. "Do me a favor," he requested, not quite ready to jump in feetfirst. "Give the boy's mother a call. You met her at a Labor Day party last year. She's Grace McLeod's twin sister."

"Oh, no."

"Yes. Ask her every question you can think of. I'll see you upstairs in twenty minutes. Here's her number." He recited it from memory, then hung up.

A real man would have called her himself. Fitz acknowledged as much, but he could feel Faith's pull on him already. Bittersweet memories of their three short months together saturated his mind. It was easier to feel nothing at all than to fluctuate between mountain-top moments and bottomless abysses.

He blew out a breath. *Please help me find the kid alive.* All he wanted was to send the kid safely home to his mother. Anything more than that—like asking for Grayson to accept him so he could marry Faith and be fulfilled—would just be greedy.

If you didn't want too much, you could never end up disappointed.

Faith knew how law enforcement worked. She'd been the wife of a state policeman for thirteen years. They didn't want civilians in the way. They wouldn't let her join them in their search for her son. It was only after pleading relentlessly that Seth agreed to take her with him as he liaised with the FBI team now handling the case.

She'd had a much easier time of convincing Grace to take over for Sonja after work that afternoon. The fact that it was Friday was proof of God's mercy, since Grace was a teacher and could watch Faith's daughters tomorrow morning without having to find a sub. Amos, her husband, would probably come over with their two boys for a fun day in the country.

On the other hand, the odds of finding Grayson, now that his cell phone had gone silent, weren't great. And the longer they looked for him, the less chance they would find him at all.

Her stomach growled, reminding her that she hadn't eaten, let alone slept, in the past twenty-four hours. Tired and overwrought, she kept silent as Seth drove them along the route Grayson had been taken yesterday according to the pings his phone had sent to nearby cell towers. The sky was overcast and dismal. A January chill pervaded the rural landscape.

As they passed the Great Dismal Swamp, the black-as-ink water lapping at the roots of cypress trees made Faith shudder. *Grayson's not here*, she assured herself. The route traced by her cell phone company suggested he'd been taken southeast, about one hour from their home.

Seth glanced over at her as he turned onto a narrow road that would cut east across the lower half of Virginia. "Would you believe we police this area, too?"

She eyed the relentlessly flat farmland surrounding them. "I remember. Jerry did an undercover job out this way about ten years ago, well before he joined the tactical team."

"That was before I joined the force."

The scenario returned to Faith. "Some guy with a gun shop was suspected of selling firearms without background checks. Jerry befriended him to find out. Sure enough, he sold a semiautomatic to a felon, and Jerry got him arrested." That memory jogged another. Hadn't a child been killed in a subsequent shootout? Jerry had been distraught for months afterward. "Hmm."

"What?" Seth prompted.

"Oh, I was just remembering what happened at the gun dealer's arrest. One of the arresting troopers was young and nervous about walking into a gun shop. The dealer's little boy popped up over the sales counter holding a water gun, and the trooper shot him dead."

Seth gaped at her. "No way. That's awful."

"Yeah, Jerry blamed himself for not communicating more clearly that the gun owner had a son. In his defense, the boy should've been in school that day." Closing her eyes, Faith willed away the tragic memory while blotting out the view of empty fields and naked tree branches.

The movement of the car must have lulled her to sleep. When she opened her eyes next, they were on a four-lane highway crossing the border into North Carolina, a mere half hour from the Outer Banks where they used to vacation every summer.

She straightened in her seat. "Oh, I know where we are." She scanned the familiar route with its quirky shops and empty market stands on either side of the road, seeking any sign of Grayson.

Minutes later, Seth put on his signal and waited for the oncoming traffic to pass before turning into a strip mall. Faith had already spotted the collection of unmarked sedans and SUVs. Her eyes widened as she took in the knot of federal agents, all wearing navy-blue jackets with *FBI* emblazoned in yellow on their backs. They stood on the sidewalk in front of a laundromat.

Faith recognized Charlotte, the leggy redhead who'd called her earlier that morning. Standing next to Charlotte, about the same height and with hair just a shade less vibrant, stood Fitz.

A gasp of surprise hitched in Faith's throat. *He'd come!* Relief and gratitude sang through her veins, causing tears to smart. She quickly blinked them back.

No sooner had Seth parked the car than Faith shot out of it, making a beeline to Fitz, who'd spotted her and fallen silent. Seven sets of eyes noted her and Seth's arrival, but Faith's attention was riveted to Fitz. She didn't miss the look of reproof that he shot at Seth for bringing her along.

Stopping in front of him, she read tension and wariness in his expression. "Any updates?" she inquired.

His lips firmed. "Not yet." Fitz's injured vocal cords made the words sound like a cat's purr. "This was the last area from which his phone pinged the nearest cell tower, but no one in these shops claims to recognize his photo."

Charlotte handed Faith one of the flyers they were distributing. It was the same picture she'd provided to Seth for the AMBER Alert. Grayson's lopsided grin as he held a newborn Mary Mae made Faith's stomach hurt. Hoping to sense her son's proximity, she noted the business in the strip mall: a liquor store, a laundromat, a Chinese restaurant, and an antique store. Only the restaurant would have been of interest to Grayson.

"Have you checked for any security cameras?"

Fitz nodded. "Of course. The liquor store has one, but it hasn't worked for years."

She turned away, hugging herself against the moist breeze as she surveyed the area. This busy stretch of highway was backed by trees and fallow fields. If Grayson was here, somewhere, wouldn't she feel it?

Hearing the agents confer in low voices, she moved toward them again, overhearing their decision to extend their search, since the pings were only vaguely reliable.

Faith waited for them to split up into three groups.

Seth caught her eye. "Have a seat in the car, Faith. We'll be back."

Ignoring his suggestion, she fell in behind Fitz and Charlotte as they peeled away from the group. The rest of the agents either headed east or crossed the highway to question people on the other side.

The small stand of trees on the west side of the strip mall was littered with trash. Taking note of Faith's company, Fitz slowed his step, then put himself between Faith and the traffic that was zipping up behind them. As a trio, they walked past the trees, between the highway's shoulder and a gully.

On the other side of the trees stood a brick rancher converted from a home into a funeral parlor. As Charlotte and Fitz marched up to the front door to make inquiries, Faith remained in the parking lot, not wanting to approach anything associated with death. Tamping down the shudders that racked her spine, she lamented the fact that Grayson had gone off in just a hoodie the previous morning. He had to be freezing.

Where are you, Grayson? Why did you come this way? The possibility that he'd run away occurred to her again. Surely he wasn't *that* unhappy.

Her attention snagged on something blue caught in the bushes just up the road from where she stood. Grayson's backpack was that exact shade of blue.

Wanting to investigate and seeing Fitz and Charlotte still occupied with the proprietor of the funeral home, Faith headed toward the object. The closer she came, the more it resembled Grayson's backpack. Her heart began to thud with cautious excitement, then with dread. She slowed her steps. What if she came upon his body? She wasn't prepared for that.

An eighteen-wheeler roared by her blaring its horn, as if the driver was angry at her for walking on the narrow shoulder.

"Faith!"

Fitz hurried toward her, a look of real concern on his face. Before he could scold her, she pointed to the object just feet away. "I think that's Grayson's backpack."

He caught her arm before she could step across the gully. "No one can touch it."

The feel of his warm hand anchoring her in place made her want to throw her arms around him and hold on tight.

As Charlotte overtook them, he pointed out the object to her while pulling on a pair of latex gloves. Charlotte took his place in holding on to Faith's arm while Fitz stepped across the gully. He reached into the branches and pulled out a backpack. Faith's knees jittered as she recognized the logo.

"It's Grayson's or one just like his." Joy and terror gripped Faith simultaneously.

Looking more grim by the moment, Fitz unzipped the main pocket, reached inside, and pulled something out—the brown bag lunch she'd made for him on Wednesday night.

Faith's head spun. Her legs went weak as a cold river of shock coursed through her veins. "I have to sit down."

Charlotte pulled her across the gully and down on the damp, dirty ground. "Put your head between your knees."

This can't be happening. But it was. As Faith breathed in through her nose and out through her mouth, she could hear Charlotte join Fitz in moving through the bushes, canvassing the area for more evidence. *Please don't find his body. Please don't.*

"I've got a cell phone!" Charlotte sang out.

Faith snapped her head up. Fitz was stepping toward Charlotte. With his gloved hand, he picked up what she was pointing to.

Faith clambered to her knees, needing to see it.

Fitz joined her by the gully. "Can you ID this?"

The battered iPhone in his hand was scarcely recognizable, but it had the same green case as the phone Grayson had received on his tenth birthday. She'd been so proud of him for never misplacing or dropping it. But now it was crushed, the glass smashed to pieces. "It's his."

Fitz eyed her more closely. "You okay?"

"Yes. We have a lead now." And no body, which meant Grayson had to be alive.

Charlotte rejoined them. "There's no sign of anyone walking through these bushes. My guess is both objects were tossed out the window of a car, headed back the way it came, which means the abductor found the phone, destroyed it, and threw it out the window after turning around."

Fitz pondered her words a moment, then checked the shoulder

—looking for tire tracks, Faith realized—but the shoulder was comprised of gravel.

"Looks like someone spun out right there, as they pulled back onto the road." He made brief eye contact with Charlotte. "Okay, let's get these items to our forensic team."

As they returned to their vehicles, he kept himself between Faith and the traffic while carrying Grayson's recovered items.

Once at their vehicles, Fitz opened his trunk and sealed the items in evidence bags of varied size. Just then the forensic team returned from their reconnaissance farther east and bent over the open trunk to examine the evidence.

Faith waited on tenterhooks, hugging herself hard as she prayed for something to be revealed by their discovery. At last, one of the forensic specialists turned to Fitz.

"Sir, there's nothing immediately apparent that would tell us anything. We'll need to take these items to the lab to look for fibers and fingerprints and such."

Faith's hopes floundered. How long would that take?

Fitz cast her a worried glance, then addressed the techs. "I want you to hop a flight from Norfolk. Every minute counts."

Hop a flight? Faith waited for the men to shoot away in their car before asking Fitz. "Where's the lab?"

"Quantico."

She stared at him, too stricken with dismay to speak. Quantico Marine Base was a good four-hour drive away.

Fitz's eyes, the color of spring grass, conveyed empathy. "Who's watching Olivia and the baby?"

It was good of him to spare a thought for her other children. "My sister."

He nodded, then grimaced and shook his head. "I understand why you're here, Faith, but it makes it harder for me to do my job while worrying about your state of mind."

"I'm fine. And I'm not leaving until I find my son." She stared at him until he looked away with a humorless laugh.

"You're a stubborn one."

"No. Grace is the stubborn one. I'm just a mother. And a mother will leave no stone unturned when her child is lost." Her throat closed up suddenly, and tears filmed her vision.

Fitz crossed his arms, as if to keep himself from hugging her. "When's the last time you ate anything?"

"I ate breakfast yesterday."

He pulled back the sleeve of his jacket and checked his watch. "We're breaking for lunch," he announced, getting looks of agreement from the others. "We can brainstorm our next move while we wait for forensics."

Stooped over, with his ankles bound to his wrists, Grayson shuffled out of the little bathroom under the stairs and froze. The shotgun was propped against Brian's chair, forgotten, while Brian himself was in the kitchen, out of sight, cooking what smelled like pasta.

Grayson's stomach rumbled, but all thoughts of eating took a back seat as he beheld the shotgun just standing there. It looked like the one his father used when hunting.

His heart began to thump. He looked down at himself. Could he raise the shotgun when he hadn't even been able to pee standing up?

Buckshot doesn't require accuracy. Just point and fire.

His father's advice sounded in his head, right when he needed it. When he was eleven, his father had taken him hunting for deer. A beautiful doe had wandered into the clearing while they were hunkered up in a tree stand.

"Just point and fire," whispered his father. Grayson had centered the crosshairs right over the doe's heart when his dad pushed the barrel down. *"Wait."*

A fawn had ambled into the clearing to join its mother. They'd

72

both stared at it before looking at each other, chagrined to have nearly killed the baby's mother. Ultimately, they'd gone home from their hunting trip empty-handed but with no regrets.

Grayson had no intention of killing Brian, either. Buckshot punched multiple holes in the target, and he didn't want to see that. On the other hand, maybe he could use the shotgun to barter for his freedom.

He shuffled closer to the chair, inspecting the weapon more closely. It was exactly like the one his father had taught him to shoot! What's more, if he sat down, he had enough slack in the rope to pick up the shotgun and hold it.

With his knees quaking, he dropped into Brian's chair. The ex-con was stirring something on the stove and didn't notice. The smell of onion and garlic made Grayson's stomach burn. He'd never been so hungry. Grabbing the barrel with both his bound hands, he hefted the shotgun, careful not to bump it on the side of the chair as he worked his hands down the frame, past the loading port, to the grip. He had just tucked the stock under his arm when Brian peeked his head out of the kitchen.

"Hey, you done in..." The man's words died. He gaped in surprise at Grayson who was pointing the shotgun directly at him.

Say something. "I want you to let me go." His voice came out fearless and confident. "If you don't, I'll shoot you." That was a bald lie, but Brian didn't know him.

To his surprise, his abductor threw back his grizzly head and guffawed.

Grayson scowled at him, trembling with frustration. Brian kept bellowing with mirth, his laughter getting louder. The man wasn't taking him seriously enough. Pulling back the bolt, Grayson went to drop a shell into the chamber to show the man he was serious. The subsequent hollow click told him the reason for his captor's glee. The shotgun wasn't even loaded.

Grayson lowered the weapon to his lap, then flinched against the back of the chair, expecting retribution.

Brian sobered, wiping a tear of hilarity from his face. But with liquid boiling over in the kitchen, he was forced to attend to it. Grayson eyed the impotent weapon. Had the shotgun ever been loaded? Was Brian carrying the shells in his pocket, or had he just used the shotgun to scare him?

If he wasn't going to kill Grayson or ransom him for money—since he didn't even seem to own a cell phone—why, then, had he bothered kidnapping him?

A terrible notion stole into Grayson's mind. Maybe Brian was keeping him here to take Tommy's place.

CHAPTER 6

aith awoke in a hotel room—in the only respectable hotel in Moyock—dismayed that she'd actually slept while her son was in the clutches of a kidnapper. What kind of awful mother was she?

It was Fitz who'd insisted on getting her a room. "Just rest for a little while. There's nothing we can do right now but question more people while we wait for forensics to get back to us."

The barbeque sandwich she'd eaten for lunch had filled her belly and lulled her to sleep in the king-sized bed. She sat up, dismayed to see a twilight sky through the open curtains. A glance at the bedside clock confirmed her realization that it was nearly evening already. She had slept the afternoon away!

Lunging for her cell phone, she expected to find an update from Fitz, but only Grace had texted her, sending a reassuring picture of her two boys playing with Olivia and another of her husband, Amos, holding Mary Mae with a smitten look on his face.

Keep us posted, Grace had written.

Faith texted her back: *No news yet except we found Grayson's backpack and his cell phone. Waiting on forensics.*

Then she called Fitz, pleased when he answered on the first ring. "What did forensics say?" *And why did you let me sleep so long?* She bit back the second question.

"Come on downstairs. We're just off the lobby in the little conference room."

His dampening tone informed her they'd made very little progress. Crushed, Faith closed her eyes as she absorbed the disappointment. "I'll be right down."

Grayson was so hungry that the soles of his shoes would have tasted good. Brian's spaghetti, made from a box of pasta, a jar of sauce, and sausage from the freezer, was every bit as delicious as the kind his mother made. Sitting at a table for four in the dilapidated kitchen with peeling wallpaper, Grayson discovered it was awkward but not impossible to eat with a fork, even with his wrists tied together.

"I grew up in this house."

Brian's admission had Grayson picturing him as a kid, sitting at this very table.

"My grandparents raised me right, but they were strict."

Grayson easily pictured him—a quiet, sullen boy wedged between a stern, older couple.

"I'm glad they died before...before everything happened." Brian stared out the window at the bleak backyard with nothing in it but a woodpile.

Curiosity got the better of Grayson. "What do you mean by everything?"

Brian looked over at him. "Before I got into trouble the first time," he clarified. "They were long gone by the time Tommy got shot by the police."

Grayson laid his fork down as he put two and two together. "My father? My father shot your son?" His appetite vanished.

Brian shook his gray mane. "No, but he might as well have. I would never have been arrested again if it weren't for Jerry. Every day he would come into my gun shop, and we'd talk. I thought he was my new friend." A sneer turned the scar on Brian's lip white. "So when he asked if would I sell a semiautomatic to some guy with a criminal record, I did it, just for him."

Staring at Brian's haggard face, Grayson couldn't help but feel sorry for him.

"You know, there's a term for that kind of trickery. It's called fruit of a poisonous tree, and it's just wrong. I was in the back room making some coffee when they came to arrest me. Tommy'd thrown up that morning, so he didn't go to school, and I had to bring him to work with me. The troopers said he popped up over the counter holdin' a water pistol." Brian's voice thickened with grief. "They shot him, thinking it was me with a real gun. Tommy caught two bullets, and I got ten years at Augusta Correctional Center."

Goose bumps scrabbled up Grayson's spine and dug into his scalp. Poor Tommy. Poor Tommy's dad.

Brian swiped the back of his hand under his nose and sniffed. "All I could think about the whole time I was there was how I was gonna make Jerry Saunders pay for what he did, trickin' me into breakin' the law."

Brian's words, spoken through his teeth, raised the hairs on Grayson's forearms.

Say something.

But the tension rolling off his abductor as he picked up his fork and swirled his noodles kept Grayson's throat clogged. He focused on Brian's beefy hand and the tattoos inked onto his knuckles, right there where he would always see Tommy's name. Grayson could only imagine the sorrow and regret the man carried in his heart. Pity rose in him.

"You could let me go, you know," he suggested softly.

Brian's head came up sharply. His deep-set eyes narrowed.

"I'll just say I ran away. Everyone would believe that. I haven't been myself this last year."

His captor's shaggy eyebrows sank slowly together. "Hush," he finally growled. "Don't lie to me, boy."

"I'm not lying. Trust me, they'll believe I ran away. I swear I won't tell anyone anything about you. I don't want you to get into any more trouble."

Brian shot out of his chair, which would have flipped backward if the wall hadn't caught it. Grayson flinched, expecting to be backhanded, at the very least.

"Dinner's over." Reaching across the table, Brian swiped Grayson's plate and fork away. He carried them to the sink, where he proceeded to scrub them viciously.

Grayson sat heavily in his chair, afraid to move. The emotion rolling off his captor filled the room with a stormy energy that warned him not to say anything. He peered out the window at what remained of the fading sunlight.

Another day gone. He'd been here for a day and a half with no indication that anyone was even looking for him yet. The rope around his wrists seemed to burn whenever he moved his hands. He wanted a bath, to brush his teeth, to lie in his own bed in his great big room and listen to the hoot owl that lived outside his window.

Brian turned off the water and wiped his hands on his grimy jeans. By the time he turned around, meeting Grayson's cautious regard, he seemed calmer.

"You ain't goin' nowhere."

Grayson swallowed hard. God help him. He might just end up living here forever.

～

Faith knew when she saw Seth and the five remaining FBI agents seated in the hotel's conference room looking at the notes scribbled across the big white-erase board in front of them that they were brainstorming, which meant they had no good leads.

"Hey." Fitz stood as she opened the door and ventured in.

At her entrance, Seth and every other agent in the room except for Fitz and Charlotte got up and filed out, heading to dinner, given their murmurs. As soon as they were gone, Fitz pulled out a chair and gestured for her to sit down.

Faith's hopes dropped another peg. He had bad news to share.

Sitting beside her, he gratified her by covering her hand with his. She latched on to it fiercely, regretting deeply having pushed him away. His warm, sure touch was the only thing preventing her from falling apart.

Charlotte, sitting on the other side of Fitz, glanced at their interlocked hands, then sent her a sympathetic grimace.

"Tell me what forensics said," Faith demanded through a tight throat.

Fitz drew in a breath and said quickly, "Just that the phone was probably discovered by the perp, somewhere in that area, and immediately destroyed. Forensics lifted a partial fingerprint, which they're running through our databases. Regarding the backpack, there were several fibers that could have come from anywhere, but nothing definitive. Prints were also lifted off the bag, but they all probably belong to Grayson."

Faith nodded. "So, we're back where we started." Jerry's death had shattered her world just one year ago. Why would God put her through this *again*?

Fitz tightened his hold on her hand while the muscles in his jaw flexed. Poor man, the weight of this investigation was resting on his shoulders. He sent her a sudden, sharp look as if something had just occurred to him.

"What?"

"I mean, it's probably unrelated, but do you happen to know

anyone who drives an old Buick, late nineties model, with a purple or burgundy paint job?"

On the other side of Fitz, Charlotte cocked her head at him, clearly wondering what he was talking about.

"I don't think so. Why?"

"Well, something happened about three months ago while I was watching the baby for you."

That had to have been the night she'd broken up with Fitz at the counselor's recommendation. "What happened?"

"Half an hour before you came home, I was in the living room giving Mary Mae a bottle, when I heard a car coming up your driveway. I thought it was you, so I went to look out the window. There was an old Buick, which stopped when the driver saw me. Before I could put the baby down and step outside, it did a three-point turn and drove off."

"An old Buick." Faith considered another moment then shook her head. "None of my clients have a car like that."

A thoughtful silence fell over the table. Charlotte was the first to break it.

"I think we should ask the store owners at the strip mall if any of their clientele own a Buick that color."

Fitz nodded and checked his watch. "I agree. Let's go now before they close."

At their description of the Buick, the proprietor of the liquor store glanced toward the windows at the front of his store as if picturing a car just like it, parked out front.

"Uh, nope." The older man looked back at him and shook his head. "Doesn't sound familiar."

The man was lying. Fitz waited, sending him a hard stare and causing the man's Adam's apple to bob. "Okay then." Pretending to accept the proprietor's word for it, he guided a frowning Charlotte and pale-faced Faith out of the store, where they were joined by Seth and the other agents who'd postponed their dinner plans, just in case.

Darkness had fallen, and the liquor store sign cast a surreal green light on their dark-blue jackets. Fitz saw Faith shudder in the damp chill.

"Charlotte, check our trunk for another jacket for Faith, would you? I'll be right back."

Charlotte frowned at him as he summoned the special operators, or SOGs, on his team to join him at the far corner of the building. Holmes and Chisolm, both ex-Navy SEALs, followed him, then listened intently as he conveyed his suspicions.

"For whatever reason, Mr. Dawson is lying to us. I know he recognized the vehicle I just described to him. Let's go elicit his cooperation."

Sometimes it took intimidation tactics to get people to be upfront—especially people with an innate mistrust of law enforcement. Not five minutes later, with the two SOGs looming behind him, displaying their harnessed pistols, Mr. Dawson confirmed Fitz's suspicions.

His expression cleared abruptly. "You know, now that I think about it, a customer did roll up here yesterday, late afternoon in a maroon Buick, older model. That's right. He bought a bottle of Old Crow whisky."

Fitz's blood flowed faster. "Was there a kid with him? The one whose picture we showed you?"

The proprietor's eyes flashed with indignation. "No, of course not. I would've told you if I'd seen the kid. I've got grandkids myself."

"Describe the driver. Do you know him?"

"Oh, I've seen him here from time to time. Burly fellow, late forties, with a head of graying hair. Sometimes he has a beard; sometimes not. He's got a scar on his lip." Mr. Dawson touched his own mouth.

Fitz scribbled himself a note. "How often does he come here and from which direction? Did he ever give his name?"

"No name. Comes here maybe once, twice a week from the eastbound lane. Told me he drives across the state line cause my store's closer than the one in Edinburgh."

"Good." Fitz made a note that the man resided in Virginia. "What else has he told you? What have you inferred about him?"

"Um," Mr. Dawson thought back, "well, he asked me once if my security camera worked. Should've told him, yes, but he didn't seem like the type to rob me, even with the tattoos on his hand."

Fitz pounced on the detail. "Tattoos of what?"

"Oh, I don't know." Mr. Dawson searched his memory. "Letters," he replied, sounding more certain. "I remember reading *T, O, M.* Couple of *M's,* I think."

"Was it a name? *Tommy* maybe?" Fitz quizzed.

The proprietor stared down at the counter as if picturing the perp's hand. "Yeah, I think there might've been a *Y* on his pinkie."

"That's good, Mr. Dawson. You've been very helpful. Now, if you don't mind, we're going to lift fingerprints off your front door and this counter here—won't take but half an hour or so."

The store owner crossed his arms and sighed. "Be quick about it. I'm bound to lose business with Feds milling around my store."

Hearing a quiet knock on her hotel-room door, Faith wondered if she'd imagined it, but she wasn't about to ignore the sound or wait for Fitz to knock again since it was quite late. *Please, let it be him!*

She padded to the door in the plaid pajamas she'd stuffed into a bag that morning.

Fitz, still in the butter-yellow polo and navy slacks he'd worn all day, regarded her through red-rimmed eyes. His wavy, auburn hair stuck up in places, giving him a boyish demeanor. "Were you sleeping?"

His tone alone told her he had news. "No. What did you find out?"

He glanced past her. "May I come in?"

She hesitated the barest second, balancing propriety against her need to be near him. "Sure." She pulled the door open, admitting him.

As he entered the room, Fitz's gaze went straight to the rumpled bed before he veered toward the desk, pulled out the chair, and sat down on it.

Faith sat at the foot of the bed close to him. His gaze flicked over her pajama-clad frame, and his lips twitched toward a smile, one that faded as he prepared to tell her his news.

"We have the perp's prints."

Elation and terror filled Faith in equal parts. "Seriously? Out of all the prints you lifted from the shop? How's that possible?"

"His were one of just two prints in the system. His name is Brian Sutton. He owned a gun shop near here, just across the border in southeast Virginia."

Faith's mouth turned dry. Goosebumps ridged her arms. She knew this story.

"A decade ago, he was arrested for selling a semiautomatic weapon to a felon. Since he had a prior record, he got ten years. He was just released from prison three months ago."

Faith clenched the bedspread to contain her runaway panic. "So, this is an act of vengeance."

Fitz frowned. "How so?"

She gripped the bedding harder as the room went into a slow spin. "Brian Sutton was the gun dealer Jerry befriended when he was working undercover." Her voice went faint with horror. "When troopers went to arrest him, Jerry said Sutton's son was in the shop playing with a water pistol. One of the troopers got spooked when the kid popped up over the counter with a water gun. They shot him, thinking it was Sutton. I'm pretty sure the boy's name was *Tommy*."

Fitz stilled, his face a taut mask. All at once, he lurched across the space between them, sitting on the bed beside her and pulling her into his arms. Clinging to him, Faith quaked with the terrible certainty that Brian Sutton was avenging Tommy's death.

"He's going to kill him." Articulating her suspicion made it even more real. Faith pushed her face into the crook of Fitz's neck and burst into tears.

Not my son, Lord. Please don't take my son from me.

Her shoulders heaved as grief tore into her heart, wrenching sobs from her that sounded like they were coming from someone else. Fitz held her tightly to him, rocking her ever so gently, saying nothing.

At last, when her sobs came intermittently, he murmured, "We're going to find him soon, Faith."

He meant the kidnapper, of course. Grayson's fate wasn't so certain.

Faith lifted her head from Fitz's damp collar to read the reassurance in his gaze.

"The man is on probation, which means his probation officer knows where he lives. We're tracking him down even now. We'll have him by morning."

The words were meant to be comforting, but they also meant by morning, she might learn that her son was dead. An eye for an eye. A son for a son. How could God let this happen? He'd always been there for her, comforting her, blessing her.

With an indrawn breath, Fitz caught her face between his hands and gazed deep into her eyes. "I know how you feel. You're not alone right now."

Through her misery, she recalled the story he'd once shared, how he'd come home one night to find his entire family dead in their beds. How could he have endured the loss of, not just his wife, but of all three children, the youngest just a baby? Yet here he was, sitting here with her now, still alive, still functioning.

"I love you." The words slipped off her tongue, uncontainable. She'd been guarding them in her heart for months now.

His fingers seemed to tremble as he stared back at her, clearly caught off guard by her confession.

"It's okay." She tried her best to smile but couldn't. Dragging his hands down to her lap, she held on to them, squeezing hard. "I know you love me, too. What I don't know is how things will ever work out for us, but I hope they will. This world is full of so much suffering. What we have is a gift."

A sheen of tears appeared in his eyes before he lowered his lips to hers and kissed her—a bittersweet kiss that, nonetheless, contained the promise of passion and permanence.

With a groan, he severed the kiss and lifted his head. "I need to get back to my team."

She nodded, releasing him reluctantly. "Please come back," she begged him. "I won't be able to sleep…"

He sent her the smallest of nods, as if reluctant to get too close but helpless to stop himself. "Okay."

Before standing, he brushed a thumb across her cold cheek, then walked briskly to the door, letting himself out. The look he shot her through the closing door enjoined her to be strong: She wasn't alone.

Even in this terrible trial, God had not abandoned her completely.

CHAPTER 7

*I*n the middle of the night, Grayson was awakened by the sound of the door on the woodstove opening. Slitting his eyes, he suffered the despair of knowing he wasn't dreaming any of this. It was real, and it would remain his reality until he was found, or managed to escape, whichever came first.

Brian was down on one knee, poking the embers in the wood-stove. Grayson realized he had never caught Brian sleeping. The man spent most of his time sitting in his chair, considering his circumstances with a look of desperation on his lined face. He had to know he couldn't keep Grayson here forever. No one could take Tommy's place.

Poor Brian was in over his head. With that thought, Grayson drifted off to sleep, the musty blanket heavy on his chest.

Hours later, light was shining through the window. Sensing Brian standing over him, Grayson lurched awake only to shrink back at the intent look on his captor's face. Cradling his shotgun like a baby, he stared at Grayson as if for the last time.

There aren't any shells in the shotgun.

No sooner did that reassuring thought cross his mind than

Brian slid a hand into his pocket and pulled out three of them. With sharp alarm, Grayson watched him load the shells one at a time.

"Get up, kid. You're goin' home." With the shotgun loaded, Brian propped it against the end table and picked up the serrated knife lying by the empty planter.

Grayson stared at the knife not moving an inch. Going home, as in *heaven*? Had Brian decided to kill him, after all?

Brian reached for him, grabbing the rope at his wrists and hauling him to a sitting position. With relief, Grayson realized Brian was just cutting off the bindings, not stabbing him. Silence fell between them as Brian sawed away at the rough rope. When it fell from Grayson's chafed wrists, Brian went down on one knee and sawed at the rope encircling his ankles. Once it was cut away, his captor pushed stiffly to his feet.

Grayson didn't move. There had to be a catch. If Brian was setting him free, then why the air of doom hanging over him?

Brian's dark eyes seemed to look straight through him. "I'm sorry, kid."

Grayson stared back, afraid to ask, "What for?" in the off chance that Brian still intended to kill him.

"You're free to go." His captor gestured at the front door with the knife he still wielded.

Something in the man's voice made Grayson loath to leave. A thickness in his words that conveyed despair.

Grayson finally found his voice. "Are you going to shoot me in the back?"

The incredulous twitch of Brian's eyebrows reassured him. "'Course not."

Then why the grim resolve in his voice?

But with hope leeching into his bloodstream, Grayson focused on himself and the future being handed back to him. Hope gave him strength to rise on legs that felt like rubber. For a second, they stood mere inches apart, and Grayson fancied he could feel the cloud of sorrow encompassing his captor.

"I meant what I said last night," he told the man. "I won't tell anyone what you did."

The ghost of a smile curled Brian's mouth.

The fear that had gripped Grayson for days eased suddenly, making room for the sympathy that had pricked him from time to time. "My dad wants you to know he's sorry, too." Then, before his courage could fade, he headed briskly toward the door, still not completely confident that Brian was letting him leave.

Beneath his hand, the door swung open, admitting a puff of chilly, wet air that smelled vaguely like the ocean. With a glance back at Brian, who wasn't even looking at him, Grayson darted onto the crooked porch and closed the door behind him. His heart began to gallop.

I'm free! He ran off the stoop and, with a fearful backward glance, broke into a jog, heading past Brian's car to lope down the long driveway. It was still early morning, and a thin mist obscured the main road, but Grayson could hear cars moving in either direction. He lengthened his stride, his heart bursting from his chest as he pushed himself to run faster.

The crack of a shotgun nearly sent him sprawling face first onto the patchy gravel as his head whipped around and his stride broke. Drawing to a stop, breathing hard, he peered back at the house, the skeletal remains of a once-quaint home.

"No." His cheeks turned cold as he realized what might have just happened—had Brian just taken his own life to avoid going back to jail? Then he hadn't believed Grayson would stick to his story about running away.

"No!" he shouted back at the house, but it was too late to persuade Brian he would keep his word. Rocking back on his heels, he pressed a fist into his empty stomach, sick at the mental picture of Brian lying in his living room with his brains blown out.

But then a movement at the front of the house caught his eye.

With an indrawn breath, Grayson spotted Brian as he stepped out of the house onto the crooked front porch, no shotgun in sight.

Dizzy with relief, Grayson raised a hand in farewell and held it there until Brian responded, slowly raising his own hand.

With a sob of nameless emotion, Grayson whirled around and resumed his escape to freedom.

Faith had been standing in the breakfast area in the hotel lobby eyeballing the unappetizing offerings when Fitz's cell phone rang. She glanced over at him, holding her breath.

"Fitz here." He put his plate of eggs and sausages down on the counter.

She could tell by the immediate shift in his demeanor that this was the call they'd been waiting for.

"Perfect. Thank you. Text that address to me now. I'll keep you advised." He hung up and met her gaze before announcing to the rest of the agents, "We have an address. Let's go, people. We'll eat later." He looked back at Faith. "You should stay here."

Her eyebrows rose. "I'm going with you."

He sighed and firmed his lips. "Only if you agree to stay in the car when we get there. It could be dangerous. I don't want you getting hurt."

He didn't want her stumbling onto Grayson's dead body. "I understand." Turning her back on the buffet, she headed for the exit.

Ten minutes later, with Charlotte driving and Fitz eyeing the map on his cell phone, they led their small convoy of unmarked vehicles toward the address supplied by Brian Sutton's parole officer. It was just six miles from their hotel.

With the feeling that she was caught up in a dream, Faith sat in the center of the back seat so she could see, though her visibility was hampered by the mist hanging in the air. Clasping her cold hands together, she braced herself for the possibility of Grayson's demise while clinging to the hope that they would find him still alive.

Charlotte could not be driving any faster as she sped them across the state border back into Virginia. Soon there was nothing around them but farmland and the occasional house. How odd that Grayson would be out here in the middle of nowhere.

All at once, Faith's watchful gaze fell upon the silhouette of a man—no, it was a boy!—walking on the other side of the road. At their approach, he waved both arms as though to catch their attention. "Wait, is that...?"

Fitz and Charlotte saw him, too, turning their heads to glance his way, but they didn't slow down.

Faith whipped around to peer out the back window. "That was Grayson!" Or was her hopeful mind just imagining things?

Fitz cast an incredulous glance back at her. "Are you sure?"

Charlotte took her word for it. Without waiting for permission, the dauntless redhead stabbed on her hazard lights, then her left turn signal, conveying her intent to the agents behind them. As they came to a crossing in the median, she slowed abruptly, sending the car into a squealing, 180-degree turn and prompting the two vehicles behind her to do likewise.

"Don't hit him, please!" Faith was already taking off her seat belt.

"Stay in the car," Fitz ordered, but she wasn't going to obey him if it was Grayson she had really seen.

Eyes glued to the side of the road, she spotted him standing just inside a parking lot for a lone Dollar General, still closed on this early Saturday morning. "There he is!"

It *was* Grayson, hugging himself from the cold, looking forlorn and scared. Dizzying relief flooded Faith's arteries. A sob of pure joy escaped her.

No sooner had Charlotte pulled into the parking lot behind

him, followed by two more cars, than Faith shot out of the back door. "Grayson!"

He turned toward her, his expression of hopefulness morphing into a look of wonder. "Mom!"

She rushed at him, then gripped him fiercely, knowing right away that he'd not showered since leaving home. His hair was lank and musty smelling, but she inhaled his adolescent body odor as if it were the sweetest-smelling flower. And given the way he gripped her back, he felt the same way.

"Mom." He burst into tears, fighting at the same time to control them.

"It's okay. You're safe now, honey. You're safe."

"I'm so sorry."

Faith was aware that all six remaining FBI agents had gathered around them, including the SOGs and Seth, waiting to hear from Grayson what had happened.

"It's not your fault, honey." She stepped back just far enough to inspect him. His face was grubby, his sweatshirt stained with what looked like spaghetti sauce, but she saw no apparent injuries. Nor did she think now was the time to question him about his captor, but the expectant expressions on the lawmen's faces told her they were itching to arrest someone.

Seth stepped forward first, as Grayson already knew him. "Son, where's the man who took you, Brian Sutton? Did you escape from his home?"

Grayson stiffened perceptibly. His gaze darted back to his mother, and his face tightened the way it did whenever he told a lie. "I don't know who you're talking about."

Seth grabbed Grayson's forearm and held it up, displaying a ring of reddened skin around his wrists. "Where's the man who tied you up, son?"

Faith gasped at the visual evidence that her baby had been forcibly restrained.

Grayson's expression turned mulish. "I wasn't tied up."

"It's okay, honey. You're not in trouble. We know about Brian Sutton, how your father got him arrested and what happened to his son."

"I ran away, okay?"

Grayson's sudden outburst silenced them all.

"I ran away because I thought I hated my life. I thought I hated our new house and how Dad was gone and now Fitz is here." He gestured at Fitz, who'd stepped closer to Faith at Grayson's outburst. "But I was wrong. I just…I just want to go home. Please." His face crumpled and tears filled his eyes.

Members of the rescue party scowled at each other, clearly disbelieving Grayson's story. It was Fitz who made the decision. "Let's get Grayson back to the hotel. Charlotte, you take him and Faith. The rest of us will join up with you momentarily."

In other words, they were going to descend on Brian Sutton, regardless of Grayson's insistence.

Grayson wasn't stupid. With a glance at the armed special operators, he caught Fitz's eye. "I *won't* press charges! I *won't* testify against him. He's just a lonely man who misses his kid."

Faith caught a glimpse of Jerry in her son as he dashed away his tears and clung to his serious, adult expression.

"What happened to him wasn't fair. He didn't hurt me." He turned his pleading hazel eyes on her. "We're not pressing charges. Promise me, Mom. He'll go back to jail for years. He doesn't deserve that. He's suffered enough."

Faith waffled. On the one hand, she wanted Sutton to pay for the terror he had put Grayson through and for her own misery these last three days. On the other, Grayson was clearly serious about this. He'd obviously gotten to know his captor on a personal level and talked him into letting him go. "But he stole you away from your home, honey. We thought you were dead!"

Grayson swallowed. "What about Tommy?"

Faith stared at her son while thinking about the innocent boy, killed in error. Jerry had been so distraught knowing what had happened to him.

"You get to have me back," Grayson pointed out, "but Brian never gets Tommy back, let alone the ten years he spent in prison. Dad didn't want that for him. I know he didn't."

Faith searched herself and realized that was true. But the mother in her wanted to hold Sutton accountable. He couldn't just go around grabbing kids off the street and tying them up, for heaven's sake! "It's not that simple, Grayson—"

"Yes, it is!" He cut her off. "What is it you've always taught me? When someone hurts you, you turn the other cheek. So, that's what I'm doing!"

The righteous light blazing in Grayson's eyes finally penetrated Faith's resistance, forcing her to ask herself, *What would Jesus do?*

The answer, as much as she didn't want to accept it, was to go along with Grayson. Squelching her desire for justice, Faith faced Fitz and said in no uncertain terms, "You can talk to Sutton if you want to, but we're not pressing charges."

While the other special agents scoffed at her decision—especially the two SOGs, who clearly couldn't wait to take the kidnapper into custody—Fitz frowned and divided a thoughtful look between her and Grayson.

"As you wish." His calm tone conveyed absolute authority. "He will not be charged with child abduction."

Faith could tell that Sutton would at least get a talking to. Or perhaps the state would seek to arrest him for violating the terms of his probation, like crossing the state line without permission.

But Grayson had taken Fitz at his word. To Faith's surprise, her son released her. She watched with widening eyes as he took a step toward Fitz and extended his hand.

"Thanks for finding me, Fitz. We'll see you around, okay?"

With a stunned, somewhat humbled look, Fitz accepted Grayson's handshake, then clasped his other hand over Grayson's to indicate how much this meant to him.

Tears sprang into Faith's eyes. It couldn't be more obvious that Grayson was saying he would welcome Fitz back into their lives.

"Rest up." Fitz pumped Grayson's hand one last time, then nodded at Charlotte, gesturing for her to take Faith and Grayson to her car.

As Faith slipped into the back seat with Grayson, it finally sank into her that all was well. So much agony and uncertainty resolved in the twinkling of an eye. God was *so* good to her!

Soon, Grayson would provide more details. But, for now, she was content to buckle herself back into the center of the seat so she could sit right next to him and hold his grubby hand.

"I love you so much, Grayson." She caught his eye. "You're the best combination of me and your father."

A beat of silence passed as Charlotte started up the car and pulled them away from the knot of lawmen talking things over.

"Dad was with me most of the time."

Faith nodded, pleased but not at all surprised to hear it. "You felt him with you?"

"He talked to me. He was, like, inside my head but also all around me. I know he felt bad about what happened to Tommy."

Faith squeezed Grayson's hand. "Yes, he felt terrible. It upset him for years."

Grayson's eyes filled with tears, and he turned averted his face to keep her from seeing them. A mile down the road, he wiped his cheeks and faced forward again.

"I want to go to the Outer Banks this summer."

She smiled at him. "Me, too." He'd refused to go the previous summer. And between their move and starting up her new business, she hadn't insisted. "Let's do it."

"Fitz should come, too, so he can help with Mary Mae. I'll keep an eye on Olivia."

The offering of help was so unlike the sullen behavior he'd exhibited before his disappearance. Faith pressed a quick kiss on her son's grimy cheek. "You're a good big brother."

He paused reflectively. "I will be."

That afternoon, Brian Sutton fought to get the ax out of the log he was splitting. Moving the handle of the ax up and down, he refrained from cursing and thought, again, about what had happened just a few hours before.

Just as he'd suspected, though far sooner than he'd thought possible, the FBI and a state policeman had descended on his house. Not wanting any more trouble than necessary, he'd come out with his hands in the air, lamenting that he hadn't found the courage to shoot himself.

A ginger-haired agent with a gentle light in his green eyes had given him the shock of his life while informing him that he wasn't under arrest. He'd asked if they could go inside, just the two of them. There, he'd asked questions that had brought Brian to tears as he confessed to abducting Grayson, to putting him in his trunk, and restraining him with rope when he tried to escape.

The agent had seemed impressed by Grayson's resourcefulness as Brian described how he'd discovered the boy's cell phone under his seat and how Grayson had cut off the zip ties and escaped from a second-story bedroom by climbing down a tree.

"Brave kid," the agent had remarked.

"Yeah. He got to me. It's hard to want to hurt a kid like that. So, I guess you're gonna arrest me now." After all, he had just confessed.

The agent drew a deep breath and said, "No. No, the boy and his mother have declined to press charges. You're still a free man, Brian."

The astonishment he'd felt at hearing those words humbled him, still. Imagine if he'd actually shot himself. He would never have known the grace that he was now receiving.

Jerry Saunders had robbed him of his life and his son. But

Grayson Saunders had showed him mercy. Humbled, remorseful, and unable to free the ax, Brian sank to his knees on the soft soil and dropped his head into his work-roughened hands.

"I'm sorry…I'm sorry, kid." He sobbed out the words. "I'm just a bitter, old fool."

His tears seemed to scald his cold cheeks. As he went to wipe them away, a dry leaf crackled under a stealthy footfall. Brian whipped his face in the direction of the sound. Not ten yards away stood a beagle, shivering in the cold. They regarded each other for the longest time.

"Well, hey, little guy," Brian finally crooned. It appeared to be male. "You lost?" Brian held out a hand, worried if he stood up, the pup would bolt. It probably belonged to some hunter, though given that Brian could see the dog's ribs under his brown-and-white coat, he'd been lost for some time. "You look hungry. Come here, boy. I can feed you."

To his delight, the beagle's tail began to wag. He came straight toward him as if he'd known Brian all his life.

Still on his knees, Brian stroked the dog's broad head, while inspecting his faded red collar for a tag. Nothing. He looked directly into the dog's soft brown eyes and knew: This dog was for him.

"Let's go inside, little fella. I got plenty of firewood for now. Come on." He kept a hand on the dog's collar just in case, but it didn't pull away as he stood, prompting Brian to let go. He started for the door, and the pup fell into step next to him.

A minute later, he had filled a bowl with scraps from his refrigerator. "There you go." The beagle homed in on it.

"Oh, you like that, don't you, Tommy?"

In the act of wolfing down his food, the beagle stopped and looked up at him. Brian's eyes filled with grateful tears. So this was what it felt like to be forgiven.

EPILOGUE

The sun shone hot on Grayson's back as he helped Olivia scrape out a moat for her sandcastle. The Atlantic Ocean rushed toward them, just feet away, before retreating. It was hard to believe that two short years ago, his father would have been the one to help Olivia, whom he'd dubbed the family artist. Grayson would have been riding the run up on his skim board, waiting for his father's attention, never realizing Jerry's days were numbered.

His father would be proud of him for how he'd changed, though. Now Grayson lived like every second counted. On February first, he'd asked Fitz for Brian Sutton's address, and he'd sent him a greeting card. Every day and on weekends, he and Cameron mucked out the barn together. While Cameron got paid, Grayson had requested that his pay be deposited into his college fund. And since he wasn't sulking at school anymore, his grades were better, and he'd made a bunch of new friends.

Hearing soft footfalls in the sand, Grayson imagined for just a moment that his dad was about to join them. When he glanced over to see Fitz wearing a huge straw hat and a white, long-sleeved shirt over khaki shorts, he sent him a sincere smile, though it was hard not to tease the man for protecting his fair skin at the beach.

Fitz's shadow folded over him as he inspected their castle. "Wow. When can I move in?"

Olivia cast him a proud grin, while displaying the gap where her missing canines used to be. "Wanna help?"

"Sure. But I need to talk to Grayson first."

Concerned, Grayson glanced toward their rented beach house. His mother stood on the main deck holding eleven-month-old Mary Mae, who wore a bonnet to rival Fitz's straw hat. "Am I in trouble?"

"'Course not. Let's go put our feet in the water."

That was about all Fitz really did, unlike his father who used to take Grayson a hundred yards into the deep blue so they could catch waves on their boogie boards.

They went to stand where the water swirled around their ankles and the sand shifted under their feet.

"I'll get right to the point." Fitz slanted him a sidelong look. "I'd like to marry your mother, but I want your blessing first."

The ocean pulled away from them and Grayson sank deeper into the sand. The words came as no surprise. Fitz had been part of their lives nonstop since his abduction. But, as far as Grayson could tell, his mother never had him up to her bedroom. Sometimes when they kissed, though, it went on and on, prompting Grayson to look away.

He searched himself for resentment or anger, but all he felt was inevitability. "Yeah, that's fine."

"Yeah?" Fitz pivoted so they were facing each other. "You sure?"

Meeting the man's bright-green gaze, Grayson realized he couldn't ask for a better father for his sisters. With "Fitzy" in her life, Olivia would forget her old daddy. And Mary Mae had never met her father. Only Grayson would hold on to the memories. But that didn't mean he couldn't rely on Fitz from time to time. He nodded while swallowing the lump in his throat. "Positive."

Fitz sent him his trademark ghostly smile. "Thank you. I had a son once," he added unexpectedly. "Well, two sons, actually, but Collin was just a baby. My older son, Rory, was about your age. He would have liked you."

Surprise and then pity stole into Grayson. His mother had mentioned once that Fitz had lost his entire family to mob retaliation. "I'm sure I would have liked him, too."

They shared a pained smile. *I could never hate this man*, Grayson thought.

Olivia's voice broke them apart. "Fitzy, come see!"

Fitz, who suffered his nickname with stoicism, headed back to Olivia. "Oh, I see. You made a drawbridge."

"So crabs can get in."

"Oh, a castle for crabs. I guess I'm not moving in." His attention fell to her shoulders, and he pulled a tube of sunscreen from the pocket of his shorts. "Time for more protection, Livvy."

"Aww." As Olivia brushed the sand off her hands and stood, Grayson watched them together, acting like daughter and father already. Jerry Saunders would have wanted that. It was like he'd hand-picked Fitz to take his place.

Is that true? Grayson put the question to his father, confident that he could hear him.

His dad hadn't spoken to him in an audible voice since the kidnapping. But a wave rolling onto the shore behind him seemed to say, "Yes," as it foamed across the sand. A seagull gave a cry of exhilaration while winging toward the water's surface. And Grayson sensed his father was smiling.

BE NOT AFRAID

PROLOGUE

*R*uby Bonheur gaped at the test strip in her hand. The shock rolling over her stole her breath as she beheld the double-pink stripes. That second line was *not* supposed to be there. She had taken precautions—well, as consistently as she was capable of being.

The test had to be wrong. Only it said right there on the box: 98 percent accurate. And she had been feeling a teeny bit sick every morning for the past two weeks.

I'm pregnant.

Her heart beat a tattoo of denial. What was God thinking? This couldn't happen now with her journalism career in full swing!

A lead investigative reporter, Ruby had exposed corruption and fraudsters all along the East Coast, including, most recently, the powerful Centurion Cohort down in Savannah, Georgia. At that point, WTKR had stolen her away from WAVY television by offering her an obscene salary just to track down every corrupt cop, corporation, or politician she could find.

For a girl who'd once wasted her degree in journalism by wait-ressing at Showstoppers, she'd sure come a long way. And she owed a lot of her success—most of it, in fact—to her new husband, Tony, and her newfound faith in God. Tony had taught her that all things were possible when she relied on God for strength. This was the first time God had let her down.

I can't have a baby.

It would ruin everything. The fabulous run on her career would come to a screeching halt the moment she shared her news with anyone. Tony would view her pregnancy as a reason for her to cut back on her hours at work. They might have to move since their beachfront rental wouldn't accommodate a growing family. And then there was her boss who would pull her off the set the minute she started showing—pregnant news reporters were bad for the ratings.

Maternity leave would be the final nail in her coffin. Ruby would be relegated to small-time reporting—no more scandals that took her beyond Virginia Beach. Then who would she be? Just a mother, and that was a job she was totally unfit for.

The light knock at the door startled the tester out of Ruby's hand. It clattered onto the tiled floor where it skidded toward the tub.

"You okay in there, *Bella?*" Tony's baritone voice conveyed worry.

A locked door had never been a deterrent to her husband. Recovering the test strip, Ruby offered the first excuse to pop into her head. "Just doing my makeup, love. I'll be out in a sec."

She and Tony had eloped while on vacation in Bermuda earlier that fall. The spur-of-the-moment ceremony performed under a moon gate seemed to have turned his mother, Anna, against her. It had taken Ruby three years to marry her son, and then she'd gone and done it without Anna in attendance.

Regret did occasionally prick Ruby for not having shared that special moment more traditionally, with Tony's family and his Navy SEAL teammates present, not to mention her older sister, Opal, and Opal's husband, Commander James Monteague. But it had felt so right, so romantic, pledging her future to Tony under a moongate overlooking the tourmaline sea. Besides, who had time to plan an elaborate wedding?

She and Tony were finally together in every sense of the word. He knew her better than anyone. He also knew she'd just lied to him because she always put on her makeup in the car. She could sense him hovering on the other side of the door, wondering what she was keeping from him.

"Listen." His voice coming through the crack made her hold her breath. "What do you think of us goin' to Mama's for Thanksgiving this year, instead of her coming down here?" His thick Philadelphia accent had faded only slightly since they'd first met. "She says her washing machine doesn't work, and she needs me to fix it. Plus, I'm worried about her health."

He wanted to go to Philly for Thanksgiving? A sudden benefit banished Ruby's dismay. Her plan to interview the lieutenant governor of Pennsylvania one month from now was clearly meant to be—not that Tony needed to know anything about that. In fact, if he found out, they wouldn't be going anywhere near Philly.

Ruby met her thoughtful reflection in the mirror. "Sure, that sounds okay."

A beat of silence answered her response. "Did you hear me right? I said, maybe we should go to Mama's for Thanksgiving." He enunciated each word.

"Yeah, why not?" She took one last look at the tester before hiding it under the sink in a tampon box, where Tony wouldn't come across it.

A subtle *click* of the lock had her slamming the cabinet shut and straightening guiltily as the door cracked open. Tony peered through the scant opening, his chocolate-brown eyes locking on her guilty expression.

Heat flooded her face. "I've told you not to do that! A woman needs her privacy."

His gaze searched the bathroom before returning to her self-righteous glare.

Ruby's toes curled inside of her high-heeled shoes.

He pushed the door farther open. "You're honestly okay with having Thanksgiving at my mother's?"

She forced herself to hold his gaze. Tony's eyelashes were so thick and dark it looked like he wore eyeliner. The first time they'd met, she thought he looked just like Joey Tribbiani from the sitcom *Friends*, but Joey didn't have Tony's lush eyelashes.

"Yeah, I'm okay with it." Unable to lie to his face, she leaned toward the sink to inspect her complexion.

Tony's eyebrows pulled together. "Then you've forgiven Mama's remark about your skinny hips?"

Ruby forced a negligent shrug even as the reminder stung her pride. "What's to forgive? She was upset that she'd missed our wedding. It's only natural that she would lash out about it."

"But she said some pretty hurtful things."

Anna's exact words had been that *it was time Ruby quit her job, put some meat on her skinny hips, and start being the wife that Tony deserved.*

"She wants grandbabies." Ruby managed to face Tony, adding magnanimously, "Who can blame her?" Guilt wrung her within, as she realized she could now make Anna's dreams come true. But she had no intention of sharing that happy news—not yet, anyway.

Her answer banished the suspicion in Tony's eyes. He put his arms around her, pulling her closer. "Yeah, maybe we can work on that before you go to work this morning."

His seductive voice had an immediate tingling effect on her body, but the musky sweat still dampening his T-shirt from his morning run prompted Ruby to squirm free.

"You're going to soil my work clothes."

"Just a kiss then." He caught her jaw before she got away, crushing his lips to hers.

As the kiss deepened, goose bumps played tag along Ruby's

skin. By the time he lifted his head, her bones seemed to be melting, and she was contemplating staying longer. She grabbed his wrist to read his watch. "Oh, shoot, I'm late."

"You're always late. What's another half hour?"

"No, seriously, I have to go. My new boss is making us sign in."

On the verge of slipping under his arm and out of the room, Ruby pressed a heartfelt kiss to her husband's cheek. "I love you so much." Tears stung her eyes.

His eyebrows quirked. "I love you, too."

She fled before he could pursue the question she'd heard in his voice. Tony knew her like nobody else did, even better than her sister. If he guessed her circumstances, if he knew she was carrying their baby, he would talk her into quitting her job and staying at home.

Over my dead body.

Exiting the bathroom swiftly, Ruby went to collect her purse and jacket from the hall closet. Being lead investigative reporter gave her the self-respect she desperately craved. Just three short years ago, she'd been indulging in pastimes that were self-destructive and living with her sister because she couldn't support herself waitressing.

And then Tony Caruso had come along. He might have been barely out of his teens and three years younger than she was, but he'd had his act together—a sound work ethic, a career in the Navy, and a long-term goal of becoming a doctor. He'd taught her to believe in God. He'd inspired her to improve herself. Finally, she felt like she was worthy of him, but only because of her job.

When he found out she was pregnant, that would change—not just because Tony would insist she alter her priorities but also because being pregnant would ruin her career.

Maybe I won't tell Tony.

The thought sneaked into her brain as she backed her cherry-red Range Rover out of their carport, careful not to sideswipe

Tony's Honda in the process. She could visit a clinic somewhere and quietly— *Oh, God, no.*

She squashed the notion almost as soon as it occurred to her.

Shame made her swallow hard as she tugged the gearshift and pulled forward onto Shore Drive in Virginia Beach, headed for the highway that would take her toward the adjacent city of Norfolk. There was no excuse for her even thinking like this. She and Tony had the means to care for a baby. And Tony, despite his young age and his plans to enter medical school, would make a terrific father. The problem was Ruby.

Maybe she could negotiate.

"Okay, Lord. I'm not ready for a baby. I mean, You *have* to know this. I'll make a terrible mother. I'm too self-centered. And the fact is, there are even worse people than me out there, manipulating the system and crushing other people just because they can. If I don't catch those criminals and hold them accountable, who will? You need me for that. And I can't have a baby and still do what I do. Right?"

She flipped down her visor and peered into the lit mirror there half expecting God to speak through her reflection. What she saw was a professional young woman in a smart sage-green jacket and cream silk top. Her vivid red-gold hair was pinned up in a loose but elegant knot. Her turquoise eyes would pop as soon as she put on her makeup.

But all Ruby saw were faint lines at the corners of her eyes, marring her porcelain complexion. She would turn twenty-nine in December.

The clock—her biological clock—was ticking.

"No." Women were having babies well into their forties. She could cling to her career for another ten years before starting a family. This pregnancy would ruin *everything*.

Steering with one hand, she felt inside her purse for her makeup. Tony's chiding voice sounded in her head. *"Bella, you don't need to do that. You're perfect the way you are."*

His nickname for her meant "beautiful" in Italian, which he spoke, in his own words, "badly."

If only she saw herself the way Tony did.

She pulled the lid off her concealer, intending to cover up the circles under her eyes. What kind of chemicals and toxins was she putting on herself? Once at work, a makeup artist would put a ton of product on her, anyway.

Ruby stuck the lid back on the concealer and dropped it back into her purse. She might be an inherently selfish person, but she didn't need to expose the secret life inside her to more harmful chemicals than necessary—assuming the little tyke would be born in eight months, wreaking havoc on the satisfying career Ruby was enjoying.

CHAPTER 1

$\mathcal{T}$ony's mother still lived in the Italian neighborhood of Bella Vista in the same clapboard row house squeezed between two others just like it, except Mama Anna's was a pretty butter yellow instead of dishwater gray. The street, as always, was lined with parked cars and littered with debris. Whenever Ruby took in Tony's old stomping ground, she couldn't help but marvel at what he'd overcome.

"You're a saint," she stated as her husband parallel parked her Range Rover between two beaters.

He issued a startled laugh. "Hardly. What makes you say that?"

How she admired his humility. Not only had Tony resisted recruitment by the local gangs while growing up here, but he'd also helped to raise his little sister when their father ran off and his mother fell ill. "Most people are victims of their circumstances. But you always take the high road, Tony." Which was why she felt like such a loser in comparison.

His purely Italian shrug sloughed off her praise. "Nah, it's a choice. Everybody has a choice."

His words echoed in her head as he set the parking brake and punched the button that killed her engine. Worry furrowed his brow as he took in his former neighborhood. "We should'a brought my old Honda. Someone's gonna key your SUV out of jealousy."

"Well, that's why I hit Opal's mailbox." She nodded like she'd done it intentionally. "Now the dent in the rear fender makes it look like all the other cars."

Another laugh burst out of him. "Oh, that's why you hit the mailbox."

"Yep." Truth was, she'd persuaded Tony to drive her car up because she thought she might need wheels to keep her appointment with the lieutenant governor, and she had yet to learn to drive Tony's stick shift.

He cut her a look as he went to push his door open. "I know why you wanted to bring your Range Rover."

She hid a gasp of dismay. Tony was the most observant person she knew. It surprised her he hadn't asked about her two missed periods yet, but how could he have found out about Katz? "Oh?"

"So you could leave if Mama hurt your feelings."

Phew! "You know me too well."

Tony put reassuring a hand on Ruby's knee and gave it a squeeze. "She'll behave herself; I promise. Besides, Corinna's here to distract her." Nodding at his little sister's lime-green Escort, he pushed out of the driver's seat.

Corinna, now a theater major at Drexel University, was home for the holiday. Looking forward to seeing her, Ruby got out and went to the back to help Tony with the luggage.

A chilly breeze and the ubiquitous smell of sautéed onions filled the air. Tony gave her the smallest bag to carry, then shut the rear of the SUV and toted their two suitcases toward his old home's front stoop. The door popped open, and Mama Anna, with her cloud of graying curls and ample figure, emerged with her arms outstretched.

"Antonio *mio!*" She ignored Ruby to embrace her son, pulling him against her apron-clad bosom and pinning him there. If his shoulders weren't as wide as they were, Anna's embrace might have swallowed him whole. "Welcome, welcome," she crooned, kissing him on both cheeks.

At last, she set him away from her and met Ruby's gaze. The thread of tension between them snapped as she threw her arms wide and embraced her daughter-in-law with equal zeal. "Thank you for coming. I have cooked all day!" Her English was perfect, though faintly accented, having immigrated from Puglia with her parents in the 1970s. "Come in, come in! It's so cold outside."

She ushered them into the house ahead of her. She hadn't even closed the door behind them before the old staircase shuddered and Corinna Caruso, with her dark ringlets streaming behind her, blew down from the upper level and collided into Tony at a full run. But he was ready for her, swinging her around to keep from staggering backwards. "Hey, Sis! How's it goin'?"

"Couldn't be better." She beamed at them. "Hey, Ruby."

Ruby smiled back. "Hey."

Tony studied his sister. "Why are you glowin'? What's goin' on with you?"

"What, I'm not allowed to glow? Maybe I'm happy to see you."

"Humph." Mama Anna pursed her lips with disapproval. "Corinna has a boyfriend."

"Mama!" The eighteen-year-old's cherry-brown eyes flashed. "I told you not to tell."

"*Boyfriend,*" Tony spat out the word like it was something filthy. "What do you need a boyfriend for? You're a student. It's your job to study, not waste your time on some schmuck."

"Tony!" Ruby elbowed him aside to throw an arm of solidarity around her sister-in-law. "You can't tell Corinna what to do with her heart. So, who's the lucky guy?"

Corinna shot her a grateful smile. "His name is Robert and he's a philosophy major."

"Philosophy, hah." Tony scowled. "What's he gonna do with that degree?"

"Go to law school." Corinna arched a dark eyebrow at him.

"Oh." And suddenly Tony had no more to say on the subject.

"Enough talk." Mama Anna gestured grandly. "Take your stuff upstairs and come to the kitchen for food."

"We just had subs on the way up, Mama." Tony hefted a suitcase in each hand and started up the stairs to his old bedroom.

Ruby followed close behind him. This would be the first time his mother let them share a bed. Considering they were *finally* married—even though Anna hadn't been invited—she didn't have much choice.

Trailing Tony into the tiny front room, Ruby deposited her purse and cosmetics bag. She hadn't dared to bring her laptop or Tony would have guessed she was working on a story. Luckily, she didn't need her laptop. The facts pertaining to her investigation were filed away in her head.

If Tony had the slightest notion that she was on a deep-sea fishing expedition, angling for a really big tuna, he'd have refused his mother's invitation to Philly and swept her off to some remote island somewhere.

Two hours later, they sat at the kitchen table under the glow of a pendant lamp, while daylight faded over the tiny, enclosed garden in the backyard, where Anna grew her vegetables. Tony's mother stood near the sink, stuffing a twelve-pound turkey in preparation for tomorrow's feast. Corinna was describing the musical production at her university, in which she'd secured a leading role, while only just a freshman.

As she listened, Ruby plotted how to finagle time to herself the following morning. At least Tony would be busy fixing his mother's washer, as they'd discussed on their drive up, as well as questioning his mother about her health.

A decade earlier, Anna had required a valve replacement and, lately, she'd been complaining of fatigue. Tony wanted her to consult her cardiac surgeon, while also persuading her to let him pay her medical bills. Neither suggestion would be an easy sell.

All Ruby needed was a two-hour window in which to get downtown, conduct her scheduled interview with Lieutenant Governor Katz, then get back to the house. Considering the famed Philadelphia Thanksgiving parade would clog the roadways, it might take even longer. That thought prompted an idea.

She waited for Corinna to stop talking, then suggested, "Hey, let's go see the Thanksgiving parade tomorrow." The only drawback was having to involve Corinna in her plans. "You know it's the oldest ongoing parade in the country, right? I've never seen it."

Tony predictably frowned. "You know I don't like you bein' in a crowd, especially without me around. Why don't you just go to a movie or something?"

"On Thanksgiving morning? The theaters aren't even open. Besides, a parade will get us into the holiday spirit. I can't wait!"

Her expectant grin had the desired effect. Tony sighed and relented. "Fine. Just don't stand by any trash cans or planters."

"We won't." Remorse pinched her for misleading him. But, as much as she hated keeping secrets from her husband, what Tony didn't know couldn't hurt him. Besides, he was too protective, too prone to imagine bad things happening to her. This way, she could conduct her interview, and he'd never have to worry.

Later, when she managed to expose Lennard Katz for the liar that he was, Tony would realize what she'd done and when she'd done it, only it would be too late to scold her.

Better to ask forgiveness than permission. That'd been Ruby's MO all her life, and she didn't see any reason to switch things up at this juncture.

∽

Tony stretched out on the length of his childhood bed, his toes touching the footboard. The double bed felt tiny compared to the king-sized monstrosity they had at home, but contentment filled him as Ruby joined him for the first time in his mama's house, snuggling close to keep from falling off the edge.

"Finally, I get to have you in my own bed. This is so nice." He smoothed a hand up her trim tummy, his palm gliding over her silken nightgown when she stiffened against him. *What was that about?* "You doin' okay, Bella?"

"Yeah, sure." Her tone was overly bright.

Suspicion lanced him. Tony pushed himself up on one elbow while turning her face in his direction. Her jewel-like eyes were lit by the glow of both the city and the streetlamp pushing through his worn blue curtains. "Did my mother say somethin' to hurt your feelings again?"

"Not at all. I'm just thinking about the parade tomorrow, looking forward to it."

"Yeah?" He couldn't imagine what was so exciting about floats and bands and crowds but whatever. "Ready to gorge yourself afterward and put some meat on those skinny hips?"

The sound she made in her throat told him that his joke fell short.

Besides, her hips weren't skinny. They were smooth and shapely. Every curve of her body fit perfectly in his hands, which he set about proving to her as he went back to caressing her hourglass figure, petting her until she arched toward his touch, her breath coming in faster.

She needed warming up was all. Tony was up for that challenge. Making her skin blaze with heat thrilled him more than jumping out of airplanes. Ruby's passion was just one of the many things he loved about her. In fact, she never ceased to amaze him.

Sure, she could be a handful. Sure, she got herself regularly into trouble by butting heads with people in positions of authority and upending the status quo. But, with Ruby, there was never a dull moment.

Pulling her closer, he reveled in the bliss of becoming one with her. Ruby was his home. He belonged with her. God willing, he would get to come home to her again and again for the rest of his life.

She reached up, furrowing her fingers through his hair. "I love you so much, Tony."

She'd been saying that a lot lately. While he could never hear it enough, the words were starting to take on a portentous quality. Was something bad going to happen? Nah, it was just his paranoid mind playing tricks on him.

"I love you, too, Bella." God meant for them to be together forever. He was sure of that.

CHAPTER 2

*R*uby rubbed her hands together briskly, wishing she'd thought to bring gloves. The beat of a bass drum filled her ears, overlaid by the cacophony of trumpets as one marching band moved on and another tramped closer. Ruby winced as the minor key of "What Child Is This" clashed with the major key of "We wish You a Merry Christmas."

She and Corinna had arrived with the parade already in full swing. Still, they'd managed to find standing room among the crowd viewing the spectacle from the long run of steps made famous by the first *Rocky* movie and leading up to the Philadelphia Museum of Art, right where the parade ended. As float after float reached the finish line, each one more colorful than the last, Ruby began anticipating the Christmas season. Holiday motifs abounded, lifting her spirits.

I'll tell Tony about the baby at Christmas. Won't that make a nice present!

The decision warmed her heart. Now she had a good reason for keeping her secret.

As last, the final float came into view, marking the end of the parade. Owned by the city council, it touted a massive, brightly decorated Christmas tree that spired twenty feet into the air. At its base stood the mayor of Philadelphia, a swarthy Italian dressed in a Santa suit. As the crowd roared with appreciation for the event that was in its 104th year, the mayor blew kisses back at them, happy to accept credit for the festivities.

His appearance was Ruby's cue to rendezvous with Lieutenant Governor Lennard Katz in the office complex adjacent to the museum. They'd planned to meet once the parade was over, with Katz requesting to keep their interview brief, as he'd scheduled lunch with the mayor right afterward.

Ruby leaned toward Corinna, who was videotaping the mayor with the fancy digital camera Tony had given her for Christmas the prior year. "Hey, I forgot to tell you I'm supposed to interview someone right after this. It'll take me twenty minutes. Stay around here, and I'll find you when I'm done."

Corinna's eyes widened with alarm. "But the parade's over. Why can't I come with you?"

Maybe that was the better choice, as Tony wouldn't like her leaving his sister all alone. "Okay. Why not? Come on." Keeping a hand on Corinna's coat sleeve, Ruby followed the disbanding crowd down the museum steps and across the thronging street to an office complex leased by the environmental advocacy group, which Katz chaired.

As they approached the building, Ruby spotted a young man wearing a wool trench coat, his cheeks ruddy from the cold, watching her with a hopeful look. "Ruby Bonheur?" he asked as they neared him.

"Yes." She had kept her maiden name to keep from losing the notoriety she had gained before her marriage. Adopting the demeanor of a top-notch reporter, Ruby extended a hand. "And you are?"

"Dave Cullum. I'm Lieutenant Governor Katz's assistant. He's expecting you." His friendly smile faded as focused on Corinna. "I understood you'd be alone."

Ruby thought on her toes. "Oh, this is my camerawoman. With the lieutenant governor's permission, we'd like to film the interview."

Cullum's gaze fell to the Nikon camera hanging on a strap around Corinna's neck, and he shrugged. "It's up to him." He turned toward the double glass doors behind him. "Right this way."

They entered a wide, echoing stairwell, blessedly warmer than it was outside. Chatting about the weather and the vibrancy of the parade, they climbed a broad marble staircase to the second level, then coursed a quiet, unlit hallway to an open door. The room beyond it was obviously a boardroom.

As Ruby's gaze lit upon Len Katz, he rolled out of the chair he was lounging in and fixed a plastic-looking smile on his face. "Ah, here she is."

"I hope I didn't keep you." The man's physique was the first thing Ruby noted about him. He was built like Tony, only taller—a former Marine but still fit at fifty-four, with broad shoulders and long, sturdy legs. Following his twenty-year career in the military, he'd served briefly with the CIA, no more than a handful of years, about which nothing could be found, despite how hard Ruby had scoured the internet.

"Not at all. I just sat down. That was quite a parade, huh?" His slate-gray eyes swiveled in Corinna's direction.

Ruby made introductions. "This is my camerawoman, Corinna. She's an intern."

"I didn't realize you'd be filming me." Katz smoothed his still blond, but thinning hair. "I thought this was just a write-up for a Virginia newspaper."

Ruby had misled his secretary intentionally. "Well, no. I work for a television news station—WTKR. We're located in Norfolk with a large military population." And while she'd intended to record his answers in a voice memo on her phone, filming Katz's reactions might reveal his lies better than a voice recording ever could.

"I see." His plastic smile returned as he gestured to the seats around the table. "Should we have a seat or do this standing up?"

"Let's sit right here where the lighting is best." Ruby pulled out two chairs, positioning them to face the light shining through the windows. Then she shimmied out of her pale-peach swing coat to reveal her Jones of New York java-colored wool suit, paired with a cream silk blouse and tailored to show off her curves.

In her peripheral vision, she noted Katz's appreciative once-over. Tony hadn't seen what she'd been wearing when she left the house, as he'd already been down in the basement, hard at work repairing his mother's washer.

As she cast her coat over the table, she directed Corinna to stand to one side of the windows and await her cue.

Playing right along, Corinna moved to the right spot and fiddled with her camera settings.

Ruby smiled at Len Katz and sought to put him at ease—for now. "Did you bring your family with you?" Katz's offices were in Harrisburg, the state capital, an hour away. He was married, with a three-year-old son.

"No, they had to stay at home. My son has a bit of a cold."

"Oh, what a shame." She pursed her lips into a frown. "I bet your little boy would have loved the parade. That Santa Claus was very convincing."

They chatted for another minute before Ruby cued Corinna with a nod to start filming. "Well, thank you for taking time out of your busy schedule to meet me, Lieutenant Governor." She pivoted her body forty degrees toward his, set one elbow on the back of her chair, and cocked her head slightly, keeping her body language receptive.

"My pleasure." Katz brandished his false smile, his gaze dipping toward her cleavage.

After tucking a curl behind one pearl-studded earlobe, Ruby

launched into introductions for the viewer and offered up standard questions, which the former Marine answered with practiced ease. He was just beginning to look comfortable when she brought up his service in the CIA. "Is it true you worked for the CIA after your retirement from the military?"

The split-second pause on his part betrayed a reticence to touch on the subject. "Well, yes. I discovered that retirement didn't suit me, and I still wished to serve my country."

Another practiced answer. She zeroed in for the kill. "But you were only in the CIA for six years. Why would you quit so early on?"

"Well, I realized I could do more for Americans by working in politics."

Here goes. "Then your decision had nothing to do with an operation in Dishu that went terribly wrong?"

The glint entering his gimlet eyes had an instant cooling effect on Ruby's skin as he stared at her, perhaps just now realizing she wasn't your average, everyday reporter. He shook his head. "I'm sorry, but I don't know what you're talking about."

Ruby touched a finger to her chin, as if searching her memory. "August of 2016, I believe it was. Your mission was to snuff out a top Taliban official, Gabir al Baldawi, who operated in the Helmand Province. He was supposed to be holed up in a private home on the west side of Dishu. You and a squad of Navy SEALs raided the building, only al Baldawi wasn't there, just five or so civilians, including a boy and his mother who ended up dead."

Len Katz had stiffened with every word coming out of her mouth. "Who told you this?" His expression remained pleasant, baffled, but his voice had cooled several degrees.

Ruby shrugged. "Like I said, I live in a military community, and that's the rumor circulating. Can you confirm or deny the story? Maybe you could clarify what went wrong?"

Katz's lips thinned and his jaw hardened. "There's not an ounce of truth to that story. I don't know where you get your information, but I'd advise you not to listen to rumors that aren't true."

"Mm." Ruby nodded with false sympathy. "So, this is just another attempt to discredit you in the eyes of the public?" She strove for a sympathetic expression. "I imagine it's because you're a candidate for the vice presidency and your opponent has made up the story hoping to ruin your reputation."

"Exactly." He seized on to her excuse immediately. "The opposition will say anything to discredit me. I assure you I have never taken part in any military operation that I wasn't proud of. Of course, I'm not at liberty to talk about those days, but my conscience is clear. I don't believe in keeping secrets."

"I didn't think so." She sent him her most charming smile, while nodding toward Corinna to signify that they were nearly done. "It's been a pleasure interviewing you, sir. I hope we can do it again sometime." She stretched out a hand for him to squeeze and noted his fingers felt distinctly clammy. The next time they spoke, she vowed she would have the proof to call him a liar. Any man who lied to cover up a murder had no business becoming the vice president of the United States. "Enjoy your lunch with the mayor." She pushed to her feet.

"I will." Katz rose also.

Gesturing for Corinna to join her, Ruby threaded her arms quickly through the sleeves of her coat as she started for the door. "Have a wonderful Thanksgiving, gentlemen. Oh, thank you, Mr. Cullum."

The friendly assistant had darted forward to pull the door open.

"We'll see ourselves out."

With a glance toward his boss, Cullum nodded. "Oh, sure. Okay. Bye."

Katz must have gestured for his assistant to stay behind with him. Ruby kept her satisfied grin contained until the door between them closed. She had hooked her big tuna. All she had to do now was to reel him in.

CHAPTER 3

*C*atching Corinna's arm, Ruby halted their progress toward the stairs and tugged her sister-in-law in the opposite direction—past the room they'd just left. "Let's wait here," she whispered, pulling Corinna around the corner with her and out of sight.

"Why?" Corinna's suspicious frown was identical to one Tony often wore.

"I want to hear what they're saying on the way out."

"But what if they catch us?" The young woman's voice conveyed dread.

"We'll say you had to use the ladies' room."

"Me?"

"You're an intern. Interns do stupid things."

Corinna rolled her eyes and huffed out a breath.

Down the hall, the office door clicked open. Ruby peeked around the corner, then quickly pulled her head back. The lieutenant governor was stepping out of the room with David Cullum on his heels, looking distinctly red-faced, like Katz had chewed him out.

"I want to know who's talking to her." Katz's lowered voice just reached Ruby's ears. "Another of the SEALs has gone back on his word."

"I thought we took care of the leak," his staff member muttered.

"Quiet! Don't ever mention that again." Footsteps echoed on the stairs, fading as they descended. The big door at the bottom clanged shut, leaving nothing but silence.

Ruby rounded on Corinna. "Did you hear that?" She resisted the urge to jump for joy. "He knew exactly what incident I was talking about." Now all she needed was for one of the SEALs in the firing squad to back her up. Only that would involve twisting the arms of two of Tony's teammates, who had a tendency to clam up around her.

"We gotta get out of here."

Corinna's anxiety diminished Ruby's triumph. "Yeah, yeah. In ten minutes or so, once we know they're good and gone."

Corinna elbowed her sharply. Looking over, Ruby found her companion staring at the discreet, domed camera overhead.

"Someone could be watching us right now." Corinna hugged her slender frame and gulped. "I can't afford to get arrested. I'll lose my scholarship, maybe even get thrown out of school."

Doubt overtook Ruby's contentment. "Well, you're the one who insisted on tagging along. Fine," she amended at Corinna's outraged glance. "We're leaving. The secret to not getting caught is to look like you belong. Shoulders back, head up. Let's go."

Together they marched down the hall toward the stairs the men had taken, but two silhouettes remained visible through the double-glass doors at the bottom. Both women gasped and quickly retraced their steps.

"Let's find another way out." Ruby marched ahead of Corinna as she searched the maze of hallways for another set of stairs.

At the back of the building, they discovered a fire exit and took it to the lower level. Their footsteps faltered as they both read the sign beside the door warning an alarm would go off if the door was opened.

Corinna whirled on her. "Great! What do we do now?"

Ruby envisioned their escape. "We'll make a run for it. The streets are crawling with people. Who's going to see us if we blend into the crowd?"

"Oh, help." Corinna rubbed her forehead.

Guilt wrung Ruby for causing her sister-in-law such distress. "Listen, we had every right to be in the building, and now we're leaving. It's no big deal. Come on. Just follow my lead. Act casual."

Throwing her weight into the door, she pulled Corinna out into the cold with her. In the same instant, a high-pitched wail floated from the stairwell, alerting the world to their exodus.

Ruby grabbed Corinna's hand and towed her straight into the crowd headed toward the art museum. Corinna's fingernails dug into the back of Ruby's hand, but no one pursued them. No one shouted, "Hey, wait!"

"See, I told you we'd be fine." Prying free of Corinna's death grip, Ruby led the way past the steps toward the far side of the museum. It was there they had parked Corinna's car, in the hotel parking garage where her boyfriend worked as a valet.

Corinna had fallen thoughtfully silent. At last, she looked over at Ruby, one slim eyebrow raised. "Let me guess. You don't want Tony knowing anything about this."

"Right. And if you tell him," Ruby searched her mind for something to hold over Corinna's head, "I won't take you to see *Hamilton* when you visit over Christmas break."

Corinna's jaw dropped and her eyes widened. "You got us tickets for *Hamilton*?"

Well, she hadn't done it yet, but she had every intention of buying tickets to the famed musical, which was coming to Chrysler Hall. Hopefully there were still some tickets left. "Yes."

"Oh my gosh, you are such a great sister-in-law. Crazy but great." Corinna grabbed up her arm as they proceeded to their destination. Her expression grew reflective. "And, by the way, that guy was totally lying when he said that story was just a rumor, wasn't he?"

Ruby smiled thinly. "He admitted it on the way out. Now all I have to do is prove he killed that boy and his mother." There had to be some way to get Tony's teammates to talk.

"You hear that?" On the verge of climbing into his sleek, black Genesis G90, Len Katz stared back at the high-rise building they'd just come from.

"It sounds like the alarm's going off." His assistant appeared nonplussed.

"Why would the alarm be going off? We were the last ones to leave the building."

"Maybe we weren't." Collum pointed toward the crowd emerging from behind the building. "Look. That's the reporter and her intern. What if they just snuck out the fire exit?"

Searching the crowd, Len finally spotted the reporter by her bright-copper curls. He narrowed his eyes. Why the sneaky little vixen! To what purpose had she hidden in the building following their interview? Suspicion furrowed into him. Had she only pretended to empathize about the circulating rumor when, in fact, she'd eavesdropped in the hopes of hearing something incriminating? He recollected Cullum's and his conversation on the way out.

Oh, heavens, Cullum had mentioned the leak they'd already addressed! He himself had said the word "SEALs."

Hurling a curse at his assistant, Len shoved him in the women's direction. "Don't take your eyes off them! Follow them on foot and call my cell when you know which way she's headed." He ducked into the back seat of his car and slammed his door shut behind him. "Mason, drive straight ahead, slowly, and await my orders."

As his elderly Black chauffeur pulled into traffic, Len gripped the seat in front of him, leaving off his seat belt to retain a 180-degree field of sight. Not two minutes later, his cell phone buzzed. "Which way?" he demanded, recognizing Cullum's number.

"They're crossing Pennsylvania Avenue, heading toward Fairmount." Cullum huffed as he tried to catch up.

Len ordered Mason to turn right at the next intersection. The roads were jammed with cars leaving the parade. They couldn't do more than creep forward one yard at a time. "Stay on the line with me, Cullum. Don't let them get away without finding out where that reporter's staying."

"Maybe at the Best Western. She's headed right toward it. Or, maybe not," Cullum added a minute later. "They're going into the parking garage."

Len raked an eye over the façade of the monstrous hotel in front of him. "Where's the parking garage?"

"Right side of the hotel as you face the entrance." Cullum was full-out panting now.

"We'll wait outside for her. Stay on the phone." He ordered Mason to pull into a handicapped parking space along the curb. Cullum would blow it for him if he showed his face. "Don't let her see you. If she drives by you, duck or something. You've done enough damage for one day."

Cullum's dismay was reflected in his silence. Then, finally, "Okay, they're getting into a lime-green Escort. Yes, they're leaving now. You can't miss them when they pull out."

"Back off and wait outside the parking garage. We'll collect you on our way by."

"Yes, sir."

Len put his phone away. Blood thrummed through his arteries; a muscle ticked in his cheek. Operation Lights Out had haunted him from the night it totally backfired. He didn't know if he'd trusted the wrong people or if the assets he'd courted for six months prior to the operation had betrayed him, but either way, he'd messed up.

Gabir al Baldawi hadn't been in the apartment building surrounded by his closest advisors. Instead, the place had been occupied by nothing but civilians. In his outrage, Len had shot some kid who wouldn't stop wailing. The bullet had gone straight through the boy killing his mother, too—so what? Things happened. He'd persuaded the SEALs in his firing squad to report the incident as an accident—either that or it'd be his word against theirs. They'd only agreed to keep silent if *he* agreed to leave the Agency.

He'd done as they demanded, so why were they betraying him now? Jealousy, no doubt. Maybe they didn't want him becoming their vice president in a year's time.

The vision of a bright-green Escort pulled him out of a cold sweat. "Follow that little green car, Mason." He pointed to it.

As his chauffeur accelerated from the curb, Len spared a glance at Cullum, who hovered just outside the parking garage, expecting to be picked up. The Escort, meanwhile, gained speed, threatening to slip out of sight.

"Leave him," Len decided. Ignoring Cullum's look of dismay, he focused his attention on keeping the smaller car in sight.

Two intersections away, the lime-green Escort turned right onto Arch Street and disappeared. "Drive faster."

They turned the corner just in time to see the Escort veering toward South Broad. When they caught sight of it again, it was turning left onto Christian Street, making its way into the old Italian neighborhood of Bella Vista.

A block ahead of them, it parallel parked in front of a series of row homes. "Pull over, quick. Don't let them see us."

Mason swung the front of the Genesis into the nearest alley, leaving the back end sticking out. Craning to see out the rear window, Len peered down the street in time to see the two women hurry from their vehicle into a clapboard home, painted pale yellow. He waited another five minutes to see if they would emerge again. When they didn't, he instructed Mason to continue down the street.

The number on the door made it easy to find again—769. Now he knew where the reporter was staying.

"Sorry for the detour, Mason." Len sat back in his seat, finally putting on his seat belt. "We can return for Cullum now."

With his jaw muscles jumping, he pondered what to do about the journalist. If he let her live, she might ruin his bid for the vice presidency. He would have to silence her the way he'd silenced the Navy SEAL threatening to expose him. And what about the intern? She was probably too young to be a threat. Certainly, nothing he'd said on camera could be used to implicate him. He could probably let her be. Besides, getting rid of people in ways that couldn't be traced back to him cost a pretty penny. Ruby Bonheur's disappearance would put him back twenty thousand dollars. *Blast it!*

As they slowed at a stop sign, Len roused from his dark thoughts and glanced at his watch. He swore aloud this time. "Now I'm late for lunch with the mayor!"

CHAPTER 4

ony emerged from the basement, intent on washing up for the Thanksgiving meal when the words *former Navy SEAL* had him turning toward the tiny television perched on one end of the kitchen counter. Ruby, Corinna, and his mother heard it, too. The kitchen, already filled with the aroma of roasting turkey, fell quiet as they all turned their attention to the news story.

". . . The rash of break-ins attributed to a gang of teens resulted in his death. John Staskiewicz left the Navy SEALs six years ago, returning to Fishtown, the neighborhood he grew up in." The photograph of a handsome bearded man in fatigues appeared on the upper-right side of the screen. "This is the first time the break-ins have resulted in murder. According to the autopsy, Staskiewicz was shot in the head while sleeping. Anyone with information pertaining to his death is requested to call the police. Back to you, Chris."

As the anchorman moved on to a new topic, Ruby turned three-quarters to send Tony a searching look. "Did you know him, honey?"

Tony shook his head while wiping the incredulity off his face. "No, not personally." He could have sworn, however, that he'd just seen the distinct name Staskiewicz written somewhere.

As he cast his thoughts back, the memory came to him of a return label affixed to a rectangular box that had been sitting on one corner of his commander's desk just the other day. Had to be the same Staskiewicz, and now he was dead. But if the police thought some young petty thieves had shot a trained Navy SEAL in his sleep, they were seriously misled. Tony filed away the incident to discuss with Commander Monteague later in the day.

"Food's almost ready, Antonio. Go wash." His mama shooed him out of the kitchen.

Ruby trailed him into the empty hallway. "Did you manage to fix it?"

He pictured the washing machine he'd worked on all morning while showing her the grease under his nails. "Not really. I gotta get a new part tomorrow when the stores reopen, but at least I know what's wrong. It needs a new tub bearing. Then the cylinder won't wobble like it's demon possessed."

"You're so clever." Ruby slipped her arms around him, using the embrace to whisper, "Did she say anything about her health?"

Figuring out the problem with the washer had been easy. Getting his mother to admit that her heart might be causing the fatigue she complained of wasn't. "Not really. She tried telling me she was just getting old. When I said I'd pay for her doctor visits, she went all quiet on me." Ruby didn't seem to be listening too intently. "How was the parade?"

"Amazing."

Her averted gaze revived the suspicion that she was hiding something. He searched her pretty face for clues, but she released him, going back into the kitchen to help his mama before he could ask her any more questions. With a shrug, Tony hurried upstairs to shower and change.

By the time he rejoined the women, the only table in the house, just big enough for four, had been set with a lace tablecloth and porcelain dishware brought from Puglia by Tony's grandparents. Their Thanksgiving feast was set out along the kitchen counter, buffet-style.

"Cut the turkey, Tony," Mama ordered. "It's time to eat."

Tony obliged, slicing up the turkey with a knife in bad need of sharpening. Mama led them in a blessing, and then they piled their plates with food and sat down to enjoy it.

His mother glanced critically at Ruby's plate. "That's all you're gonna eat?"

Ruby looked down at her meal and up at Tony. She had loaded up on green beans and white meat, the kind of lean foods she usually ate to keep her figure trim for the cameras.

He rushed to intervene. "She'll get seconds, Mama. Have some cranberry sauce on your meat," he suggested, passing Ruby the cut-glass relish plate.

Ruby took it with an inscrutable expression, dished up a spoonful of sauce, and plopped it next to her meat.

"Potatoes," Mama insisted, still frowning. "How're you supposed to make babies when you're so skinny?"

"Mama," Tony interjected on a warning note.

Corinna piped up, "I'll eat her portion of the potatoes. And her portion of pie, too."

"Oh no you don't." Ruby surprised them by jumping up and spooning a heaping mound of mashed potatoes onto her plate, before dousing it with gravy. Tony held his breath as she retook her seat. Was she playing games? Calling his mama's bluff?

To his surprise, she proceeded to eat every last bite of food on her plate. She even had a slice of pumpkin pie.

An hour later, they lay across his bed, too replete to do anything but take a nap. Ruby lay with her head on Tony's chest, talking on her cell phone to her sister and then to her two-and-a half-year-old nephew, Ryan, who was astonishingly verbal for a toddler.

Tony wanted to speak to his commander. "Is Monty there?"

With a curious glance at him, Ruby asked Opal if she could put her husband on the phone, and then she relinquished the call to Tony.

"Evening, sir." Tony greeted his SEAL Team Six commander with a mix of familiarity and formality. As his brother-in-law, he got to call him Monty, but never on Dam Neck Naval Annex where the team trained. "How was your Thanksgiving?"

"Great. And yours?"

"Excellent. My mama outdid herself this year."

"So did Opal. We've got my folks visiting."

"That's what I heard." He cut to the chase. "Actually, I have a question for you. Did you ever know a SEAL named John Staskiewicz?"

The silence on Monty's end supplied an answer even before his CO confirmed it. "We served in Afghanistan together. Why do you ask?"

"You know he's dead, right?"

"What?"

Tony cringed at the dismay in Monty's voice. "I'm sorry. I just heard it on the news."

"How'd he die?"

"Good question. According to the media up here, he was shot in his sleep by a gang of teens who've been breaking into houses, but you know as well as I do that's not likely." Realizing that his wife was listening avidly to their conversation, Tony transferred the cell phone to his other ear so she couldn't hear Monty's response.

"When was this?" The CO sounded more suspicious now than dismayed.

"Probably two nights ago since they already did an autopsy. I, uh, I saw his name on that box on your desk." Tony held his breath at the confession.

Monty went strangely silent. "Listen, Bambino."

Tony could hear him withdrawing to a private area of his house. Bambino had been Tony's code name in the Teams ever since he became the youngest SEAL to graduate from Basic Underwater Demolition/SEAL training.

"What I'm about to tell you stays between the two of us. Can Ruby overhear us?"

Glancing down at Ruby, Tony saw that her eyes were closed. She was pretending to doze, but, knowing her, she was straining to overhear every word. He doubted she could hear James's voice, but he thumbed down the volume, just in case. "No, sir."

"I worked with John Staskiewicz about ten years ago, as did Chief Harmony and a SEAL named Saul Wade. The four of us formed a firing squad sent to Dishu to eliminate a high-profile Taliban chief. We were working under the direction of a CIA case officer, who must have gotten his intelligence wrong because the target wasn't in the building when we hit it, just a bunch of families, mostly women and kids. One kid wouldn't stop crying and the case officer wigged out and shot him. The bullet went through the kid and killed the mother, too."

"Whoa." The visual in Tony's head sickened him. If Ruby hadn't been listening intently earlier, his reaction guaranteed she was listening now. He turned down the volume one more notch.

"The case officer then threatened to turn the tables on us if we reported him, so we made him a deal. We'd write off the incident as an accident, so long as *he* promised to leave the Agency. We figured that would be the end of it. Unfortunately for everyone, he went into politics, and now he's the lieutenant governor of Pennsylvania, Lennard Katz."

"No way." Tony let his incredulity show.

"What's more, he's on the short list to becoming our next vice president. When Staskiewicz realized Katz's political ambitions, he decided to go back on his word and write an exposé. And now you're telling me he's dead."

Tony struggled to digest that a politician determined to protect his reputation had murdered the former SEAL. "So, what are you going to do with that box, sir?" Monty hadn't said as much, but Tony guessed it contained the dead SEAL's exposé.

"Well, I could just turn it over to NCIS, but Katz has so many powerful people in his back pocket, nothing would probably come of it. I guess *The Washington Post* is my best route. I'll have to think about that. Anyway, thanks for telling me about John. He was a solid guy." James blew out a breath on his end. "I'm going to make some phone calls and try to find out where and when his funeral will take place. I'd like to attend it."

"Probably be up here in Fishtown where he lived. It's not far from my mother's house."

"Yeah, Stasky had a similar accent to yours."

Tony could hear the sorrow in James's voice. "I'm sorry about the news, sir."

"Thanks. It's sobering, but I appreciate you telling me. See you Monday."

"Hooyah." As Tony lowered the phone from his ear, Ruby's head popped up. He'd known she wasn't sleeping.

She propped a hand under her chin and searched his gaze avidly. "How well did James know him?"

Tony feigned ignorance. "Know who?"

"The SEAL who was killed, of course. Did they work together?"

Tony shrugged. "He said he'd worked with the guy back in Afghanistan."

"Hmm." She didn't look too surprised to hear it.

With only twenty-five hundred active-duty SEALs worldwide, most SEALs had at least heard of each other.

"But he didn't know this Stasky guy was murdered till you told him," she accurately guessed.

"Staskiewicz," Tony supplied. "It's Polish."

"Right. And Staskiewicz gave James a box? Any idea what's in it?"

Tony heaved an exasperated sigh and closed his eyes. "You know I can't talk about this."

"But this is a civilian matter because Staskiewicz retired from the Teams, and *then* he was killed. The only reason why you couldn't talk about his death was if it related in some way to— Oh. It *is* a military matter."

He opened his eyes again. "Yeah. And like I said, I can't talk about it."

"Then I'll torture you until you do talk." With a determined look on her face, Ruby delved a hand under his shirt and proceeded to tickle him.

Tony didn't so much as flinch. "You can't break me. I've been trained to resist interrogation."

"Oh yeah?" She jumped to her knees and redoubled her efforts.

Tony bore the torture for as long as he could stand it. Bursting into laughter, he grabbed her wrists, flipped her onto her back, and rolled on top of her.

"Oh." To his alarm, she blanched, then whispered, "I have to throw up."

He lifted his weight off her, watching with concern as she hung her head over the edge of the bed while covering her mouth.

"Trash can!" Tony sprang out of bed to retrieve it. By the time he shoved it under her, she was drawing deep breaths, some of her color returning.

"I'm okay now. I think I just ate too much."

He left the basket by the bed just in case, then sat next to her. "You didn't have to eat that much just to please Mama, you know."

"I know." She averted her gaze and gnawed her lower lip, making him think she might say something more on the subject of his mama's overbearing attitude. "I'd better take a nap," she declared, instead. "All that turkey made me sleepy."

"Tryptophan. You're not the only one." He crawled back over her, putting his back against the wall and pulling the blanket over them.

With a contented little sigh, Ruby snugged closer as he spooned her. "You sure you won't tell me what James said?"

Tony smiled a little. "You're relentless. Listen, I'm gonna put that new part in Mama's washer tomorrow morning, and then I think we should head home by noon to beat the traffic." Ruby stiffened in his embrace. "What, you want to stay longer?"

"I'm thinking we should go to the Staskiewicz's funeral first, if it's this weekend."

"Why? I never knew him."

"But James did. You should go to represent the Teams."

Since when had manifesting solidarity mattered to Ruby? "We'll see. What would you do tomorrow if we don't leave till Saturday or Sunday?"

"I'll take Corinna to Macy's tomorrow for their Black Friday sales. Maybe I can get all our Christmas shopping done early."

"Hmm." She'd never been one to do anything early. "Just be careful out there on the streets. Remember this city is bigger than what you're used to. You know how easily you get lost."

"Macy's is a mile and a half away, Tony, and Corinna will be with me. I can't possibly get lost."

"Well, keep your phone turned on so I can find you." The best thing he'd ever done was put Ruby on his cell phone plan. It gave him peace of mind to know he could find her anywhere with the Find My service.

"Stalker." Ruby's slurred reply was scarcely comprehensible. In the next instant, her slow, shallow breaths suggested she was sleeping.

CHAPTER 5

*C*orinna heaved a sigh, prompting Ruby to look over at her from the driver's seat. With the heater in Corinna's little car on the fritz, Ruby had decided to drive her Range Rover. "What's wrong?"

Corinna lifted the phone in her hand to show her a text. "Robert was just told to take the day off."

On the verge of pulling her SUV away from the curb at Mama Anna's, Ruby considered her sister-in-law's long face. "You want to cancel our shopping trip so you can be with him?"

"No, no. Tony wouldn't want me to ditch you."

"Hmm." Considering her options, Ruby proceeded to pull into the street, headed in the direction of Macy's. The drooping corners of Corinna's lips made her recall how desperately she had longed to spend time with Tony back when they were dating. "Well, what if Tony never found out?" She glanced over at Corinna as they neared an intersection.

Her cherry-brown eyes had widened hopefully. "What do you have in mind?"

Slowing down only slightly, Ruby looked both ways before

gunning through the four-way stop. *Shoot.* She really needed to improve her driving habits for the baby's sake. But the rusty Volvo behind her also ran the stop sign, lessening her remorse.

She glanced back at Corinna. "How about I drop you off somewhere close to Macy's? Robert can meet you there, and you two can hang out while I shop. Then I'll pick you up again on my way home, and Tony will assume we spent the morning together." With an impulse to browse the maternity section, she had good reason for wanting to shop alone. "We won't even have to lie to him."

Corinna bit her lower lip, thinking. "Well, there's a Starbucks right around the corner from Macy's. Maybe Robert and I could hang out there."

"Perfect." Ruby sent the car riding her bumper a dirty look. "I turn right here, don't I?" she asked as she neared a stoplight.

"No, not yet. Two more blocks. Are you sure about this? I don't want you to feel neglected or anything."

"Sure, I'm sure. I remember what it's like to be in *love*." She waggled her eyebrows at her sister-in-law.

Corinna smirked back at her. "That's because you and Tony are still in love."

Ruby hummed her agreement. "True." But then doubt nagged at her. How might a baby change Tony's and her relationship? They hardly had any time together as it was.

Seeing the next light about to turn red, she slowed down instead of speeding up, and the Volvo nearly plowed into her back end. She started to whip her head around to glare at the driver, but then she remembered how she'd met Tony—by crashing into the back of *his* Honda. It wasn't that long ago that she'd ridden people's bumpers.

Should I have told him about the baby last night?

The question tormented her as she waited for the light to turn green. She'd been too distracted by how Staskiewicz's murder tied in so neatly with her exposé on Katz. Even though Tony kept turning down the volume, she'd overheard enough of James's words to fire her imagination. What were the odds that Staskiewicz was part of the firing squad, along with Monty and Ben Harmony?

Corinna looked up from her iPhone, flushed with anticipation. "Robert says great. He can meet me at Starbucks in five minutes. Just turn right at the next light and it's on the right side."

Ruby followed her directions, and soon they were nearing the familiar green Starbuck's sign. The long line at the drive-through was blocking the entrance.

"You want to just drop me off?"

"Sure, but you'll have to give me directions to Macy's." Ruby flipped on her turn signal, hoping the Volvo that still dogged her would finally pass. Instead, it stopped right behind her as she pulled up next to the cars parked along the curb.

Corinna pointed. "Okay, so turn left right there at the corner. That's the Wanamaker Building where Macy's is. Go past the main entrance and look for the Wanamaker garage that's underneath the building. There should still be parking this early in the morning." Pushing her door open, Corinna hesitated. "You sure you won't get lost?"

"I'm sure. Out you go. Say hi to Robert for me."

"Okay. Call me when you're almost finished, and I'll come to you, so you don't have to circle back. You have my number, right?"

"Of course." Frustrated with the Volvo, Ruby stuck her hand out of her window and waved for the driver to go around her. Instead, he beeped his horn at her. "What a jerk!"

The instant Corinna shut her passenger door, Ruby punched the accelerator, determined to shake the annoying driver off her tail.

Ten minutes later, she had yet to find a parking spot. Nor had she managed to distance herself from the Volvo that pursued her as she circled the parking garage, going down, down, down into the very bowels of the Wanamaker Building. The Volvo finally vanished from her rearview mirror. *Good riddance!*

At last Ruby spotted an empty space that had been shunned by other drivers since it butted up against a cinder-block wall, making it hard to turn into. Confident of her parking abilities, she swung wide and eased her SUV between the wall and a white Cadillac.

"Hah. I win." She killed her engine, unlatched her seat belt, and lifted her purse off the floor. Before slipping out of her SUV, intent on some serious shopping, she verified that her phone was turned on, her ringer set on high.

She locked her SUV and started up the sloped garage ramp, headed for the elevator that would take her up to Macy's. As her gaze alighted on the prominent forehead of the driver of the Volvo locking up his own vehicle, her steps slowed.

When he glanced over, she summoned an uncomfortable smile. "Oh, good. You found a spot. That one's even better than mine."

He acknowledged her words with a nod and nothing else.

A cagey feeling danced over Ruby's skin as she noted the man's tense jaw, his rigid stance. This was not your normal, easygoing holiday shopper. Unwilling to get into an elevator alone with him, she pretended to have forgotten something, threw her hands up, and started back toward her Range Rover.

She hadn't taken three steps when the sound of running feet had her looking back in alarm. The man crashed into her, banding an arm around her from behind. Ruby shrieked as he lifted her against his broad chest and jabbed something sharp into her upper arm, straight through the material of her swing coat.

With a gasp she looked down. A syringe glinted in the man's gloved hand as he withdrew it, tossing it down onto the cement floor. Shock kept her frozen.

He just stuck a needle in my arm!

He snatched her purse from her limp grasp and tucked it under his arm, then dragged her toward her Range Rover. The heels of her boots scraped over concrete.

I'm being abducted! The realization encased her in ice. It paralyzed her. Or maybe it was the drug because her field of sight was shrinking. With her vision tunneling, she willed herself to scream. But nothing more than a whimper issued from her throat.

Finding her keys in her purse, the stranger unlocked all four doors of her Range Rover, as if he owned it.

Fight him! Tony had taught her dozens of ways to defend herself, but her body refused to cooperate. Her head, too heavy to hold up, dropped onto the man's shoulder.

The ceiling of the parking garage became the ceiling of her SUV as her attacker lowered her onto the rear seat. He grunted, pushing her farther into her car across the trundle seat in the middle, until he could bend her legs and stuff her feet inside, shutting her in.

Ruby lay on her right hip with one foot dangling over the edge of the seat. A seat belt buckle gouged her rib cage. Her head was propped against an armrest.

Stay awake! she ordered herself.

The part of her brain still capable of functioning came to an appalling conclusion: This wasn't some random abduction. This had to do with her interview with Katz yesterday—she just knew it.

He's going to kill me!

That certainty preceded utter darkness. *Tony!* Her heart cried out in remorse. God forgive her. She ought to have told him the truth—not just the truth about her interview with Katz but also the truth about their baby. Now, he would never guess what had become of her, unless Corinna gave him clues.

Oh, Corinna, please tell Tony. Tell him everything!

CHAPTER 6

*C*orinna checked her cell phone, only to frown at the empty display. It was 12:15 P.M., and Ruby had yet to call her. They'd promised Tony they'd be home by noon. At this rate, they would return late, making her brother worry for no reason.

"I'd better call her." She released Robert's hand so she could access Ruby's number and put her phone to her ear. Ruby's voice mail answered in lieu of a ring, and Corinna frowned. "That's weird." With a prickle of concern, she A prickling of concern, she finished her mocha Frappuccino in one big gulp. "Something's wrong. Her phone's not even turned on."

Robert met her statement with skepticism. "She's probably listening to the organ recital. Maybe they ask people to turn their phones off."

"I doubt that." Macy's giant organ, the largest functioning pipe organ in the world, gave a thunderous Christmas recital every two hours during the holiday season. A ringing cell phone wouldn't begin to disturb the sonorous performance. Corinna's phone buzzed and she immediately snatched it up, only to cringe as she recognized Tony's number. "Hello?"

"Yo, where are you girls? You said you'd be home by noon. Mama's got lunch ready."

"Uh..." Dread strangled Corinna's vocal cords. She pushed a reluctant confession through her tight throat. "I'm not actually with Ruby right now."

"What?"

His confusion inspired guilt, though she wasn't about to bring up Robert. "She...she said I could go to Starbucks while she finished her shopping, and I haven't heard from her since." The silence on Tony's end had her holding her breath.

"Have you tried calling her at all? Has she answered her phone for you?"

"All I get is her voice mail. Maybe her battery died."

"She charged it all night. You were supposed to stay together."

The reproach in his voice made her face burn. "What about your Find My service?"

"I'll try that now. Then I'm gonna come pick you up and we'll go looking for Ruby. You still at Starbucks?"

"Yes."

"And the keys to your Escort are where?"

"On my dresser in my room."

"Give me ten minutes. Stay inside until you see me pull up."

"I will." Ending the call, Corinna met Robert's watchful gaze. "You'd better disappear. My brother's on his way, and you don't want to meet him right now."

Robert's eyebrows quirked. "Does his wife do this often?"

"Enough to make him crazy. Hopefully he'll find her using his own phone. I just...I have a bad feeling." Ruby's interview with Katz yesterday stood at the forefront of her mind. How far would Katz go to keep Ruby from pursuing the rumor she'd brought up?

"Let me know if I can help."

"Thank you." Corinna slipped off her stool, hugged Robert good-bye, then went to wait by the door for Tony.

Out the corner of her eye, she could see Robert studying her in the same protective way Tony watched her. He didn't go anywhere, just watched over her as she waited for Tony. She dialed Ruby's number again, getting the same result. When her Escort pulled into the parking lot minutes later, she sent Robert a tiny nod, dashed outside, and slipped into the passenger seat.

If the set of Tony's jaw was any indication, the Find My service had told him something bad. "What did you find out?"

"She's not shopping."

"What? But she was all excited about the sales at Macy's."

"Her phone is somewhere off the highway. See for yourself." He plucked his iPhone out of the cupholder and handed it to her.

Corinna found herself staring at a map with a blue dot near an access ramp leading to I-95 North. "I mean, there's a little dog park there. She probably drove right past the Wanamaker Garage and got lost, and now she's asking someone for directions."

"I've told her never to get out of her car. It's not safe." He took the phone back and wedged it into the cupholder again.

Since when did Ruby ever play it safe? Corinna swallowed the question.

Tony turned left at the light, then right on Race Street, making the street live up to its name by accelerating way past the speed limit and whipping through traffic. A glance down at the phone showed them closing in on the blue dot, which hadn't moved.

Corinna looked up. "She ought to be right on this ramp coming up."

"Yep."

Instead of slowing down, Tony pulled them onto the tight-turning ramp at a speed that caused her tires to squeal. But Ruby's Range Rover didn't suddenly appear. In fact, the ramp was completely empty. Tony glanced down at his phone, then slowed abruptly, pulling them close to the guardrail before parking. He picked his phone up while cracking his door.

Vehicles were whizzing past them. "Stay in the car, seat belt on."

With a glance in his mirror, he vaulted out of the driver's seat, went around the idling Escort, and stepped over the guardrail into the clumps of dead grass growing between the ramp and the tall chain-link fence hemming in the dog park. A glance at his phone had him doubling back along the fence line.

With her breath sawing in and out in the quiet car, Corinna watched him. How could Ruby have vanished in the scant time they'd been apart? Craning her neck to keep an eye on her brother, Corinna spotted him bending over. Her breath caught when he straightened with something in his hand. His expression turned thunderous. As he marched back to the car, her stomach swiveled unpleasantly.

A puff of cold air accompanied him as he got back into the driver's seat and slammed the door shut. "Found her phone." His voice was hoarse, his complexion gray with worry.

Corinna stared at the brand-new iPhone Tony cupped in his hand. It must have been turned off when he found it because it was still coming back to life. As he waited with grim calm for it to come online, Corinna pictured Katz's assistant chucking Ruby's phone out the window of their moving car.

At the verge of entering Ruby's passcode, Tony glanced her way and did a double take. "What?"

"I might know who's behind this," Corinna admitted.

His dark pupils seemed to expand as they focused on her. She had his full attention now. "Talk," he ordered with so much intensity that she had to swallow to find her voice.

With her car's windows fogging as it idled, Corinna relayed the story of their interview of Katz the day before. Her halting explanation made Tony pale even more. She told him how they'd hidden in the office building after the interview and how they'd overheard Katz's assistant say that they'd taken care of the leak.

Tony covered his eyes with a hand and whispered, "Sweet Jesus."

Knowing how spiritual he was, she interpreted the exclamation as a prayer for help. "I filmed the whole interview. I have it at home on my camera," she added in case he wanted proof.

Tony dragged his hand down his face. Corinna thought he might call 911 or drive like a madman to their mother's house. Instead, he accessed his contacts on his phone and placed a phone call. "Sir." His strained voice radiated alarm. "Tell me you didn't give Stasky's book to *The Washington Post* yet. I just found out Ruby interviewed Katz yesterday." He relayed what Corinna had just told him. "And now she's missing. I found her phone lying in the grass off an exit ramp leading to the highway. You think this guy is capable of—" Tony's voice cracked. He cleared his throat. "I think he just snatched Ruby."

Tony couldn't believe the words coming out of his mouth. This wasn't the first time Ruby's actions had left him bathing in a cold sweat. But it might well be the last.

His CO's voice seemed to come at him from a great distance. "How could she know anything about Katz?"

"I don't know." Ruby had a nose for corruption. Tony didn't ask why or how. "She just knows. She questioned Katz yesterday about an incident in his past."

"Are you sure she's missing?"

"Pretty sure. I'm gonna backtrack, see if she ever even made it to Macy's, where she was headed. It's possible somebody just stole her phone, then threw it away when they realized it could be traced."

"Call the police if you don't find her."

James's calm, implacable voice helped to focus Tony's splintered thoughts.

"Report her disappearance, but don't say a word about Katz or we'll lose the advantage of surprise. Call me back with any updates."

"Yes, sir." Tony thumbed in the passcode to Ruby's phone, then handed it to Corinna. "Look up her texts and any recent phone calls. Tell me what you see."

With an eye on his mirror, he threw the car into Drive and accelerated up the ramp, continuing onto the highway.

"There's nothing here," Corinna reported a minute later.

Tony was busy making his way back to City Center. "You sure? No text, no calls, nothing?"

"Nothing."

While giving him zilch to go by, Corinna's reply eased the worry that Ruby had lied about wanting to shop the Black Friday sales. Realizing she'd already lied about wanting to see the parade made his stomach hurt. If only she'd told him she was interviewing the lieutenant governor of Pennsylvania. Tony would have heard James's story last night and immediately put two and two together. He would have protected Ruby, and this horrible fear that something irrevocable had happened wouldn't be fisting his intestines.

Stifling a curse, he slapped the steering wheel, causing Corinna to startle away from him.

"Sorry." He swooped off an exit ramp in order to double back to Macy's. "I just don't understand why my own family is keeping secrets from me."

Corinna hugged herself, looking miserable.

"Did she tell you not to say anything?"

"Sort of. She said she wouldn't take me to see *Hamilton* over Christmas break."

"Ugh." Tony shook his head in disgust. That sounded exactly like something Ruby would say. "She has no idea how dangerous this guy is."

"He shot a kid and his mother." Corinna's voice wobbled. Tears brimmed in her lovely eyes.

Tony glanced at her, dumbstruck. "You know about that?"

"Ruby asked him about it directly."

Oh no. "What did he say?"

"He denied it. Said it was the opposition making up stories to discredit him. And yet we overheard his assistant mention a leak they'd taken care of. Of course, he didn't know we were listening."

Tony pictured Ruby hiding out of sight, eavesdropping on the man she'd interviewed.

Staskiewicz. That had to be the leak the assistant was talking about.

Tony blew out a breath as panic threatened to impair his thinking. Everything James had told him over the phone last night Ruby already knew. Boy, was she clever! But she'd bitten off more than she could chew this time around. "We gotta call the cops." But first he needed to give them something to work with. "When's the last time you actually saw her?"

"Um. When she dropped me off at Starbucks."

Tony swung an incredulous look at her. "You didn't even go *shopping* with her?"

"Robert had the day off," Corinna blurted, clearly on the verge of bursting into tears. "Ruby knew I wanted to see him, so she dropped me off."

"Your *boyfriend* is to blame?"

Corinna's eyes flashed as her own temper ignited. "Don't you dare put this on him!"

"Unbelievable!" Tony gripped the steering wheel so hard his knuckles hurt. *Focus.* He ground his molars, forcing himself to think. "Where did you tell Ruby to park?"

"I gave her directions to the garage under the Wanamaker Building."

He was approaching the latter right that second. Flipping on his turn signal, Tony headed into the underground parking area, where he was forced to stop at an automated gate and get a ticket. Ruby would've had to do the same thing. "Look for cameras," he instructed Corinna. "And keep an eye out for Ruby's car."

Maybe they would find it parked here. Maybe she was somewhere inside of City Center shopping and having a grand time, completely unaware that her phone had been stolen. But who would steal a phone, only to throw it away almost at once?

The tires on Corinna's Escort squealed on the smooth cement as Tony circled his way through the parking garage, eyes peeled for Ruby's Range Rover.

Nowhere. He didn't see it anywhere.

There was one car, an old Volvo, that caught his eye because its license plate was missing.

He executed a three-point turn on the lowest level and started back toward the entrance, where he intended to call the police. He drove around a syringe some junkie had tossed down onto the cement. That really ought to go into a trash can.

As he neared the elevator, his gaze landed on a trash can not twenty yards away with trash overflowing from it, including a license plate of all things. He almost drove right past it, but when his intuition niggled, he jammed on the brakes.

Someone had tried to wedge not one, but two completely good Virginia plates into a trash can overflowing from Thursday's parade. Tony pulled them out and stared, acid burning his esophagus. They didn't belong to the Volvo. They were Ruby's plates.

Corinna had one foot out of the car and was staring at him over the top of her Escort. "What'd you find?"

Icy with shock, he held up the personalized plates, I XPOZ U, for her to see as he walked automatically toward her.

Corinna's jaw had dropped. "Somebody took the plates off her car and stole it?"

They should never have brought her Range Rover to Philly. "Whoever drives that Volvo put his plates on her Rover." The words he was saying actually encouraged him since the police would jump all over a stolen vehicle, whereas they'd wait twenty-four hours to take action on a missing person's report.

Dropping back behind the wheel, Tony took out his phone and tapped three numbers with a tremor in his fingers.

"911. What is your emergency?"

"I'd like to report a stolen vehicle and a missing person."

By the time he hung up, Corinna was crying quietly, her face in her hands. She lowered them to raise her tearstained eyes at him. "This is all my fault!"

Tony palmed the back of her head and pulled her into his arms, taking as much comfort from her fierce embrace as he was giving. "No, it's not." In fact, if the women hadn't gone their separate ways, Corinna might have been kidnapped, too. "I'm thinkin' it's a good thing you had coffee with your boyfriend."

At his comment, Corinna pulled back far enough to search his expression. "You think we would've both disappeared?" The color drained from her face.

"Yeah." If this was anyone's fault, it was *his*. Clearly, Ruby didn't trust him to support her investigations. She didn't see him as her teammate, which put her at serious disadvantage. Tony faced danger with his fellow SEALs, but Ruby worked alone. She kept her business to herself because Tony had a habit of overprotecting.

But his fears were well founded. Powerful men did not take lightly to having skeletons dragged out of their closets. Just look at what had happened to Staskiewicz.

God, please don't let that happen to Ruby.

If Ruby ended up murdered…Tony refused to consider the possibility.

CHAPTER 7

"*S*ir, you have a personal call on line three." The voice of Lennard Katz's secretary purred over the speaker on Len's office phone in Harrisburg, Pennsylvania.

Personal call? Working his way through proposed legislative revisions, Len tore himself from the tome lying open on the desk in front of him. His heart gave a funny flip as he considered whether the call might have anything to do with Ruby Bonheur's disappearance—of course not. No one would have connected him to her abduction, and Cullum would have called his cell phone, as he'd done earlier to report the abduction successful.

Brushing off his prickle of concern, Len punched the correct line and picked up the receiver. "Katz speaking."

"Len, this is a blast from the past. James Monteague here. We worked together in Afghanistan, when I was with SEAL Team Two. You knew me as Monty, remember?"

However friendly sounding, the baritone voice of the golden-haired lieutenant who'd followed his orders in Operation Lights Out doused Len in uneasiness. "Monty." He searched for his usual glib tongue. "Of course. What a great surprise. How the heck are you?"

"Well, I've been better, Len. Don't know if you heard about it, but one of the guys in our old squad was murdered just down the road from you, in his old neighborhood in Philly—John Staskiewicz, went by Stasky. Remember him?"

Len's mouth went desert dry. "Sure, I remember Stasky. I hadn't heard that news. What happened?"

"Some thugs broke into his house and shot him in his sleep."

"Oh, wow, that's terrible."

"Yeah, I'm on my way to his funeral. It'll take place Sunday at eleven at Palmer Cemetery in Fishtown, where he's from. Now that you know about it, maybe I'll run into you there."

"Oh, well, I'd have to look at my calendar. Awfully nice of you to pay your respects, though. I take it you and Stasky have stayed in touch?" What if all the SEALs had collaborated against him and not just John? The phone went slippery in his sweating hand.

"No, not really."

Relief left Len weak.

"But, you know, we're a tight-knit community, which is probably why John left me this book he'd written. I'm not sure what to do with it."

The blood in Len's veins turned to ice as his fears became manifest. That exposé John Staskiewicz had threatened to write if he became lieutenant governor—it must have made it farther than Stasky's computer, stolen and destroyed the night he'd been killed. Len had acted too late.

"Oh?" His voice cracked.

"It's all about that op that went bad, Operation Lights Out."

Len cringed. This couldn't be happening.

"Stasky described you as a cold-blooded killer, Len. You know we SEALs take the code of silence seriously, but John didn't care much for your politics. It's pretty clear he intended for his book to halt your ascent up the political ladder."

Len drew a shaky breath. "What are you going to do with it?"

"Well, that depends. As it turns out, you've got something I need. Maybe we can strike a deal."

"What have I got?" Sweat made Len's shirt stick to his back. The man had the gall to blackmail him?

"The journalist, Ruby Bonheur. I'll give you the manuscript in exchange for her safe return."

The walls of Len's office seemed to shimmer like the sand in the desert. "I've never heard of her." His thoughts raced. How had Monty put two and two together so quickly? Perhaps the four-man firing squad had planned to betray him all along and they'd recruited the journalist to help them publicize their allegations.

"You know exactly who I'm talking about." Monty's voice hardened. "Unfortunately, what you didn't know when you arranged to make her disappear is that Ruby Bonheur is my sister-in-law."

Len swallowed hard. Right. He hadn't known that.

"And as much as I'd like to honor John's memory by seeing his book published and your career go up in smoke, my wife would throw me out if I didn't get her sister back safe and sound. So here's my offer, Len…"

With Monty's ultimatum sounding in his right ear, Len stared dazedly out the window.

"You show up at Palmer Cemetery on Sunday morning with Ruby Bonheur sitting safely in your car; I'll show up with the manuscript, and we'll do a trade. How's that? You get to salvage your career, and I get to salvage my marriage. Fair enough?"

Len gave one more stab at protesting his innocence. "I already told you this, Monty. I don't know what you're talking about."

"Then you leave me no choice. I'll make copies of the manuscript right now and mail them to *The Washington Post* and *The New York Times*. You'll be a political pariah by Sunday morning. Good talking to you, Len."

"Wait!" Len blurted the word before he'd decided what to say.

"How do I know you haven't made a copy of the book already, or that you won't expose me later?"

"Gee, I hadn't thought of that." Sarcasm dripped off Monty's words. "I guess you don't know, but my priority is my wife's happiness. Yours is your career. Return Ruby Bonheur at the funeral on Sunday, in pristine condition, and I'll let you finish your term as lieutenant governor. I won't finger you as Stasky's killer, provided you decline your candidacy for vice president."

Len could smell his political ambitions starting to smoke. "You can't pin Stasky's murder on me. I had nothing to do with it!" His voice climbed a full octave.

"Best to be on the safe side, Len. Come to Stasky's funeral. I'll give you the manuscript, and you'll release Ruby Bonheur. Then I'll leave you alone if you leave politics alone. You have my number," the man noted. "Call me if you wish to accept my offer."

Pride kept Len mute. He flinched as the phone clicked in his ear, signaling an end to the call. On autopilot, Len lowered his arm until the receiver clattered into the cradle.

Fury burned in him. He ejected from his chair and stalked toward the window. The gray, inhospitable sky spewed sleet down on the city of Harrisburg. *What do I do?*

His popularity might survive the rumor that he'd shot a child and his mother out of sheer frustration. Certainly, he wouldn't go to jail for that as he'd had license to kill whomever back in those days. But he didn't doubt for a second Monty would find a way to ruin him if he stayed in politics.

Resentment made Len's face burn. He'd worked too hard to get where he was just to give it up now. But neither did he wish to be constantly looking over his shoulder, dreading the appearance of three wrathful Navy SEALs. That left him with two choices: either he quit politics for good, or he only pretended to, while eliminating the obstacles in his way. It would cost him quite a bit of money to have all three SEALs killed.

Len ground his molars together, thinking. First, he would withdraw his name as a potential candidate. Then, he would double down on a couple of business ventures that had come his way and make enough money to pay off a mercenary like Yordan to pick off the remaining SEALs, first Monty, then Ben Harmony. Saul Wade, once America's top sniper would be the last and the hardest to kill. It might take a few years before Len could return to politics, but he'd be back.

And the journalist? Not long after he surrendered her in exchange for Stasky's book, she would be the first to die.

Len rubbed his palms together, mollified, before spinning toward his desk to stab the intercom button. "Michelle, get the last caller back on the phone with me, will you?"

"Of course. Just a minute, sir."

Brutally efficient, she got back to him in half that time. "Sir, I have Commander Monteague on line one for you."

Len hit line one, and with a smirk in his voice, said, "I'll see you at the funeral."

He slammed the phone into the receiver, then opened his desk drawer and withdrew his cell phone, putting a call through to his assistant.

"Yes, sir?"

"I've changed my mind. Call Yordan and tell him not to harm the package. He'll have his chance at her later. I need you to collect her from him tomorrow and keep her at the office for twenty-four hours. Nobody will be there on a weekend."

"Me, sir? I don't really want to—"

"Shut up and listen. I'll pick her up early Sunday morning. Just keep her tranquilized. Yordan will show you how."

Len hung up on Cullum. He could care less whether his assistant felt squeamish about babysitting. Len had been far more inconvenienced than Collum. The jangling of his cell phone made him jump. Cullum was calling him back. "What?"

"Yordan wants to know if he'll get paid the same."

"Only if the package is unharmed."

He hung up on Cullum a second time, then hurled his cell phone across the room. By luck, it landed on an armchair, then bounced harmlessly onto the Turkish carpet.

If only he'd restrained himself back in Dishu when his temper got the better of him. Then none of this would be happening. He couldn't let them destroy everything he'd worked for. He wouldn't.

In a couple of years, he'd be back in politics. Who knew? Once the SEALs and the journalist were out of the picture, he might even run for president.

The sound of a rough male voice roused Ruby from a drug-induced sleep. Exerting every ounce of strength at her disposal, she managed to slit her heavy eyelids and glimpsed the salt-and-pepper head of her abductor in the driver's seat before her eyes slammed shut.

The man had been holding a cell phone to his ear. She could hear him speaking in a strong Eastern European accent. "He needs to pay me the same, regardless."

Pay me. Oh, help. He was discussing his fee for killing her! *Regardless.* Regardless of what?

A whimper escaped Ruby's unresponsive lips, and the car wobbled. Managing to peek through her lashes again, she saw the driver angle his rearview mirror to look back at her, and she snapped her eyes shut, playing possum.

How will he kill me? Quickly and painlessly, she hoped. Or would he torture her first to elicit the names of her sources? Of course, Katz already knew the names of the SEALs who had worked with him in Operation Lights Out, but he might wish to know if *others* knew.

No one yet. Ruby'd gotten her information by eavesdropping at her sister's Halloween party, where James and the bald chief petty officer, Ben Harmony, had been reminiscing about their service with Team Two, not knowing Ruby lurked just around the corner, her ears pricked in hopes of hearing a juicy story.

"As long as he doesn't name us in his book, Stasky can say whatever he wants to," James had been saying to Ben. *"What's Stasky got to lose now that he's retired?"*

"True. And someone had better drag Katz off his mountain before he climbs any higher." Ben's voice roughened with disgust. *"Man, I'll never forget the way he just turned and shot that kid and his mom like it was nothing. I never dreamed he'd go into politics."*

"I hear he's on the short list for vice president." James's grim tone made it clear he didn't like that prospect.

"No way. Tell Stasky to go ahead and write his book. I'll hand-sell it for him. We thought Katz was dangerous working for the CIA? Wait until he's next in line to be our commander-in-chief."

Ruby had been in journalism long enough to know Stasky's murder was no coincidence. The coincidence was that Katz, Staskiewicz, James Monteague, Ben Harmony, and a SEAL named Saul Wade—if Ruby'd overheard the name correctly while eavesdropping on Tony's phone call—had all worked together to eliminate Gabir al Baldawi. Only their termination of the dangerous Taliban leader hadn't happened. Instead, some terrified kid and his mother had been shot dead by Katz for no good reason.

The SEALs must have been so reluctant to cover up the truth. Stasky, the first SEAL prodded by his conscience, had ended up dead. Which meant that Katz would stop at nothing to keep his faux pas out of the public eye.

I am so dead.

Terror gave rise to a wave of nausea. Battling the need to hang her head off the edge of the seat and vomit, she held as still as possible while drawing deep breaths. If she so much as moved, her abductor might pull over and hit her with another crippling injection. God only knew what was in that stuff and what it was doing to the fragile little life in her womb.

My baby! Oh no. I can't let my baby die with me.

As the car veered off the highway, banking onto a tight-turning exit ramp, Ruby adjusted her position surreptitiously. Their speed slowed, giving her hope that they would pull up to a gas station where she could draw attention to herself by kicking the window. But then she remembered—Tony had topped off her tank right before arriving at Mama Anna's on Wednesday evening. Her Rover wouldn't need fuel for several hundred miles.

It wasn't any wonder her assailant had stolen it. Only two years old, candy-apple red, loaded with features, and immaculate—except for the dent she'd made with Opal's mailbox—it was worth at least fifty thousand dollars. Her kidnapper hadn't been able to resist it.

Ruby realized she'd rolled against the seatback which meant they were headed uphill. As the car continued to climb, performing hairpin turns in the process, she consulted her inner map to determine where they were. The Pocono Mountains were about two hours northwest of Philly. Unless she'd been unconscious a lot longer than that, the Poconos was where they had to be.

And that made perfect sense. After all, her captor had a job to do, and the mountains provided him the privacy and space to do it.

I don't want to die. The feeling overpowered her fear.

She had way too much to live for, not the least of which was a lifetime with Tony. But, more than that, her death would mean their baby would never have a chance. That wasn't what God wanted for either of them.

I refuse to die!

All she had to do was escape before her captor killed her.

CHAPTER 8

"*M*ama, you mind leaving us so we can talk?"

Tony's mother, who'd been setting out left-overs for the two Navy SEALs who'd pulled up to her home half an hour earlier, firmed her lips and started out of the kitchen. With an astute glance at Tony, Corinna trailed her.

"Not you, Corinna. Actually, go get your camera and bring it down here."

As she hurried off to fetch it, Tony gestured to the spread laid out by his mother. "Help yourselves. You must be hungry after your drive." It was ten o'clock on Friday night. The police had scoured the city for Ruby's stolen Range Rover to no avail. The tag-less Volvo had turned out to be stolen, itself. If its original plates had been transferred to Ruby's SUV, that might make it easier to find her. But there was no guarantee that was the case.

Mama's kitchen had never felt smaller with three SEALs filling the space. Monty was six-foot-three, and Ben was built like a WWF wrestler. They loaded up their plates with leftovers before taking seats at the little round table. Tony waited by the door for Corinna to bring her camera down. He'd already watched the interview with Katz, his gut churning as he beheld the man's false charm, sensed the evil lurking beneath it.

When Corinna returned and placed the camera in his hand, he chucked her under the chin. "Get some sleep, princess." He then listened for the sound of her footsteps on the stairs before joining his teammates at the table. He found the video, started it, then set the camera down so they could watch Katz's interview as they ate.

Monty stopped eating with half his food still on his plate. He laid his fork down. Ben kept eating, but his eyes were glued to the screen.

The burn scar that marred the right side of the CO's face paled to a white seam, while Ben's ears turned a deep pink, which they only did when he got angry.

"Liar," Monty muttered as Katz denied all knowledge of the rumor Ruby had brought up.

When the interview ended, Tony took back the camera and powered it off. "According to my sister, she and Ruby hid themselves in the hallway and overheard Katz's assistant talk about the leak they'd take care of. Pretty sure he was referring to Staskiewicz."

Ben finally put his fork down.

Monty leaned back his chair, folding his arms across his chest. "What have the police found so far?"

The hollow feeling in Tony's gut expanded. "Nothing. No sign of her or her vehicle."

Silence filled the small kitchen, interrupted only by the faint clicking of the clock on the stove and the sounds of the bustling city beyond the darkened windows.

With Monty's whisky-colored gaze resting on him, Tony struggled to maintain his composure.

"I spoke with Katz right after you told me what happened to Ruby. He tried to deny he had anything to do with taking her, but he agreed to my deal. I promised if he returns her to us at Stasky's funeral, I'll hand over the manuscript Stasky mailed me."

Tony drank in his CO's words like they were life-giving elixir. "You really think he'll bring her?"

"Yes, and in pristine condition, as specified. Plus, I suggested in no uncertain terms that he leave politics, or the manuscript may still come back to haunt him."

Relief knocked on the door of Tony's armored heart. "You mean, if he brings Ruby back, we're gonna let him get away with Stasky's murder?" The mere idea made his stomach hurt.

Monty sat back in his chair, threading his large hands together over his flat stomach. He turned his head, meeting Ben's blue-eyed glower. "No. While Katz's actions as a case officer can't be prosecuted, he can certainly be charged stateside for kidnapping Ruby and for ordering Stasky's murder. I already made a copy of the manuscript. We're going to gather any other evidence that comes our way, then hand it all over to the FBI to conduct their own investigation. That way Katz goes to jail instead of seeking reprisal and going immediately back into politics."

Tony pictured Fitz, the special agent who'd worked the ricin case in which Monty's wife, Opal, had been victimized. "Does Opal know what's happened to Ruby?"

"Not yet. You want me to tell her?"

"No." The fewer people who felt as miserable as he did, the better. "We'll tell her when it's over." That was assuming everything went as planned.

Monty stretched out a long arm and gripped Tony's shoulder. "I know what you're going through, Bambino. Don't forget Ruby's a fighter. You know she's unstoppable when she makes up her mind to do something."

Oh, I know. And while James meant for his words to be reassuring, they only notched Tony's anxiety higher. It would be so like Ruby to undermine their rescue attempt by trying to escape on her own. The very real possibility that she could end up getting hurt, even killed, pushed tears of distress into his eyes.

Monty removed his hand to check his watch. "We should probably get going. Ben and I are headed to Harrisburg tonight to surveil Katz, make sure he doesn't leave the country or something. We'll return Sunday morning for the funeral." He pushed back his chair and stood, prompting Ben to do likewise.

Tony followed suit. "Just leave your plates. I'll clean up."

But Ben ignored him, scarfing up both his and Monty's place settings and carrying them to the sink. On his way to the door, he met Tony's gaze. "I have some items in the car for you."

"Oh, good."

Tony had requested Ben pick up what he needed for the funeral. Hoping Ben had brought his sidearm as well as his dress whites, Tony followed his visitors back down the hall and out the front door into the cold night air. Ben's new vehicle, a black GMC Yukon, big enough to carry the three boys he was legally adopting, gleamed under the streetlamp.

While Ben reached inside and pulled out the uniform hanging in a garment bag, Tony kept his eyes peeled for strangers. Dried leaves fluttered along the sidewalk, but nothing seemed out of place. Ben handed him the garment bag containing his uniform, then reached back inside for a bulging sack.

"Here are your dress shoes and your sidearm with a spare mag. Sorry, I couldn't find the right socks."

"No worries. I'm just glad you found the hide-a-key." He kept one hidden in his carport as Ruby locked herself out regularly.

Ben ruffled Tony's hair, his expression sympathetic. "Hang in there." Then he spun away, rounding the SUV to get into the driver's seat.

Monty waited by the passenger door looking vigilant. "We'll see you at the funeral, Tony, if not before. Try to get there an hour early—or will you need a ride?"

Sunday seemed like a lifetime away. "I think I can use my sister's car."

"Just let us know." Both SEALs stepped into the vehicle.

As the engine gave a throaty rumble, Tony backed away, struck by a thought. If Katz had been gutsy enough to kill Staskiewicz, might he not seek to murder the remaining members of his old firing squad?

The Yukon pulled away. Once its taillights disappeared, Tony went back inside, locked the door, hung his uniform over the top of the closet door, then dug in the plastic bag for his sidearm, taking reassurance from its familiar weight. Tonight, he would be sleeping on the sofa in the front room with his SIG Sauer close at hand.

Both Mama and Corinna came creeping down the stairs. At their long faces, he hurried to reassure them. "We got a plan in place. Supposedly Katz is gonna bring Ruby to Staskiewicz's funeral and trade her for the book Stasky wrote."

The relief in their expressions was immediate. But doubt still sat like a boulder in the pit of Tony's stomach. No way was it gonna be that easy.

CHAPTER 9

*I*t's wearing off again.

Ruby blinked away the sticky weight that kept her eyelids shut. She lay face down across a soft surface, drawing on fractured memories of the last time she'd been conscious long enough to make sense of her situation.

She remembered her Range Rover stopping. The second the engine died, she'd sat up, determined to catch her captor off guard. Only, she hadn't moved fast enough. One minute she'd been pawing at the door handle, fumbling to release the lock, and the next she'd fallen into his arms. A light snow had flecked her cheek.

She'd gleaned a fleeting impression of tall pine trees and cold mountain air just before the sharp prick of a needle pierced her triceps for a second time. The last thing she remembered was being hauled out of the car and tossed over her captor's broad shoulder.

Where am I now?

A thread of silver light pierced two dark panels—curtains?— suggesting the presence of a window. Turning her head the other way, she spied a brighter beam of light at the bottom of a closed door. From beyond it came the sound of a television program, complete with canned laughter. The blanket under her nose emitted the odor of mothballs.

The brief glimpse of her whereabouts earlier had confirmed her guess that she was being taken to the Pocono Mountains. And now she was in a log cabin, given the lumpy walls. Was this where her captor meant to kill her, in some remote lodge where no one would hear her screams? If so, why hadn't he done it already? Perhaps he was waiting for her to regain consciousness. That made sense if he was after information.

Not going to happen.

She tried to move. Her limbs felt weighted and clumsy. Well, no wonder. Both her wrists and her ankles were bound together with plastic zip ties. In fact, it was the numb fire licking up her arms that had awakened her, not unlike the two separate times, years before, that she'd awakened in the middle of a medical procedure —first at twelve years old, when her tonsils were being taken out, and then again at eighteen, when her wisdom teeth were extracted.

"It's her red hair," the orthodontist had informed his horrified assistant. Apparently, Ruby needed more anesthetic than most people.

Well, in this case, waking up was a good thing, only her captor had better not overhear her, lest he commence with his interrogation or jab her with more of the sedative.

Stifling a moan of pain, Ruby rolled onto her back. She then jackknifed to a sitting position and took closer stock of her whereabouts. Her eyes, now adjusted to the dark, made out a small but decently appointed room with a raftered ceiling. There was a bed, a dresser, and a mirror. Perhaps there was something she could use to cut herself free?

An object resembling her purse had her looking back at the dresser. Would her captor be so careless as to leave her purse, with her phone inside it, sitting right next to her?

Tony! She could call for help.

She scootched as quietly as possible to the edge of the mattress. The bed beneath her squeaked. Then she stood slowly, not altogether certain her legs would hold her weight. When they did, she gave a shaky little hop and then another.

She leaned over the dresser and tried to open her purse. Using her lips and teeth, she succeeded in freeing the snap that kept it closed. She nosed her way into the main pocket, searching desperately for her phone. But it wasn't there. Her abductor must have removed it, maybe even thrown it away so they wouldn't be traced.

He wasn't careless, after all. Or was he?

Seizing the whole bag with her teeth, she hopped back to the bed and dropped it there, causing the contents to spill out. Then she sifted through them with her nose—makeup, wallet, lipstick—ah ha!—fingernail file. She turned around, sat next to it, and groped behind her back to pick it up. She would use it to cut herself free.

This looks a lot easier in the movies.

But hope and desperation lent her dexterity. Back and forth over the plastic strip Ruby sawed, cutting through it one millimeter at a time. With a snap, the cuff around her wrists fell away. *Ay, ay, ay.* She shook the blood back into her arms before going to work on her ankles. Outside her room, the television program gave way to advertising. At any moment, her captor might get up and check on her.

Having injected her twice now, he was clearly aware that the drug only worked for a limited amount of time on her. He was probably gearing up to inject her yet again—or worse yet, keep her awake for questioning and torture.

But it wouldn't come to that if she could help it. She was getting the heck out of here.

All things are possible through Christ who gives me strength!

That Bible verse had changed her entire life. With another snap, the second zip tie fell away from her ankles. Ruby jumped to her feet. Straining to hear over her galloping heart, she swept her belongings back into her purse, looped the strap over her head, and tiptoed toward the window. On her way there, she glimpsed her coat hanging over one corner of the footboard and hurriedly donned it, fingers fumbling to button herself up. It would be cold out there.

She had just reached the window when the television fell silent. Terror spiked, causing her to freeze on a gasp, ears pricked to the sounds beyond her door. Her captor seemed to be listening, also. Any minute now, he would get up to check on her. She couldn't afford to tarry.

Stretching out a hand, she felt behind the curtain for a window latch. There it was, in the middle of the window, icy to the touch. The mechanism was simple. With a swipe of her thumb, she flipped it open, then went to lift the window. On the other side of the door, the slow thud of approaching footsteps goaded her into reckless action.

Now, Ruby! But the window was stuck. Ruby strained with both hands and, with a pop, it rumbled upward. Frigid air blasted in. At least there was no screen to contend with.

The doorknob turned. *Should have locked that.*

With the silhouette of her captor filling the opening door and his shout of warning abrading her ears, Ruby threw herself head-first out the opening, diving into the darkness. More than halfway out, her upper thighs caught on the windowsill.

For a terrible second, she hung suspended, clutching her purse as the strap slipped. Her captor had grasped her legs while the ground outside was just feet away. *Good thing I'm on the first floor.*

With a mighty kick, Ruby freed herself. Her captor's grunt of pain mingled with her own as she toppled onto the hard ground, hands outstretched to break her fall. To keep from striking her head on the frozen soil, she tucked her chin, rounded her spine, and rolled just like she'd done in gymnastics as a child.

To her amazement, she came right up on her feet, losing her purse in the process. No time to pick it up now. Injured wrist tucked close, she ran blindly into the darkness, only to discover that the shadows in front of her were the pointy ends of many branches.

Ruby squeezed her eyes shut and pushed blindly into them. They clawed at her clothing and her hair, yet she escaped unscathed out the other side.

The earth rose sharply under her pumps, forcing her to ascend a densely wooded slope, one with unseen boulders that jutted out of the earth. One such boulder tripped her. She fell to her knees on a bed of pine needles, pain lancing her wrist anew, and struggled up again.

Behind her, she could hear a door slamming and the tramping of feet.

As expected, her captor was coming after her. He'd seen which direction she was fleeing. The beam of a flashlight strafed the darkness.

Hide! She cast about for a bush to squirm beneath. There wasn't any underbrush in sight. As he neared her, she darted behind the wide trunk of a tree and froze.

He slowed, breathing heavily as he panned the light around.

Ruby tried to stop panting. She could hear Tony in her head, teaching her how to breathe the way Navy SEALs did—*"Inhale for the count of three, through the mouth, hold for one second, then slowly exhale."* But her chest convulsed in fear, turning her exhalation into a sob.

The light grew brighter. On the other side of the tree, twigs snapped under her captor's heels. *Run!* But she was frozen in fear.

"Thought you could get away?" Her captor pounced without warning.

She screamed.

"Quiet!"

The slap came out of nowhere, sobering her with its force.

Holding his phone between his teeth, the man spun her around and prodded her back in the direction of the house. "You want to get me in trouble." His accented English was as foreign as this bizarre situation.

Ruby played the last card left to her. "Whatever Katz is paying you, my husband will double it."

"I don't know who's payin' me, and I don't care."

"He's the lieutenant governor of Pennsylvania, Lennard Katz."

"Quiet. I don't want to know. I just do what I'm told."

"Then you're just a puppet."

"I said, *quiet!*" He gave her a push that sent her plowing face-first into the nearest tree trunk. Her injured wrist throbbed as she caught herself. Rough bark abraded her cheek, leaving it stinging.

Her captor jerked her back against his side. "You gonna hurt yourself, and I'll get the blame." He grabbed her by the hair and led her downhill toward the house.

The telling words seeped into Ruby's consciousness. Wait, he would get into trouble for hurting her? Relief edged aside her despair.

Well, that was reassuring...or was it? He might be selling her to human traffickers.

The log cabin came into view, gilded by moonlight and resembling something a seasonal hunter might use. No other structures were in sight—no signs of other people anywhere.

He shoved her through the open door into warmth, kicked it shut behind them, then drew her toward the refrigerator. "Don't move." With a warning glare, he released her to open the black plastic case inside.

Ruby touched a finger to her stinging face and discovered she was bleeding.

When he turned around, her captor was sucking clear liquid from a capsule into a syringe.

She backed away, shaking her head. "Oh, don't do that. You're going to hurt my baby with those drugs."

Her captor paused, giving her hope that he would simply tie her up again. But then a sneer curled his upper lip and he lunged toward her, seizing her by her coat. The needle pierced the thick material, just as it had done two times previously.

In a matter of seconds, Ruby slumped against him. The room turned gray, then black. Why was he keeping her alive? *Please God, not human trafficking. I just want to go back to Tony.*

CHAPTER 10

"**E**at your sausage, Antonio," Tony's mother insisted.

"I'm not hungry, Mama." He pushed away the plate that had been there since breakfast that morning. Though he'd stayed up most of the night guarding his family, Tony still seethed with restless energy. If only he could have joined Monty and Ben, he wouldn't be feeling so useless.

With his mother puttering around him, he watched Ruby's interview with Katz again on the Nikon's previewer, unable to take his eyes off the man.

Katz looked so clean cut, so upstanding. It was bad enough the man had shot a little boy dead, just because he'd gotten bad intel and the crying kid had gotten on his nerves. To have abducted Ruby—Tony's clever, glittering Ruby—made Tony want to wrap his hands around the man's neck and squeeze the life out of him. That was what Katz was doing to *him*. Tony couldn't think, couldn't breathe, couldn't eat a thing.

Swallowing a bitter taste in his mouth, he wished someone had tried to hit his house last night. Not that he'd wanted Corinna or his mother in harm's way, but he'd been stewing for a fight. Still was.

"Are you going to kill him?"

The fearful question brought Tony's attention back to the present. He'd forgotten Corinna was sitting in the chair next to his, keeping him company. The dark smudges under her eyes and the pallor of her olive complexion told him she had hardly slept a wink herself. "No." He frowned at her. "'Course not. I'm not a murderer. *He's* the murderer."

Corinna nodded, her eyes watering. "But you wish you could kill him."

Tony examined the words with a pinch of shame. Wanting to kill someone was just as bad as actually killing them. What he ought to do was pray for Katz to come to his senses.

The tear rolling down Corinna's face tore him from his introspection.

"Hey." He lifted a hand to her soft cheek and wiped it away. "This isn't your fault, Corinna. No matter what happens, you remember that. Ruby does what Ruby does. You didn't force her into anything, did you?"

She shook her head, unable to answer him.

Just then his cell phone buzzed, and he snatched it off the table, his pulse leaping to see his CO calling him. "Whatchu got, sir?"

"Nothing yet."

The dampening news kept his expectations low.

"Just wanted you to know, I'm watching Katz's home, and Harm has a bead on his office. If anything happens on our end, I'll update you."

"Thank you, sir." Monty had to be hearing the agony in Tony's voice.

"Anything to report there?" His own voice was full of sympathy.

"No, sir."

A short pause. "I'll be in touch."

As Monty hung up, Tony lowered the phone to the table. A great weight sat on his chest. "I'm gonna go work out in the basement." His old punching bag still hung from a beam down there. He pushed his chair back. Mama and Corinna regarded him with identical expressions of worry as he headed for the basement stairs. "Call down for me if you need me."

He was going to beat the punching bag to a pulp. And then he was going to pray that Katz repented of his evil ways. He could only hope his prayers heaped burning coals onto Katz's blond head.

Ruby roused to the feeling of being moved. There were hands under her arms and a second set of hands around both ankles. Another person had joined them! She tried prying her heavy eyelids open and managed a quick glimpse of a well-dressed young man walking backwards as he carried her lower extremities toward a snow-dusted vehicle.

"Since when did you drive a Range Rover?" he asked.

Recognition shot through Ruby. Cullum's voice! Why was Katz's assistant getting involved?

"Had it for a while now." Her captor tried passing her car off as his.

Liar. She was dying to call him out, only she couldn't speak, couldn't move. God knew how her tiny baby was responding to the drugs in her body.

What could Cullum's arrival at the hunting lodge signify? Ruby racked her foggy brain. He didn't strike her as a killer.

He transferred her ankles to the crook of one arm as he opened his car door. Through her lashes, she saw him toss her purse onto the floor mat before lowering her feet next to it. Wow, so she still had her purse. Dead women didn't need purses.

Her captor grumbled as he slung her into the seat itself. "Be easier to put her in the trunk."

"Are you nuts? She'd freeze to death. I told you, the boss wants her unharmed for now. Just look at her! And what's with her wrist? Did you do that?"

"No. She threw herself out the window. She's crazy, this one. And she needs more sedative than most."

Cullum said nothing to the kidnapper's warning. The door closed, leaving Ruby in the much warmer car by herself. Her head lolled forward, causing her hair to fall around her face, hiding her fluttering lashes from both men.

"I want my money." The kidnapper's Eastern European accent was distinct. "Your boss hasn't paid me yet."

"I don't have anything to do with that, Yordan. Sorry. I'm–I'm sure he'll transfer the sum soon." Sounding afraid of her captor, Cullum rounded the car to the driver's side.

Yordan. Ruby filed away the name she'd overheard.

The driver's door opened and Collum got in quickly, his jerky movements communicating fear. The engine roared to life, and he executed a swift U-turn before pulling away. As they started downhill, Ruby's upper body tipped toward the dashboard. Her face was going to hit it.

"Whoa there." Cullum threw out an arm, catching her forward momentum in the nick of time. Whispering anxiously to himself, he slowed the car to a stop, then reached across her to draw the seat belt over her and snap it into place.

Her body still tipped forward.

With a grunt, he reached across her lap and hit a button that lowered the back of her seat until she was reclining.

"There." Breathing heavily, Cullum put the car into Drive again and started forward.

Ruby slit her eyes, taking stock of her situation. Unless Cullum looked back at her, he wouldn't notice her return to consciousness. They were wending their way down a slick, steep road. Given

Cullum's white-knuckled grip on the wheel and the feel of the tires slipping on ice, the going was treacherous.

The digital clock read 2:03 P.M. Both her wrists and her ankles were bound again. She knew from her previous returns to consciousness that it would take another hour before she could move. But her fear was fading. Cullum was a far less dangerous adversary than the man who'd kidnapped her. She could probably persuade him to remove the zip ties. Confidence thrummed in Ruby.

Then, at just the right time, she was going to make a run for it.

Tony regarded his bloodshot eyes in the bathroom mirror. Having prayed as sincerely as he could for Katz to change his ways, his desire for vengeance had surprisingly subsided. But perhaps that was because he'd punched his old punching bag until his knuckles bled. Now he just felt gutted.

His thoughts kept drifting back to the day he'd first met Ruby. He'd been slogging through traffic, headed back to the Beach after dropping off some equipment at the Naval Base in Norfolk. Even before the rusty Oldsmobile behind him tapped his bumper, he'd known the driver wasn't paying attention. With his Italian temper at a simmer, he directed the young woman with a pointing finger into the breakdown lane, intending to scold her before getting her insurance information. One good look at the flame-haired beauty dressed in a mesh sweater and ripped jeans, and he could tell she didn't have insurance. He told her he would settle for a date— which had ultimately taken every ounce of determination he had to actually get, as Ruby hadn't wanted anything to do with a younger man.

But Tony kept showing up and, little by little, she'd become his best friend first, then his girlfriend, then his beautiful wife.

His nostalgic smile in the mirror vanished as he remembered

she was gone. He tried to blink back the grief that welled in his eyes like a geyser, but then his chest convulsed. He sank onto the edge of the bathtub with his face in his hands and silently sobbed.

God, please keep her safe. Bring Ruby back to me, alive. I don't want to live without her.

CHAPTER 11

*W*ith her head lower than the windows and the dash, Ruby couldn't tell where they were headed. The road had grown smoother and flatter, with traffic sounds suggesting a return to civilization. Cullum listened to classical music, of all things, on XM radio. The car he drove was a BMW, according to the logo on the steering wheel—older model because there wasn't any kind of computerized display. He could be driving her to Timbuktu, for all she knew.

When a tall green sign came into view with the word *Harrisburg* emblazoned on it, she must have gasped out loud because Cullum's head whipped in her direction.

Ruby snapped her eyes shut, forcing her body to grow lax and praying he couldn't see her heart thumping through the material of her buttoned coat. Hearing nothing from Cullum, she dared to crack her eyelids a moment later. He'd turned his attention back to the road. And there, filling the windshield, was the skyline of Harrisburg, backdropped by pinkening clouds as evening descended.

She had vanished from Philly well over twenty-four hours ago, closer to thirty hours. Corinna might have spilled the beans about Katz. But that was the only reason anyone would think to look for her in Harrisburg.

Tony was probably scouring the wrong city. Picturing him, she closed her eyes against the urge to weep. Her husband was such a good man—too good for her, too good for the world, even. For that very reason, she had fretted since getting to know him well that God would want him back in heaven where he belonged. She could picture him so easily as one of God's archangels, complete with wings and a sword.

Guilt gnawed at her. If something happened and this was it, she would never get to prove her worth to Tony. If only she'd told him about both Katz and the baby. None of this would be happening. Tony wouldn't have let her interview Katz in the first place, especially if he'd known two of his teammates had once worked with the man. But, after hearing about Stasky's murder, Tony, Monty, and Ben would have dealt with Katz in their own way. Katz would have gotten his comeuppance from them, and none of this bad stuff would be happening.

But now...Now she might never have a family with Tony because she'd put her job and her self-interests before their relationship and before their baby's safety.

Oh, God, forgive me.

Hopefully, if she ended up dead, Tony would never discover she'd been pregnant. That would be too much for him. Beneath his tough guy exterior, his heart was pure mush. He didn't deserve that kind of anguish. And she didn't deserve him, never had.

Startling awake to the sound of a car door slamming, Ruby realized she must have lapsed into unconsciousness again. Her pulse sped up.

Where am I now? Not another parking garage!

Her door opened on a puff of cold air, and the dome light flicked on. Ruby kept her eyes closed as Cullum thrust his head and shoulders into the car directly over her. He unfastened her seat belt, looped her purse strap over his head, then heaved her out of the car with a hand under each arm.

He wasn't a small man by any means, but he wasn't as strong as either Tony or the kidnapper, Yordan. With a lot of huffing and puffing, Cullum managed to wedge a shoulder under her stomach before lifting her into a fireman's carry.

His vehicle gave a beep that echoed in the enclosure. With her head dangling halfway down his back, Ruby battled a sudden onslaught of nausea, only vaguely aware he was carrying her toward a heavy door. She was more conscious of the bony shoulder pressing painfully into her lower abdomen, which was full and tender anyway. Unable to take it anymore, she grabbed the back of his coat to alleviate the pressure. "Please, put me down, please. I'll walk."

Startled, Cullum nearly dropped her. When he set her abruptly on her feet, she discovered she could stand, as well as talk.

Looking terrified, Cullum fumbled in the pocket of his jacket, no doubt searching for more sedative.

She held up a hand to forestall him. "Oh no. Don't drug me again. I'm pregnant. You'll hurt the baby." Saying the words out loud filled her with a raging determination to do whatever it took to keep her baby safe. She would fight to the death if he tried to inject her again.

For the longest moment, he gaped at her, his lips parted, his expanded pupils reflecting the weak light shining through the door's window insert. Then he swallowed, finding his voice. "This isn't my idea."

"I know. You're not a killer." Trying to outsmart him when her brain was so foggy wouldn't be easy. "I'll walk. Take...take the zip tie off my ankles. It's not like I can run."

"I don't think that's a good idea."

"Then what's a good idea? Doing everything Katz tells you to?"

"Shh." He glanced fearfully about, punched a code into the keypad, then pulled the door open. As he dragged her into the warm, dimly lit lobby toward an elevator, the heels of her pumps left skid marks as they slid across the marble foyer. His hold cut off the circulation to her arms, causing her sprained wrist to throb in protest.

"You're hurting my arm." He'd seemed upset by the sight of her swollen wrist earlier.

"Sorry."

His immediate adjustment assured Ruby that Cullum had no intention of killing her. He probably wanted nothing to do with craziness. Hope pulsed in her anew. Maybe she could talk him into letting her go.

Between steady supplications to God and nightmares that snatched him from his fitful slumber, Tony attempted to catch some shut eye on his mother's couch. The buzzing of his phone in the middle of the night roused him from a light sleep. Ben was calling him. "Hello?"

"Hey, Brother."

At Ben's alert and encouraging tone, Tony sat straight up. The streetlight shone around the living room curtains Mama dropped at night. Tony pricked his ears even as he checked his watch. It was minutes past midnight, and Mama and Corinna were sound asleep upstairs. "What's up?"

"Just wanted you to know I caught a glimpse of Ruby in Katz's office. I'm looking at it from a rooftop across the street."

Joy flooded Tony's heart. Given the way Ben was talking, he was trying to keep his teeth from chattering. It had to be freezing on a rooftop outside. *Thank You, God!* "She's in Harrisburg?"

"Yep, and she looked okay. Definitely there against her will but—"

"What do you mean by that?"

"Well, she didn't walk into the room. She was...brought in by some tall, well-dressed office type—not Katz. Maybe an assistant. I only got a glimpse of them before he turned off the lights. Now there's just a dim light shining, and they're not by the windows. Hard to see much. Still, I thought you should know she's in Harrisburg, which means Katz appears to be on board with the plan. I'm sure he'll pick her up in the morning and bring her to the funeral."

Tony sagged against the cushions, phone still pressed to his ear. A portion of his joyful relief faded. What if Katz's assistant was a monster like his boss? "I guess you can't break into the building and get her back tonight?"

Ben's grunt sounded sympathetic. "Maybe if I'd been waiting in the parking garage, but the place is locked down like Fort Knox, so I went across the street where I could see any lights that came on. Let's give Katz a chance to do the right thing tomorrow."

"Yeah." Tomorrow would be here soon enough.

"But she's okay. Just wanted you to know that."

She's okay. The words thawed a portion of the ice in Tony's chest, but he wouldn't fully relax until Ruby was safely in his embrace.

Fighting the urge to drift off to sleep, Ruby sensed Cullum bending over her. She reared back with a gasp as something cold and wet touched her cheek.

"Relax." He held a wet paper towel in his hand. "I just want to clean your face. You've got an ugly gash there."

"Please, just take off these zip ties. I need to use the restroom badly. I'll wash my face myself." She knew exactly where the bathroom was—right near the office door they'd entered several hours earlier.

Cullum straightened with a frown. "I'll free your hands but not your ankles." He set aside the paper towel, then slid a hand into a trouser pocket and pulled out a jackknife. Ruby held out her wrists while making note of which pocket held the blade.

"Ow." She hissed in a breath as his sawing on the zip tie put pressure on her tender wrist.

"Sorry." Cullum grimaced.

Since she couldn't run with her feet bound, she would have to talk him into letting her go.

"Okay, stand up." Cullum grabbed her by her good wrist and pulled her to her feet. Then he stepped behind her, looped an arm around her rib cage, and hoisted her slightly before dragging her across the room.

"This is ridiculous," Ruby protested. "Just free my feet. It's not like there's anywhere I can go."

Cullum didn't answer. Instead, he left her at the bathroom door to shuffle inside under her own steam. Ruby locked herself inside and flicked on the light, flinching at the glare of the sconces, then grimacing at her reflection. The side of her face that had struck the tree trunk the prior night was bruised and flecked with dried blood. Her hair was a riot of curls. Dark circles rimmed her eyes.

Helping herself to the toilet, she noticed a tinge of blood on her underwear and her heart stopped. *No!* She checked to see if she was still bleeding, but the blood appeared to be just a spotting, not an actual flow. She dropped her face into her hands. Dread made her heart pound. *Please, God.*

What she wouldn't give to be able to tell Tony she was pregnant. Now it might be too late.

She raised her head and sniffed. Anything was possible. All she had to do was get away from Cullum, whom she could hear in the office talking on the phone. Standing, she adjusted her clothing as she pressed an ear to the door, hoping to overhear any plans for her fate.

"Yes, sir. But is that really necessary? She says she's pregnant. It could hurt the baby."

Ruby held her breath. Cullum seemed to be asking about the need to drug her.

"Yes, sir. We'll see you at eight, then. Bye."

His tone of resignation failed to reassure her. His call must have ended because footsteps were now coming her way. She flushed the toilet, washed her hands, then helped herself to the stack of paper towels to dab at the abrasion on her face. Would Cullum really inject her again? She had to have her wits about her if she was going to outsmart him or convince him to do the right thing.

He gave a light knock. "Almost done in there?"

Ruby tossed the paper towel into the garbage, thinking the police could use her DNA as evidence later. She drew a steadying breath while unlocking the door. "All done."

The door swung open. Cullum's weak blue gaze went straight to her cheek. "That's better."

She was about to ask, "How long have you worked for Katz?" as a lead-in to winning him over, when Cullum seized her good arm. Something flashed in his other hand as he steadied her. She felt the sting of the needle even as she gasped in disbelief and tried to yank free of his grasp.

"No! I told you. You're killing my baby!"

"I'm sorry." His face was the very picture of remorse before it went blurry.

The sedative sluiced through her veins, debilitating every muscle. She felt herself falling as the darkness closed in.

CHAPTER 12

Only a handful of people had gathered for Stasky's funeral. Apart from Tony and Monty, a cadre of Marines, resplendent in their dress uniforms, had appeared to bestow military honors on the veteran. The only civilians were a doleful-looking middle-aged man who'd told Monty he was Stasky's roommate, a woman around forty who also claimed to have been a friend but might have been a love interest for how miserable she looked, and an older woman who claimed to be his landlady.

A bearded bagpiper, dressed in a kilt that left his bare knees ruddy in the cold, kicked off the service by filling the late-morning stillness with a heartfelt rendition of "Danny Boy." Behind him, a chilly gust tore the last golden leaf from a nearby maple tree. Tony watched it spiral though the air before settling atop the flag-draped coffin, as if Mother Nature wished to pay tribute to the fallen warrior.

Tony noted the others' expressions as thoughts bounced like ping-pong balls through his brain. Did anyone else wonder why a man of Polish descent was being buried in a Lutheran cemetery to the strains of "Danny Boy"?

His alert senses registered everything: the smell of pastries wafting from a nearby bakery, the warmth of the sun dispelling the sharp edge to the late-autumn air, the fact that Katz was nowhere to be seen. That didn't mean he wasn't here, necessarily. After all, Ben, who was acting as their scout, was here, but no one could see *him*.

Katz was going to show, Tony assured himself. According to Monty and Ben, who'd arrived later than planned, Katz was right behind them when they'd left Harrisburg. Monty had followed Katz from his residence at eight that morning when he'd driven straight to his office, allegedly to collect Ruby. Both Monty and Ben and seen her in the back seat of Katz's Genesis G90 when they'd driven past it. As Katz had been heading toward Highway 76, pointed toward Philadelphia, they'd assumed he would show up right behind them.

Only he still wasn't here.

Doubts assailed Tony. What if Katz had driven to the airport with Ruby and put her on his private jet? He could be flying her to Mexico right then. The thought made his knees wobble. He locked them, gripping his cell phone tighter. Ben would text him the minute Katz showed up.

The bagpiper fell quiet, and the Lutheran pastor addressed the small gathering. Tony barely heard the man's words. With his stomach in knots, his thoughts still racing, he checked his phone. Still nothing. Lifting his gaze, he searched for the family crypt and the large bush between which Ben was tucked, invisible to the eye but with a clear view of the parking lot.

Tony persevered, rocked by the beat of his heart. What if Katz wasn't coming?

"Ashes to ashes and dust to dust."

The pastor's sermon ended. As one of the Marine's lifted his trumpet to belt out "Taps," the rest of the Marines stepped forward, lifted the flag off the coffin, and proceeded to fold it, meticulously tight, into the shape of a tricorn hat, like those worn in the American Revolution.

Following Monty's cue, Tony released the catch on his Trident pin with clumsy fingers. They both approached the casket, atop of which Monty pounded his pin, Tony right behind him.

Anxiety roiled in him. What did it mean that Katz wasn't here?

The Marines were now taking up their rifles.

Boom. Tony had to steel himself to keep from startling at the three-volley salute. *Boom. Boom.*

The phone in his hand finally vibrated. Relief clobbered him, leaving him light-headed. He elbowed Monty, holding out his phone so the CO could see Ben's message. *Katz is here.*

Instead of the high-powered Vortex Optic scope Ben usually carried into battle, the sniper was hunkered behind the viewing end of a military-issue, long-range camera. He would film the impending exchange, which Monty would share with the FBI, along with his testimony, after they returned to Virginia.

The Marines were presenting the flag to Stasky's female friend, one of them intoning, "It is my high privilege to present you this flag, ma'am. Let it be a symbol of the grateful appreciation this nation feels for the distinguished service rendered to our country and our flag by your loved one."

The priest swept a compassionate eye over the small assembly. "Thank you all for coming. If you wish to remain here and pay your respects to the departed, the coffin will not be lowered until sunset."

Monty met Tony's gaze as he pivoted toward the parking lot. Following right at Monty's heels, Tony's searched for and identified the elegant black Genesis G90 parked alone on the far side of the cemetery. Even from a distance, he recognized Katz from Ruby's interview. The man was built like Monty, tall and imposing but with wide cheekbones that gave him a brutish look.

No sign of Ruby. Would Katz try to pull a fast one?

Tony wiped his damp palms on his thighs while missing the

reassuring presence of his sidearm. But open carry was forbidden in Philly, and he wasn't in combat, even if it felt like it. After all, things could still go wrong, affecting the outcome of his life, dictating his destiny, threatening his identity as Ruby's husband.

With measured steps, they neared the luxury, full-sized sedan. The lieutenant governor lounged against it, remarking their approach while striving to look relaxed. But his gaze was locked on the box tucked under Monty's arm like he couldn't wait to get his hands on it. As they paused in front of him, he pushed off the car.

"We meet again, Monty." His voice dripped with disdain. "I always knew one of you would go back on your word."

Monty ignored the taunt. "Where is she?"

Katz tipped his head toward his Genesis. "In the back seat. Is that the book?"

Tony tried peering through the car's tinted windows, but they were utterly opaque.

"It is."

Katz held out a hand. "Hand it to me. Then you can take what you came for. And just so you know, if you plan to screw me over in the end, I'll take you down with me."

Monty shrugged nonchalantly, giving no indication at all that he wore a microphone synched by Bluetooth to Ben's camera. "I won't be pressing any charges, Len. Let's just let bygones be bygones."

Katz's dark-gray eyes narrowed at the intentional use of his first name. "Same thing goes with the journalist," he tacked on. "You mess with me, and she'll be the first person to disappear."

Nice. The threat had to be a misdemeanor at least.

"I hear you. We'd like her back now."

With a smirk on his handsome face, Katz pulled open the rear door. Tony's heart soared at the familiar sight of Ruby's copper curls, only her head was lolling, like she was sleeping sitting up. He rushed to her side.

"Bella!" Ducking into the car, he lifted her chin to gauge her condition. His training as a medic kicked in. The minor laceration on her cheek made his blood boil, but it was nothing. Her eyes were slightly open, like she was struggling to wake up. Their glassiness suggested sedation.

He pulled his head out of the car. "What did you give her to knock her out?"

Katz's shrug was an imitation of Monty's. "No idea. My assistant was responsible."

Biting his tongue against a retort, Tony ducked back into the car, freed Ruby from her seat belt, then scooped her up like a baby and pulled her out, leaving her purse for Monty to recover. Without a backward glance, he marched toward the nearest bench, where he sat with Ruby still in his arms, her head heavy on his shoulder. "I'm here, Bella."

A small part of him was aware of Katz's immediate departure, of Monty clasping Ruby's purse as he came to stand over them. "Does she need a doctor?"

Tony, upon checking her pulse, had found her wrist swollen and discolored. His temples throbbed with fury. Palpitating her other wrist, he was comforted by the steady pulsing of her vein beneath his fingertips. He was conscious of Ben joining them, shucking off the ghillie suit that had kept him camouflaged.

He caught Tony's helpless gaze. "We've got some great footage."

Ruby's eyelashes fluttered, garnering Tony's full attention, especially as she mumbled his name, her tongue clearly impaired by the sedative. "I'm sowuh."

Sorry? The word arrested him from counting her heartbeats. A fat tear rolled out of the corner of one eye.

"It's okay. You're safe now, Bella. No one's going to hurt you again."

At his assertion, her face crumpled into a picture of misery. With a cluck of dismay, he adjusted his hold on her, then lifted her in his arms, intending to take her home.

"Wait." Monty threw a hand up. "She's bleeding. There's blood on your pants."

Horror electrified Tony. He sat abruptly on the bench again, searching automatically for a wound and discovering the lining of her coat was drenched. She was bleeding *down there*. But he knew exactly when she got her monthly flow and that would have happened over a week ago, though come to think of it, he couldn't remember it happening any time recently.

He lifted a stricken gaze at Monty, whose expression had turned thunderous.

"Yeah." Tony's voice was like gravel. "She needs a doctor."

Ruby kept her eyes closed, feigning sleep, even though the effects of the tranquilizer had worn off completely. Her sprained wrist throbbed within the bandage that now kept it immobile. The sounds of the bustling hospital, audible through her closed door, assured her she was safe, reunited with Tony, whom she couldn't bring herself to even look at.

Her pregnancy was a thing of the past. How had something she hadn't wanted at first become so precious to her? And now it was gone. Her joy lay in a dark and muddy puddle, and the fault was entirely her own.

She didn't have to open her eyes to know that Tony was sitting in the reclining chair next to her, brooding as he waited for her to wake up. Only if she woke up, she would have to explain to him why she'd kept their baby a secret.

Just talk to him, you coward. She owed him an explanation. She owed him way more than that, but it was too late now.

Dreading the conversation to come, she drew a bracing breath, opened her eyes, and rolled her head on the pillow to meet his bloodshot gaze.

Gosh, if he looked *that* bad with deep brackets around his

mouth and dark circles under his eyes, she would hate to see herself right then. "Hey." Her voice was like sandpaper.

"Hey, yourself. How're you feelin'?" His chocolate-brown eyes bored into hers.

"Sore." She swallowed against a dry throat. "Could I have a drink of water?"

"Sure." He stood and held the large plastic cup for Ruby to sip out of through a straw. As she nursed the chilled water from the straw, she tried to think of what to say.

Tony didn't give her the chance to start first. "How long did you know?"

Ruby flinched from the disillusionment in his voice and lowered her head. The loss of her baby lanced her heart afresh. The doctor had spilled her secret, telling Tony she was miscarrying before she had the chance to explain.

"Almost two months." She couldn't meet Tony's gaze.

Stunned silence followed her reply. "*Two months.*" His voice rasped with betrayal.

"I was going to tell you at Christmas. I wanted to surprise you."

"And your investigation of Katz? When were you going to tell me about that?" He laid aside the cup but remained by the bed, looming over her. "I haven't slept or eaten or even breathed in over forty-eight hours because you didn't tell me what you were up to. Because you're keeping *secrets* from me. If I'd known, I could have *protected* you. None of this would have happened!"

Remorse twisted through her, wringing tears from her. "You're right. I'm so sorry." Tears gushed at the thought that Christmas wouldn't be the joyful day she'd been anticipating. The poor little life inside her never stood a chance. But it wasn't all her fault. "Is Katz—will he get in trouble for what he did to me?"

"Eventually." Tony swung away from her, stalking to the window. "Monty wants the FBI to investigate him. That way Katz doesn't blame us...or you."

Alarm penetrated her misery at the thought of Katz seeking vengeance.

An aching silence fell between them. Tony kept his back to her. She watched his shoulders rise and fall as he fought to bring his emotions under control.

She managed to tell him in a strangled voice, "I promise you, Tony, if I'd known Katz was going to try and kill me, I would never have taken chances with our baby."

He turned his head at her assertion, not all the way, as if he couldn't bring himself to look at her. Perhaps he'd finally realized what she'd known all along—that she wasn't the woman he thought she was.

But then he finally swung around and marched back to her. "You shouldn't have interviewed the lieutenant governor without telling me. That's the part that hurts me. But what happened to you isn't your fault, Bella." Taking her good hand in his, Tony held it gently. "Katz is evil. You couldn't have known how evil he is."

Once again, Tony was taking the high ground. She agreed Katz was a monster, but Tony was wrong about the miscarriage. She'd put her exposé first and her baby second, and now she deserved to suffer for it.

"I want to go home." She needed Opal, who'd been like a mother to her ever since their own mother died young, leaving just their father to raise them.

Tony stretched out a hand and tucked a ringlet of her hair behind her ear. "I'll take you home, Bella. Just as soon as the doctor clears you." Bending over, he dropped the lightest of kisses on her lips. "Now try and rest while I find us a rental car."

Her beautiful Range Rover was gone, as was her Christmas surprise for Tony. Ruby closed her eyes to hide the tears welling in her eyes. *I'm so sorry. I'm so, so sorry.*

CHAPTER 13

*T*ony slanted his wife a worried look. Seated next to him in the passenger seat of the rented Malibu, she'd spoken scarcely more than a word since he'd checked her out of the hospital on Monday morning. He'd driven her first to Bella Vista to collect their luggage and to say their farewells. His mother and Corinna had both been as subdued as Ruby was.

An hour outside of Philly, with hours to go before they reached Virginia Beach, Tony yearned for some color to come back to Ruby's cheeks, for the devil-may-care sparkle to return to her lackluster eyes. But she remained silent and subdued, almost... penitent, which wasn't a word that had ever applied to her before.

"You warm enough, Bella?" The slate-colored clouds were starting to dust I-95 with shimmering snowflakes. He had set the heat as high as he could stand it, but Ruby still looked like she was freezing with her peach-colored coat buttoned to her chin. She sat there hugging her injured arm like a bird with a broken wing, a look that didn't suit her one bit.

"I'm fine." She stared unseeing at the road before them.

Maybe she only needed reassurance. "Katz isn't going to get away with what he's done, if that's what's worrying you."

"It's not." Her distant voice did little to reassure him. "I could care less about Katz. Every bad thing he's ever done is going to haunt him soon enough."

The sad certainty in her voice made Tony shoot another worried look at her. "Bella, you gotta stop blamin' yourself for what happened. If the baby's gone, then it wasn't meant to be born yet. We'll have a family one day. Maybe now's just not the right time."

She didn't immediately reply, giving him hope that his words had comforted her. But then she said, "That's what I thought too, at first. I thought having a baby now would ruin my career. That's why I didn't tell you right away. I didn't want it to happen. Only later, when that man named Yordan kidnapped me, protecting my baby was all I could think about. I just...I can't believe how selfish I am..."

"Don't say that, Ruby. You risked your life to keep Katz from climbing any higher."

"Some other nut job will replace him. I could spend my whole life exposing criminals, but there's always more out there."

He laughed without humor. "Yeah. Now you know how I feel."

As she lapsed into silence again, Tony thought the discussion was over. The snow frosting the highway had turned into icy rain, forcing him to switch on his windshield wipers.

Ruby spoke up again, jarring his concentration with her words. "I'm going to stay with my sister for a few days."

What? The steering wheel wobbled in his grip. "Why?" A sick feeling rolled through him. Was this the beginning of something insurmountable between them?

"I just need...some time away from us."

Us? He had to tear his horrified gaze off her profile to keep from crashing into the guardrail. After stabbing on the hazard lights, Tony edged their rental off the highway and into the breakdown lane, where he turned in his seat to face her. "I don't understand. You gotta know I love you, no matter what. Ruby, I forgive you for not telling me about the baby. It's no big deal."

Oh, those were the wrong words.

Her eyes had turned into turquoise ponds that overflowed. Her chin quivered adorably. "I love you, too, Tony. But right now, I don't love myself. I kept you in the dark when I shouldn't have."

"Ruby."

"Just let me talk. I don't deserve you, Tony. I never have."

"Please, don't say that." His heart thudded with dread that she would end their marriage over this. He tried groping for her good hand, but she pulled it out of reach. "You're amazing, Bella."

She averted her gaze while shaking her head and staring at bare-limbed trees beside the highway. "I just need some time."

Tony put his hands back on the steering wheel and wrung it, his emotions swingingly wildly. "Fine. But you need to know I can't imagine my life without you. I don't even want to."

He watched her swallow, but she didn't even acknowledge his words.

Shocked into silence, Tony stared at the cars tearing past them. They had four more hours on the road before they got home. Something told him four hours wouldn't be enough time to change Ruby's mind. They'd stumbled upon a glitch in their bond as husband and wife, one that made him quail for how little he understood it.

Being a SEAL, his first impulse was to tackle the problem head-on, to unravel the knot, then smooth things out between them. But this was a matter between Ruby and her conscience. He couldn't fix it. All he could do was hope she came to her senses while spending time apart from him.

With his heart as heavy as a boulder, Tony merged back into traffic. God had brought them together. He wasn't going to let this incident tear them apart.

~

"Dat's a lickwish cawd," Ruby's not-yet-three-year-old nephew pointed a pudgy finger at the spot where Ruby's gingerbread man was about to land. "You skip."

"Are you sure?" Ruby reached for the licorice card and turned it over. "Huh, you have the cards memorized."

Ryan had trounced her at a memory game earlier that day, and she didn't even know how he played those games on his iPad. The precocious toddler reminded her of Tony for how smart he was. Loss wrung her heart. Their baby would have been the same way.

For the fifth time that day, she caught herself wanting to text her husband. Separation put a perpetual ache in her chest, but distance gave her the perspective she needed. Was she *really* the right person for Tony, or was she the weak link in their marriage?

One thing she'd realized that she wanted Tony to know: She was actually good with her nephew. Monty had pointed out that she had a special way with kids—though come to think of it, that might have been Monty's idea of a joke about Tony's age relative to hers.

No, she *was* good with Ryan. If she wasn't, he wouldn't want to play with her all day instead of going to day care. Could God be trying to tell Ruby something?

As the afternoon wore on, Ryan yawned. Time for his nap. They went up to his dinosaur-themed bedroom where Ruby stayed by his railed bed until he fell asleep. Then she nipped downstairs, hoping to watch an episode of some reality TV show— anything to distract her from missing Tony. As she dropped onto the couch, reaching for the remote control, the door from the garage door opened, and Opal entered the mudroom, visible from where Ruby sat.

She blinked at her big sister. "Oh, you're home. I didn't hear the garage door open."

"I finished early today. Is Ryan napping?"

"Yep, just put him down."

"Oh, good. I was hoping for the chance to talk to you." Opal shook off her outer coat, military issue, and hung it on the hall tree in the mudroom, along with her purse. A physical therapist at the Portsmouth Naval Medical Center, she always went to work in uniform.

Ruby mentally reviewed the past few days. What might she have done wrong?

"So." Opal sank onto the opposite end of the couch, kicked off her pumps, and propped her stockinged feet on the coffee table. "I have an observation. Correct me if I'm wrong, but you seem to be…punishing yourself for your miscarriage."

Ruby gulped down the guilt that immediately clogged her throat. "I mean, it's basically my fault for putting my work first. For not telling Tony."

Opal sent her a commiserating smile. "I can tell you feel bad about that. You've told him as much?"

"Yes?"

"And have you," Opal kept her tone light, "asked God's forgiveness?"

"Oh yes." Ruby had shed copious tears in the process.

Opal's copper hair, straight as a pin, shifted as she cocked her head. "But you're still beating yourself up."

Ruby tucked her chin to her chest, not answering.

Silence hung between the sisters before Opal broke it. "Honey, I know exactly what you're going through. Don't forget, I accidentally killed Admiral Jenkins's hitman while trying to escape from him."

"That's different. You didn't mean to do it, plus he'd have killed you."

"But I still felt guilty. I felt like I had to do something good after that to exonerate myself. Only later did I realize, while volunteering for duty overseas, that I was already forgiven."

Ruby averted her gaze. "You deserved to be forgiven."

Her sister sighed. "Honey, what was the point of Christ's suffering on the cross if you're not going to honor His sacrifice?"

Ruby kept quiet.

"I mean, can you imagine the agony He must have felt, hanging with all His weight on the spikes driven into His hands and feet? Hours and hours of slow suffocation, not to mention a stab wound that probably punctured a lung. He could have walked away from all that. He had the power to walk away. Instead, He put Himself through unbelievable torture, so we don't have to torture ourselves. What He did was a gift for all of mankind. Rejecting that gift is like saying it wasn't good enough."

Ruby envisioned the scene as Opal described it. She watched Mel Gibson's movie *The Passion of the Christ* with absolute horror. "I never thought of it that way."

"I know. And I don't mean to preach to you. I'm just saying you don't have to beat yourself up anymore. If you asked God for forgiveness, then it's over. It's done. The slate has been wiped clean."

The words were slow to sink in.

"For what it's worth, I think you should text Tony or, better yet, call him and put him out of his misery. He's been blowing up my phone with all his texts."

"He's been texting you?" This was news to Ruby. Her heavy heart buoyed with gratitude for his continued love and forgiveness.

"Every hour on the hour. That man is completely invested in you, Ruby." Opal lowered her feet back into her shoes and stood. "I'm going to go change and take a walk with Ryan when he wakes up."

It was clear Opal wasn't expecting Ruby to join them.

She sat a moment, keeping the television off, thinking. Far be it from her to behave like Jesus's sacrifice wasn't good enough. What more of Himself could He have given? Maybe Opal was right. Honestly, when had her big sister ever been wrong? Both of them had snuffed out a life without intending to. Neither act was done intentionally. Ruby was certain God had forgiven Opal. Maybe it was time to accept that she'd been forgiven, too.

So why was she sitting here still beating herself up?

With a spark of relief, Ruby snatched up her cell phone and texted Tony, as she'd been longing to do for days now. *Hey, what do you feel like for dinner tonight?*

Less than five seconds later, he responded. *Just your smile.*

That pulled a smile right out of her. Tony always said the sweetest things. *You got it.* She sent him three taco emojis. *I'll stop at Pepe's on my way home.*

EPILOGUE

"*H*appy Valentine's Day, darling!" Ruby greeted Tony at the door in a red silk kimono dotted with black hearts and tied at the waist with a silken sash. His stunned gaze fell to her bare feet, toes painted to match the scarlet wrap.

He shut the door hastily, not just to keep out the damp February air, but to prevent every man driving down Shore Drive from gawking at his beautiful wife.

"Well, hello to you." Recalling, at last, what he held in his hands, he thrust the bouquet of long-stemmed roses at her. "Sorry I'm late. I had to run over an old man and steal these 'cause all the stores were sold out."

She tsked her tongue. "Poor old man." Accepting the bouquet, she took a long, dreamy sniff. "They're lovely, thank you. How was work?"

He kept his eyes on her as he shook out of his parka, leaving him in just his Naval Working Uniform. After hanging up the parka, he unlatched his webbed belt and sidearm and hung them inside the closet, also. "Busy." After 5:00 A.M. wake ups every day this week, he'd been feeling worn out, but not anymore.

As he shut the closet door, the odor of burnt food hit the back of his throat. "Oh. What's that smell?"

"Dinner." Disappointment tugged at her lips before she turned and padded down the hall to their open-concept kitchen and living area. "The scallops didn't come out the way I expected." She made a beeline for the sink to tend to the flowers, hiding how crushed she was.

Tony hid a wry smile as he followed her. Her attempts at cooking usually ended in failure. "It's the effort that counts, Bella. You'll get the hang of it one day."

"Doubtful." She ran the stems under the faucet while hacking several inches off with their kitchen scissors.

Tony retrieved the vase from the cabinet that was too high for Ruby to reach.

"Thanks." She took it with a smile before adding water, flower food, and then the roses. Keeping her gaze averted, she set the vase on the windowsill overlooking the Atlantic Ocean.

Tony put his hands on her silk-clad shoulders, turning her to face him. "Don't worry 'bout the scallops, Bella. We can always get takeout. So long as we're together, I really don't care what we eat."

Following her gaze to the dining room table, he discovered it was laid out for two, with the china inherited from her namesake, Grandma Ruby, a bottle of wine, and two tall candlesticks.

Her lower lip trembled slightly. "But I wanted it to be perfect."

"It *is* perfect."

She brightened slightly. "At least the salad turned out okay."

"And I'm on a diet anyway." He patted his rock-hard abs. "You want to eat now or later?"

"Later." She lowered her lashes demurely, adding, "I have a present to give you."

Guessing the gift she had in mind, Tony scooped her up, eliciting a squeak as he carried her toward their gas fireplace and the flames casting warm lights all over the room. Ruby had draped a fur throw over their L-shaped couch. "Nice." He laid her gently atop it, his lips like a heat-seeking missile homing in on hers.

"Mmm. Wait." One hand pushed against his shoulder, urging him off her. The other sank into his short, crisp hair, pulling him back for another kiss.

He chuckled against her lips. "I'm getting mixed signals."

"You're distracting me! I really have a gift to give you. It's right there on the coffee table."

Tony looked over, spying what looked like a box of chocolate wrapped in red cellophane and topped with a white bow. "You want me to open it now?" His hands went to the silken belt around her waist. "I'd rather unwrap you first."

She hesitated, her porcelain complexion blushing slowly to rose. "Later then."

Many minutes later, Tony collapsed along the length of the couch, pulling her with him and flipping the extra length of the fur throw over her bare back to keep her warm. He kissed her forehead. "I just love our life together." The only thing that could have made it better was for Katz to be in jail already, but the FBI had assured them that would happen soon. Not only had David Collum, the assistant, cracked when the FBI questioned him, but Yordan had been caught at a sobriety checkpoint driving a stolen vehicle. He and Collum had both promised to testify against Katz.

Ruby tilted her head back and smiled rather smugly. "I'm about to make it even better." She stretched out an arm, snagged his gift off the coffee table, then placed it on his chest. "Open it."

He gave it a shake. "Intriguing." What he'd thought was a box of chocolates proved too light. Using his teeth, he tugged off the sparkly white ribbon, then flicked off the lid and lifted out a white plastic test strip inside. Two pink lines suggested she was positive. "You have COVID?"

Ruby cast her eyes to heaven, but she clearly knew he was teasing her.

"You're pregnant."

She beamed. "Correct."

Astonishment, then wonder, then worry broke over him in successive waves, keeping him silent. This world was not a safe place.

"Seven weeks already." Her eyes glimmered like aquamarine jewels.

"Oh, man." Tony had never doubted they would get pregnant again, just not this soon.

"I know you'll just be starting med school. But at least we don't have to move, and my job gives me some flexibility."

The Navy was paying him to attend Eastern Virginia Medical School so long as he reenlisted for eight more years.

And Ruby now had an older male assistant to accompany her on interviews and to lighten her workload. Plus her Range Rover had been returned to her, so life couldn't get much better.

"Right." Tony nodded. God would watch over them. "I'm just processing, that's all."

Her quirked eyebrows betrayed a trace of worry. "Are you happy, though?"

He was only ever happy when Ruby was happy, which she really seemed to be, so— "Yeah, I'm ecstatic." He looked back at the two pink lines, marveling at what they represented. "We're gonna have a kid!"

"I hope he's smart like you."

"I hope she's beautiful like you." Tony slid a palm down her smooth stomach, until it rested over the slightest suggestion of a baby bump. "Wow, Mama's gonna be ecstatic."

Ruby pointed a warning finger at him. "Don't you say a word about it until I reach eleven weeks. That's when it's safe to tell people, and I get to be the one to tell Anna, not you."

"Of course." Tony grinned. His mother would never snipe about Ruby's skinny hips again.

BE STILL

PREFACE

The characters and premise for this novella were presented in my latest novel, *All Things Together*, Book 6 in the Acts of Valor series. Since that book's release, readers have clamored to discover what happens to poor McKenzie Jones after she is swept off into witness protection. Will she and Miles ever get their own happily ever after? Well, readers, fast-forward three years and see for yourselves!

PROLOGUE

cKenzie charged out of the employee elevator, then hurried down the hotel corridor toward the house-keeping cart being pushed by her colleague. The Sea Dip Hotel stood nearly empty on this weekday morning with few guests coming to Myrtle Beach so late in the season.

At the sound of her approach, Jamila glanced over, then slowed the cart to wait for her. "Caroline!" Her face reflected surprise. "What are you doin' here, girl? I thought you were off today."

McKenzie had scarcely grown accustomed to her latest alias. "I was off." She caught her breath while tightening the loose strings on her apron. "But Nadia called this morning to say she wasn't feeling well, and she talked me into taking her shift."

"Shoot, she ain't sick." Jamila rolled her dark eyes. "You know she just drank too much last night, right? You shouldn't let her use you like that."

"I know, but I need the money."

Jamila ran an assessing gaze over McKenzie's petite figure. "What's a classy girl like you doin' workin' in a place like this, anyway? You should be sellin' time-shares or somethin', not cleanin' up other people's messes."

McKenzie avoided eye contact. "It's as good a job as any. I don't need to be rich."

"Shoot."

What would Jamila think if she knew McKenzie had been wealthy all her life—until three years ago? When wealth came at the expense of other people's fortunes, it was an empty luxury. Her father, head of the Centurion Cohort headquartered in Savannah, Georgia, had taught her that bitter truth. Luckily for McKenzie, she'd inherited not only her mother's decency but also Genevieve's journals which detailed the crimes her husband had committed. Ultimately, those journals had been used by the FBI to send Jared Jones to prison, where he'd mysteriously died.

"True, but it ain't no sin to use what God gave you." Jamila gave her a pointed once-over. "With a face and body like that, you could snag a rich ol' man and never have to work another day again."

McKenzie shuddered inwardly. How close she'd come to being forced into marriage with her father's friend! "I like to work." She pushed the cart forward, cutting their conversation short.

Working made the time go by faster. What's more, her face and body were the last things McKenzie wanted anyone to take note of, lest she be recognized. As a client of the U.S. Marshal's witness protection program, or WITSEC, she had taken on an entirely new identity and appearance, coloring her dark ringlets auburn and growing her hair way past her shoulders where she used to wear it. WITSEC determined where she lived, and, in places like Myrtle Beach, a menial job was the only one she could find.

At the next hotel door, McKenzie pulled the master keycard from her apron pocket and picked up a stack of freshly folded towels. "I'll take this side." She waited for Jamila to nod before knocking on the door with the *Make Up Room* sign dangling from the doorknob. "Housekeeping."

As expected, the room was empty, with the curtains flung open and sunlight streaming in. Throwing herself into the mindless task of stripping the bed, McKenzie realized she'd been cleaning rooms at this mid-priced hotel for almost five months now. Little chance of her running into her father's entitled friends in a place like the Sea Dip, that was certain.

It beat her first job in Omaha, inspecting cans in a food-processing plant. The best job she'd found so far had been in Portland, Oregon, working as a veterinarian's assistant, but she couldn't stay there, either. It was all WITSEC could do to stay one step ahead of the well-networked Centurion Cohort.

While her mother's journals had put hundreds of members in jail, others had escaped imprisonment due to good lawyers, or possibly thanks to a fellow Centurion sitting in the jury, protecting his kind. It was the men who'd avoided jail time who sought McKenzie's ruin, keeping her on the run.

Down on her knees in the bathroom, she worked to scrape purple bubble gum off the tiled floor. *The wages of my father's sins are still being paid.*

And the debt was a heavy one. Heavy and lonely.

But God still loved her. She reminded herself of Jeremiah 29:11 every day. *"For I know the plans I have for you...plans to prosper you and not to harm you, plans to give you hope and a future."* It was just a matter of time before McKenzie could live her life again without this constant fear of being found.

CHAPTER 1

*I*t was something McKenzie could not get used to—sitting at a public bus stop in a tourist town without feeling like she might be recognized. Listening to Jamila talk nonstop about the trials of raising teenage boys, McKenzie leaned back against the wooden bench and forced herself to relax.

No one here knows who I am. She repeated that mantra to herself each and every day.

On this mild afternoon in the middle of the week, tourists streamed out of hotels to enjoy the late-September sunshine. Teenagers, just out of school for the day, cruised the strip in their souped-up cars, windows lowered, music blasting. A bright sun kept the cooler air at a perfect temperature. McKenzie tipped her head back, drew a deep breath of salt-laced air, and closed her eyes. When she opened them again, she was looking straight into the eye of a high-powered telephoto lens, aimed down at her from a hotel balcony across the street.

She jerked upright, then peered around hoping to identify something close to her that explained the need for a photo. But there was just a parking lot on one side, a street on the other.

Suspicion skewered her as she looked back at the camera. Its owner swiveled, disappearing back into his room.

McKenzie's scalp tingled.

Why would he have taken pictures of the bus stop? To capture the lifestyle of the working class in Myrtle Beach? Or to positively identify her?

"Caroline? Hey, there!" Jamila's face swam into view. "You're looking all peaked, girl. You best not be gettin' that flu. You know your friend Nadia won't cover your shift like you cover hers."

"I know. No, I'm not sick. I'm just..." *Scared. And probably paranoid.*

But this was how it always started. Men she'd never seen before started taking an interest in her, following her around. It had happened twice before. In Omaha, a young man had been filming her at work, and WITSEC had swept her away the very next day. In Portland, she'd been chased down a dark alley on her way home from work. That same night, WITSEC had moved her clear across the country. McKenzie's stomach cramped. *Not again.* "Actually, maybe I am sick."

"Don't breathe on me, honey, 'cause I can't afford to be ill." Jamila slid farther down the bench, putting space between them.

Tears pressured McKenzie's eyes. Jamila had been her first and only friend in Myrtle Beach. She'd taken McKenzie under her wing, made her feel welcome. *I don't want to start over, Lord. Please, this has to stop.*

A bus rolled up with a screech and a cloud of noxious fumes. McKenzie made a quick decision. Standing abruptly, she met her friend's startled gaze with regret. "Jamila, I might not be here tomorrow. Thank you for your friendship."

Jamila gawked at her. "That's not your bus, girl! Where're you goin'?"

If she moved fast enough, maybe she wouldn't be followed. With a grimace and a wave, McKenzie bounded onto the near-empty bus, took a seat by the door, and peered back up at the balcony. Her pulse skipped to see the man standing there again, this time with a cell phone plastered to his ear and his eyes fixed on the bus she'd just boarded.

She dug in her purse for her own cell phone and dialed her case handler.

"Higgins," he answered after three rings.

"Some man just took my picture while I was sitting at the bus stop." McKenzie pitched her voice low, though the nearest person to her sat several rows away.

"You think he recognized you?" Higgins didn't sound too worried.

"I don't know."

"Are you being followed?"

Now he sounded like she had no right to worry, even though she'd been relocated twice already.

McKenzie turned in her seat, peering down the length of the bus and out the back window. Any one of the cars dogging the bus might be following her. "I don't know."

Her handler grunted. "Look, just go home and set your alarm. If it goes off, enter your safe room immediately and call me from there."

WITSEC had installed a tiny room at the back of her closet. Reinforced with steel and padded with Kevlar, it was supposedly unbreachable. While the safe room assured protection from immediate danger, it failed to banish the suspicion that the Centurions had found her yet again, and that wasn't supposed to happen. The trade-off for giving up her old life was the guarantee of not having to live in constant fear, so why was she still afraid?

"Okay." Putting an end to the call, McKenzie looked outside to get her bearings. Her stomach churned with uncertainty.

At the main terminal, she would have to switch busses to get on the bus that went to her neighborhood. Apparently, it was up to her to lose whoever might be tailing her.

Shifting her head on the pillow, McKenzie checked her bedside clock. It was 2:00 A.M., and no one had attempted to kill her yet.

A good sign. Maybe the man with the camera hadn't been singling her out, like the guy with the cell phone in Omaha or the man in the alley in Portland. Except instinct warned her she was still in danger.

Restless, she rolled out of bed and padded to her kitchen.

As always, she took in the tiny bungalow she called home with contentment. She'd painted a mural on one wall of each room—nothing personal enough to betray her identity. If forced to move again, the landlord would paint over all of them, since the bungalow wasn't really hers. Having graduated from the Savannah School for the Arts, painting murals inspired by her late mother's garden was her dream job. *One day, I'll paint them for a living.* No more cleaning hotel rooms or inspecting cans on the assembly line or soothing panicked animals.

She heated a mug of water in the microwave. Steeping a bag of chamomile tea in the hot water, she carried the mug into her living room to brood.

In the dark room that surrounded her, not a single object was a memento from her past, except, perhaps, the mural of her mother's favorite camellia bush. The shawl she wrapped around her slim shoulders only resembled the one her mother used to use before they'd gone into witness protection together. Genevieve had died in her sleep later that summer. Since then, McKenzie had been on her own, without a single relic or photo of her mother, her past, or even…

Memories of Miles drenched her mind like snow melting on the first sunny day in spring. The recollection of his toe-curling kisses made her stomach swivel pleasantly.

She would never forget the day she had stumbled on her mother's journals and realized their incriminating information could free her from her father's dominion. Giddy with relief, she had kissed Miles, thinking he was just their gardener—handsome, clever, and only eighteen years old. Half in love with him already, she'd had no idea he was a twenty-six-year-old undercover agent working in the FBI's Criminal Investigative Division.

Falling in love with Miles had changed her life, but not in the way she'd hoped. Yes, her father and many of his associates had gone to jail. But Miles's and her relationship had been nipped in the bud. Communication between them was forbidden. As always, to comfort herself, she replayed their last shared words when he'd stuck his head into the back seat of the U.S. Marshal's vehicle.

"Once I'm sure it's safe, I will find you again. I promise, McKenzie."

She had thought that day would have come by now. Only, it wasn't here yet.

Did she still love Miles, whose youthful features she could scarcely recall? Her heart said yes. But to expect that he would wait all this time was just naïve. After three long years, he had surely moved on with his life, found someone else to love.

The thought deepened the chasm in her heart.

Resolved to try and sleep again, McKenzie plodded back to the kitchen with her half-empty cup. She had just placed it in the sink when a flicker of movement made her spin toward the moonlit window, where the silhouette of a man leapt onto her lowered shade.

McKenzie startled back, and the man disappeared.

Had she just imagined him?

A scratching at her back door nixed that optimistic hope. Someone was attempting to break in! In the next instant, her home security system started to wail.

Recalling Higgins's advice, McKenzie scuttled to her bedroom. She snatched up her purse and her cell phone, then headed straight for her closet, where she felt inside for the tiny button that triggered the door to her safe room. With a hiss and a glow of ultraviolet light, the door slid open.

She dived into the four-by-six-foot space, hit another button, and sealed herself inside.

The supplies at her feet, the retractable latrine, and the mat all meant she could survive here for up to a week if she had to, but it wouldn't come to that. The alarm would bring the U.S. Marshals to her rescue in half an hour, at most.

Higgins had told her to call him if her alarm went off. *Let him worry a bit.* Her pounding heart rocked her. He should have taken immediate action to protect her.

Through the ventilation shafts that tunneled under the house, she heard her alarm go abruptly silent. They had to have gotten inside to turn it off. Putting her ear to the steel wall, McKenzie strained to hear anything over her shallow breaths. Muffled voices reached her, sounding like they were being spoken under water.

"She's not here." The deep voice summoned an image of a large man.

"You sure this is the right place?"

The first man said something about following her home.

So, she *was* followed. She gulped against a dry mouth.

"Look under the bed. She has to be here."

They'll never find me.

"Call that number you got from her friend. Let's see if her cell phone rings."

What? Jamila would never have given her number to a stranger —oh yes, she would, if the man resembled Prince Charming. Hands trembling, McKenzie set her phone to Do Not Disturb.

"You hear anything?"

Sweat filmed her upper lip.

"Nah. She must be staying somewhere else tonight. Girl that pretty has to have a boyfriend."

"So, what do we do? We can't stick around. The alarm's gonna bring the Feds."

"I guess we follow her more closely tomorrow, see where she's going at night. Come on. Don't touch anything on your way out."

As the voices grew fainter, McKenzie sagged against the enclosure, her fear draining away.

Any minute now, the U.S. Marshals—possibly Higgins himself—would be here to whisk her away. Again. She couldn't stand this. They'd had their chance to keep her safe and they'd blown it. How was the Cohort finding her over and over again?

Higgins had blamed the last two incidences on McKenzie, who'd admitted to making phone calls she shouldn't have. But not this time. She hadn't called anyone from Myrtle Beach. So maybe *she* wasn't the problem. Maybe there was a *leak* in WITSEC. Or maybe Higgins himself had betrayed her location.

McKenzie swallowed hard. As her father used to say, every man had a price.

Among the supplies in her hiding spot was a change of clothing, flip-flops, two water bottles, trail mix, and some cash she'd been saving up, just in case she had to split. That possibility had been rooting in her mind since the second incident. Now she was grateful for her forethought. She had just enough to get shelter for a night or two.

Hefting the bag that held her supplies and her money, she dropped her phone and purse into it, slipped on the flip-flops, then pushed the button to leave her safe room.

The lights dimmed as the door swept soundlessly open. Headlights strafed the walls of her bedroom as she stepped from her closet. That was either the hit men leaving or the U.S. Marshals coming to see why her alarm had gone off. Either way, she would slip right past them by sneaking out of her window. All she had to do was remove the bar that kept intruders from sliding it open from the outside.

Touching down on damp grass, she took off running as fast as the flip-flops allowed through her backyard and then through her neighbor's, putting her a block away. She followed that street to a thoroughfare lined with cafés and souvenir shops. At the first public trash can she came across, she took her phone from the bag and, gulping down her misgivings, threw it away.

Out of necessity, she would remain Caroline Dillard, since she had the ID to prove it. But one day, she would get to be McKenzie Jones again. *God, You have to help me survive. I can't do this on my own.*

~

"I'd like a room, please."

With a thinning of his lips, the motel clerk took McKenzie's wad of cash, but he kept his thoughts to himself.

She wore pink plaid pajamas and one flip-flop, having lost the other one running across a busy street to avoid being struck by a car. Her face was flushed with exertion. Heaven only knew what the young man was thinking.

His neutral tone gave nothing away as he slid a keycard toward her. "Checkout's at eleven."

"Thank you." With her knees jittering, McKenzie rode the elevator to the third floor. To think she'd actually gone and done it, broken away from WITSEC and struck out on her own.

Locating her room, she let herself in and locked the door. What else could she do but call Miles? She crossed straight to the phone beside the king-sized bed and sat beside it. Miles was the only soul she trusted; the only person who knew her circumstances and could give advice. Trepidation filled her as she pulled the phone closer.

The morning he'd turned her over to the U.S. Marshals, he'd pressed a business card into her palm, whispering in her ear, "Memorize my number, but don't call unless it's life or death."

She'd memorized his number on the spot. Weeks later, she'd bought a prepaid phone card so she could place that life-or-death call if the need arose.

Desperation had tempted her to use it twice already—once in

Omaha, the night her mother died, and again in Portland on her twenty-sixth birthday. She'd admitted as much to Higgins who'd grilled her after Centurions had found her in both places.

"But I never even spoke," she'd insisted. "How would anyone know it was me?"

"It doesn't matter. They're obviously still watching Miles. Do you want to put him in harm's way? Don't call him again."

But Higgins had to be wrong because she'd never called Miles from Myrtle Beach; yet the Cohort had found her here, regardless. So they couldn't be monitoring Miles's calls. *Lord, please let that be the case.*

Mastering the tremor in her fingers, she tapped out the numbers on her calling card, followed by Miles's phone number, all memorized. Her heart seemed to stop beating as she waited for his phone to ring.

Then it rang and rang.

Just as she was sure her call would go to voice mail, he picked up.

"Ellis. Hello?"

Three years of loneliness, fear, and regret strangled McKenzie's vocal cords. She clutched the receiver with both hands, pushing his name through her tight throat. "Miles."

His mattress creaked. "Don't hang up." He sounded suddenly wide awake. "Please don't hang up this time. You hear me, Angel?"

Angel. That was his special name for her since she used to minister to the homeless men at the shelter where they'd met. How quickly he'd recognized her voice!

"That's it, now tell me what's wrong."

Where to start? "C-Centurions came for me again. This is the third time it's happened."

"What's the program doing about it?"

"Nothing. I ran away. They're not keeping me safe like they're supposed to."

"Where are you now?"

"In a motel room in—"

"Don't say it. All I need is the room number."

"Um…" It took her a moment to remember. "314."

"Got it. Now, don't go anywhere. I'll be there as soon as I can."

"Wait, h-how will you find me?" Panic made her heart race. "When will you get here?" What if she never heard from him again?

"Soon, Angel. Believe me, I could find you anywhere."

His answer assured her that there was no Mrs. Miles Ellis lying in bed next to him. *Thank goodness.* Miles was going to rescue her, just like he had three years ago when she'd been faced with an arranged marriage to her father's friend Ashton.

"I'll be here," she promised.

Her only answer was a beep as he ended their call.

CHAPTER 2

*M*iles forced himself to hang up. God knew he didn't want to. McKenzie's voice was manna to his hungry heart, and she so clearly needed him to stay on the line with her.

But he couldn't risk the off-chance that the Centurion Cohort was listening to his calls—not that he could see how. His cell phone had been issued by the FBI. Uncle Sam had deemed it secure and untraceable. On the other hand, his affection for Jared Jones's daughter had been no secret to the Centurion leader, now deceased. If Centurions thought McKenzie might contact him someday, they'd keep tabs on him for as long as it took to avenge Jared.

Miles should never have given her his phone number. But love couldn't bear separation and, luckily, she'd only called him twice—at least, he'd assumed it was her by the aching silence that had echoed his greeting.

This last call had been from Myrtle Beach. Opening a special app on his cell phone, he was able to pinpoint the exact location of the Hilton Garden Inn where she was hiding.

Miles leapt out of his bed, located in the basement apartment of his mother's home. He'd moved back in after his parents had split because he didn't want his mother living alone in the home he'd grown up in, located a stone's throw away from the nation's capital in Arlington, Virginia. Stripping off his sleep pants on his way to the bathroom, he then jumped into the shower while replaying McKenzie's words in his head.

How could the Cohort have found her in the first place, let alone *three* times? WITSEC had a flawless record. No one in their protection had *ever* been targeted—until now. Obviously, something was amiss with the program. Could it be the man who'd been protecting Jared Jones from within the Bureau had access to the U.S. Marshal's database? Was The Architect, as he was called, truly that powerful?

As he toweled off, Miles pondered the fastest way to reach his rescue target. Driving to Myrtle Beach from Northern Virginia would take about nine hours. A commercial flight, with all the hassles of airport security checks, would consume at least five. McKenzie needed him *now*.

Dang it, he would have to ask his father for help. Drake Ellis was, in many ways, Miles's boss. He was also the section chief of White-Collar Crimes and reported directly to the executive assistant director of the CID. It was bad enough Miles had to answer to a father who'd walked out on his mother two years ago, after twenty-seven years of marriage. Asking his father for a favor was the last thing Miles wanted to do, but Dad had a pilot's license and his own small aircraft, two things Miles desperately needed.

Swallowing his pride, he dialed his father's number and set his cell phone on his dresser in speaker mode while starting to dress.

Drake answered on the first ring. "What's wrong?"

Clearly there had to be a calamity for Miles to call his father—sad, but so true. "I need a favor." He strapped his gun holster to his calf and reached for his jeans.

"What kind of favor?"

"I need you to fly me to Myrtle Beach tonight, right now. It's a matter of life and death." He stepped into his Levi's one leg at a time.

"Whose death?"

"Mine." Considering his life wouldn't be worth living if anything happened to McKenzie, it was only a slight exaggeration. His father heaved a sigh. Miles buttoned his jeans and pulled the zipper up. "Yes or no? I don't have much time."

"Fine. I'll meet you at the airport in half an hour."

Pleasantly surprised, Miles pressed his luck. "Any chance you can make that twenty minutes?"

"I'll try." His father hung up on him.

Stowing his phone in his rear pocket, Miles turned toward his closet to pack a bag. Having no idea what he was up against, he tossed a hodgepodge of clothing into his black duffel, along with a dozen spare magazines for his Glock, just in case.

Then he fetched his shaving kit and toothbrush from the bathroom. For the first time in years, the young man looking back at him didn't look depressed.

"Please God." He spoke the words aloud, even as goose bumps sprouted on his forearms. "Keep her safe until I'm there to protect her."

Miles had to give the old man credit. He'd filed a flight plan, fueled up, and completed a preflight check by the time Miles joined him in the cockpit of his Beechcraft Bonanza.

Drake eradicated Miles's feelings of goodwill by cutting him an impatient look. "Took you long enough. Let's go."

Like it was Dad's idea to fly to Myrtle Beach at four in the morning.

The clear, crisp weather alleviated a portion of Miles's concerns as the two-seater ascended into the predawn sky and banked south. A full moon and a tail wind blowing out of the north would get them to South Carolina in two hours.

"Are you going to tell me what this is about?"

The impatient question came one hour into the flight. Miles had hoped the audio on the headset he was wearing wasn't working. Apparently, it worked fine. His father had just waited until they were three thousand feet up in the air to interrogate him. Typical.

Miles kept his gaze fixed on the thin veil of moonlit clouds. "Nope."

"Does this have anything to do with your current assignment?"

Miles spent his weekdays down in Freeport, Bahamas, posing as a yacht salesman in an FBI-coordinated effort to curb drug smuggling out of the Caribbean and into the United States. "Nope."

"Did you tell your mother anything?"

Miles whipped his head around. "I left her a note." He fought to keep his resentment from bubbling up, but it boiled over suddenly. "Which is more than you did when you abandoned her."

His father sighed, tiredly. "You have no idea what happened with me and your mother."

"I don't need to know."

Dad went back to fiddling with his instruments. Miles studied him out the side of his eye. Where his father was tall and broad shouldered, Miles had inherited his mother's petite stature along with a baby face that made him ideal for undercover jobs but sometimes kept people from taking him seriously, his father included. Considering his older half-sister was a fearless CIA case officer, Miles often doubted he would ever measure up.

Focusing back on the indigo sky, he marveled at the brilliance of the stars. God created the stars for a purpose, just as He'd created Miles for a purpose. If that was to rescue McKenzie Jones from the remnants of the Centurion Cohort, then so be it. God willing, they could finally be together again.

Please, Lord. I don't like to trouble You with much, but this is important.

An hour and a half later, the two-seater came to a standstill at Myrtle Beach International Airport. The sky was just beginning to lighten. Worry simmered in Miles's stomach. McKenzie had been alone all this time.

As the single-piston engine wound down, he hung up his headset and unbuckled his seat belt. At least her hotel was just a ten-minute drive away.

As he left the cockpit, he tossed over his shoulder, "Thanks for the ride."

He had unlatched the door and was stepping out onto the wing when a large hand clamped down on his shoulder. As fast and strong as Miles was, his father outmatched him in pure muscle. He had no choice but to halt his exodus. "What?"

"That's it? You're going to go off on your own? I thought you were smarter than that."

Considering the trouble Miles might be walking into, he knew he could use his father's help. But Dad could get fired for simply not stopping him, let alone helping him outright.

"I guess I'm not that smart." Wresting free of his father's grip, he leapt to the spongy ground with his duffel bag, then took off at a brisk walk toward the bright lights of the General Aviation Terminal. The humid air smelled of salt water and cypress. At the same time, he placed a call on his cell phone to Hertz Car Rental. His alias, Tom Keane the yacht salesman, would have a vehicle waiting by the time he reached the lot.

Miles figured his father would fly off in disgust shortly. Leaving was what Dad did best, after all.

CHAPTER 3

*M*cKenzie dozed in fitful spurts, waking periodically with her heart in her throat. Had she dreamed someone was knocking on her motel door, or was it real?

She rolled groggily out of bed and stumbled past her lit bathroom. Wiping a grain of sleep from one eye, she peered through the door's peephole with the other.

The familiar sight of Miles wearing a hoodie made her heart leap with joy. He had dressed like that while posing as a teenager at the Centurion Men's Shelter, the place where she'd volunteered so much time and effort, thinking she was doing a service to her community. Her father, meanwhile, had used the shelter to launder money as well as to recruit and groom the men who would become his followers.

With a dry mouth and fingers that could scarcely unlatch the safety chain, McKenzie hauled the door open. *Miles!* Her cry of anticipation curtailed abruptly as the light from her bathroom hit the caller's face. *Not Miles.* She was letting in a total stranger.

She tried slamming the door on him, only the stranger stuck a boot out, keeping the door from closing. Forcing his way inside, he pinned her against the closet with his sturdy frame. A moist cloth came out of nowhere, covering her mouth and nose and stifling her screams.

Caustic fumes scalded McKenzie's airways. She caught her breath and fought her captor's cruel grip, but he was stronger. In her panic, she saw two more strangers slip into the room, one of whom resembled the man on the balcony. Ordering the third man to fetch her belongings, he watched with a smirk as McKenzie's lungs convulsed for air. Cloying vapor seared her throat, and darkness gathered at the edges of her eyes.

How did these men even find her here?

Anguish speared her as the darkness took over. Now she might never get to see Miles again.

Once inside the elevator at the Hilton Garden Inn, Miles pushed the elevator button for the third floor, then jabbed the Close-Door button until the elevator finally lurched upward. Adrenaline juggernauted through his bloodstream. Anxiety twisted his intestines.

Three years. He had dreamed so often of the moment when he and McKenzie would be reunited; every one of those dreams had been impossibly sweet—not like this. Foreboding robbed him of any real anticipation.

For Centurions to have found her *three* times, WITSEC had to have been infiltrated by none other than the Architect. Who would keep McKenzie safe if WITSEC couldn't?

I can.

He pictured them running away together to a place like Morocco, where his sister was assigned. Imagine finally marrying McKenzie, getting to watch her graceful interactions with the locals, with their own children! On one hand, it sounded like paradise. On the other, could he bring himself to walk away from his mother like his father had?

The doors parted with a chime on the third floor. *This is it.*

Drawing a deep breath, he marched onto the landing and turned left toward 314. At the end of the hallway, two men were pushing through the emergency stairwell exit, and one of them was carrying a woman small enough to carry like child.

The unsettling sight broke Miles's stride.

The woman had long auburn hair, not dark brown like McKenzie's, but she could have colored it. He couldn't see enough of her face before they stepped out of sight to be sure it was her, but her scent—a blend of gardenia and honeysuckle—seemed to hang in the air. Given the way her head had lolled on the man's shoulder, she had to be passed out, cold.

They'd gotten to her first!

The realization had him pausing to retrieve his Glock 36 from under his pant leg. Pistol in hand, he knocked on room 314 just to be sure. When silence answered him, he pursued the two men, slipping stealthily through the fire door. Several levels below him he could hear footfalls and low-pitched voices. There were three of them now, not just two.

Silencing his pursuit as much as possible, he flew down the steps after them. But they were already on the ground floor, exiting the building.

As the door clanged shut behind them, Miles bounded recklessly down the remaining stairs. He couldn't let them get away. How would he ever forgive himself?

Reaching the ground floor, he barreled through the exit and found himself by a parking lot gilded by a pewter sky. Less than thirty feet away, the man who'd been carrying McKenzie had just unloaded her into the back of a van and was about to climb in himself.

"Hey!" Miles yelled at him.

The man swiveled to face him, and Miles raised his weapon,

stalking the van with determination. "FBI! Put your hands in the air and step away from the vehicle."

The man assessed the immediate area, saw no one else and, with a shout at the driver, jumped into the cargo area, slamming the doors shut behind him. The engine roared and the van peeled away.

Oh no you didn't. Aiming his weapon at the left rear tire, Miles fired. But in the gloom and with the van in motion, he missed, howling with frustration. His rental vehicle was parked near the front of the hotel. His odds of catching up with the van were slim, at best.

But then a second pistol barked, and the van wobbled, though it didn't stop. At a hampered pace, it continued to make its getaway.

Miles edged around the building looking for the other shooter, as well as for his car. Seeing it closer than he thought, he raced toward the dark-blue Taurus without spotting whoever'd helped him. With a rev of the engine, he peeled out of his parking space, having parked tail-end-in.

As he neared the road, a silhouette detached itself from beneath the hotel's raised sign and marched toward him. "Dad!"

Sure enough, it was. His father had followed him here and helped him.

Too grateful to be upset, Miles slowed just long enough to let Drake slip into the passenger seat. Before his father's door slammed shut, he took off again. Even in the dim light, his father's scowl was evident.

"So, I think I know what's going on. You don't have to explain it."

Really? How could his father guess without knowing McKenzie had called him? But, hey, if he didn't want to talk about it, that was fine with Miles. Besides, the less his father knew, the less he might get in trouble for helping him.

Keeping an eye on the dark shape of the van bumping up the four-lane highway a hundred yards ahead of them, Miles tried to think through his fear. Where would Centurions be taking her? Wouldn't their intent be to kill her? Ice cycled through his veins as he tried to close the distance between them.

He glanced at his silent father. Even if Dad had guessed this was about McKenzie, didn't he even want to make sure? "Look, I appreciate you helping me out back there, but it would probably be best for you if I let you out right here. I'm about to step way out of my jurisdiction."

Dad gave an easy shrug. "I don't think so. They're heading toward the highway, by the way."

"I can see that." Gunning through a red light, Miles managed to avoid losing sight of the van completely as it lurched up a ramp off Harrelson Blvd. onto Route 17. As followed it, gratitude sat like a fat pill in Miles's throat—necessary for his health, but hard to swallow. Miles sped up as he spotted the van again.

His father shot him a frown. "No, no. Hang back. Let's keep the element of surprise here."

Miles didn't agree, but he'd always heeded Dad's advice. It was hard to avoid being noticed on the scantily populated six-lane highway, especially with the sun brightening the eastern sky. Hiding behind a semitruck first, then changing lanes to get behind a car, Miles hung back as far as he dared.

As they passed a strip of rubber lying in the road, Dad shook his head. "I can't believe they're driving on a flat tire." A minute later, he added, "Whatever you do, keep the LE out of it."

LE was local law enforcement. The comment told Miles his father had guessed accurately that he was dealing with Centurions. The quasi-religious, civic organization had been around since the late-nineteenth century. Springing up first in Savannah, Cohorts were seeded throughout the south, preaching clean living and closed mouths while collecting pledge money that lined the pockets of the corrupt elite. New pledges were encouraged to seek careers in law enforcement, where they protected their own kind from prosecution.

"Gotcha." With Myrtle Beach just 227 miles from Savannah, there might well be former Centurions staffing both the county and state police. "So, what's the plan?" He wasn't too proud to ask for his father's input.

"Let's just see where they're headed."

"Next exit, apparently."

The van was signaling an imminent exit off the highway. Miles edged his rental into the left lane, making it look like he planned to continue straight. At the last second, he horsed across two lanes of traffic and up the ramp, just in time to see the van turn down a long, tree-lined road. The last of the tire was peeling away, and the rim sparked on asphalt.

Braking at the stop sign, Miles waited for the van to disappear behind a stand of trees before accelerating after it. The sun was now cresting the treetops, turning the leaves incandescent.

When they next glimpsed the van, it was slowing before a brand-new building overlooking an elegant, modestly sized marina. Tall sailboats and several yachts were moored to a wide pier.

Farther inland, boats had been pulled out of the water for maintenance. Miles drove the car slowly past them until his father cautioned, "Better pull over."

Miles complied, nosing the sedan in the shadow of a landed sailboat. "Why is there a marina this far inland?"

"We're next to the Intracoastal Waterway."

"Oh." Miles had to admit Dad knew more than he did about most things. The bottom fell out of his stomach as he realized, "They're trying to take McKenzie out of here by boat." It was the first time he'd mentioned his rescue target, but Dad didn't seem surprised.

As Miles tore off his seat belt and jumped out of the car, his father followed suit, whispering for him to slow down. Desperate to keep McKenzie within view, Miles did not slow down. He wove his way through the large, landed boats, heading straight for the brand-new marina store and restaurant, both closed at this early hour, with his father right behind him. Beyond the dredged inlet, the Intracoastal Waterway was a glimmering ribbon of dark water cutting through a forest.

The van had backed right up to a pier. One of the three kidnappers was carrying a slack McKenzie toward the large, sleek yacht moored at the very end of the L-shaped pier and buttered in morning sunlight. His two companions went to work changing their flat tire.

Concealing himself behind the building, Miles peered around the corner, his hungry gaze fastening onto McKenzie. Even dressed in pink, plaid pajamas with her curls a dark auburn hue, he would never have mistaken the delicate beauty for anyone but his angel. His heart swelled with longing. He had to get her back.

Dad, a good six inches taller than Miles, peered over his head. They both watched a thick-set gentleman with sparse silver hair emerge from the yacht's cabin to welcome his visitors. The man's yellow Bermuda shirt and white slacks screamed of wealth, as did his aristocratic accent that just reached their ears.

"There you are. Bring her aboard."

Recognition rocked Miles back on his heels. "That's Ashton Ravenel!"

Surprisingly, his father hushed him. Once again, he didn't seem surprised. Being well acquainted with the Centurion Cohort, Dad knew as well as Miles did that Ashton had been Jared Jones's close friend and the man McKenzie was supposed to marry. As the public corruptions section chief, Dad had worked hard to pin racketeering charges on Ravenel. It looked like he'd succeeded. Yet, in the end, his evidence had simply vanished, and the man had walked free.

Miles stole another peek around the corner of the building. McKenzie disappeared into the yacht's enormous galley, still carried by the goon.

Pulling back, he met his father's sharp gaze while considering their options.

"What do you want to do?"

Wait, Dad was letting *him* call the shots? This was a first.

Miles took another look at the setup. The odds weren't particularly good right then, but the men fixing the tire looked like they were planning to leave any minute. "Once the perps take off, we board the boat, unless, of course, it pulls away first."

His father's green eyes narrowed. "Okay."

Miles waited for him to point out all the flaws to his decision. Instead, he produced a Glock from under the tail of his button-up shirt and loaded it with a fresh magazine. Miles quickly followed his example.

The slamming of the van's doors had them peering simultaneously around the building. The flat tire had been replaced with a spare. The two who'd worked on it were back in the van, waiting for their companion to come off the yacht so they could leave.

A pulse throbbed in Miles's temples. How he longed to get on that boat, to pull McKenzie into his arms, and tell her everything would be okay.

At long last, the big man came out of the cabin, still stuffing money into his pocket. He crossed the short gangplank and strode swiftly up the pier toward the van. As he climbed into the back, Miles and Dad retreated to the back of the building to avoid detection as the van tore past them.

At the back of the building, they discovered the best way to approach the pier unseen was to continue around the building toward the water. The hope that Ravenel and McKenzie were the only two on board the yacht was shattered as they emerged to find two young men hoisting the gangplank. Miles groaned as a third man, older and burlier than the boys, appeared in the wheelhouse on the yacht's third level, where he fired the boat's engines.

At motor's throbbing, Miles's heart began to race. "We can't let them leave." He might never see McKenzie again.

"Yeah, but…" His father hadn't removed his gaze from the man piloting the craft. "I bet you that man is armed. And a boat this size probably has an arsenal."

An idea occurred to Miles. "We're not fighting our way on board. Come on, follow my lead." He didn't leave his dad much choice. Darting from behind the building, Miles marched toward the pier with his head up, shoulders back. He could hear his father right behind him.

As they stepped onto the pier, the deckhands took note of their approach, glanced at each other, then up at the wheelhouse. "Hey, Skipper."

The man in the wheelhouse looked toward the boys, then frowned at the interlopers.

"Morning." With a friendly smile, Miles stepped right up to the stern of the *Julius Caesar* while trying not to roll his eyes at the pompous name. "I hope I'm not late."

The young men stared at him, then looked at each other again. "Late for what?" asked the one with bad acne.

Miles feigned puzzlement. "Didn't Mr. Ravenel tell you? It must have slipped his mind." He took out his wallet and fished out a business card, holding it up. "I'm Tom Keane, with U.S.A. Yacht Sales. Mr. Ravenel asked me to stop by this morning and appraise his boat, and I brought my mechanic with me."

Not waiting for an invitation, Miles leapt aboard to thrust his business card at one of the boys, all the while aware that the skipper had just cut the engines and was making his way down toward them. Miles waved his father over. "Hop aboard, Daniel. Mr. Ravenel's a faithful client of mine."

As his father joined him, the two deckhands turned with relief toward the skipper, who was just coming off the tanning deck. "He says he's here to appraise the boat." The boy passed the business card to the older man.

Miles became the object of the skipper's narrow-eyed appraisal as he looked up from the card. The man's street-tough demeanor warned Miles that they were looking at trouble.

The skipper turned to the deckhands. "Did the boss say anything to you about this?"

They both shook their heads. "But he gets a new boat every year, don't he?"

Miles jumped on the detail. "He does, actually, and he gets them from me. I'm sure it just slipped his mind that I was dropping by. He did say he was busy lately. How about I take a quick look around, then you can fetch Mr. Ravenel when I'm ready to assess the cabin? I brought Daniel my mechanic with me." He jerked his thumb toward his father, who sent the men a nod.

The skipper's hard expression had Miles holding his breath. He didn't exhale until the man said, "What do you need to see first?"

"Well, if you could show my mechanic the engine room, that'd be great. I'll get busy on the upper decks."

"Fine." Skipper jerked his head at Dad. "Follow me."

Given the look his father sent him, Dad wasn't happy getting stuck with the skipper. But, hey, Miles had the two young-'uns to deal with.

Pretending to look around, he waited for his father and Skipper to disappear belowdecks before he pulled a couple hundred-dollar bills from his wallet, walking back to the teens. "Hey, guys. I'll give you each a hundred dollars to walk up to the marina store and wait there until we leave."

The boys looked at the bills in his hand, then looked at each other and shrugged. After taking the money, they jumped off the boat, all the while whispering between themselves and sneaking backward glances.

Miles turned around, his heart pounding with purpose. Now to find McKenzie.

CHAPTER 4

A throbbing pain brought McKenzie's hand up to her temple. She cracked her eyes open only to squeeze them shut again as nausea roiled and the pounding intensified. *Oh, no.* Why was she lying on her back in so much discomfort?

The memories came flooding back—how she had foolishly opened the door to a stranger, been overpowered, and forced to breathe some kind of noxious fumes. She jerked upright, only to be yanked back by something biting into her right wrist.

Rolling her head on the pillow, she stared with rising alarm at the handcuff chaining her wrist to a bar on the brass headboard. She whipped her face the other way and took in the odd dimensions of an unfamiliar bedroom. The built-in cabinetry and rounded window made it apparent she'd been stowed aboard a boat. The telltale rumble of the boat's engines brought a gasp of protest to her lips. Was the boat moving yet? It didn't seem to be.

One of her father's favorite methods of disposing of problematic people was taking them out to sea—and never bringing them back. "No."

Yanking at the handcuff, she tried desperately to slip her hand through it, only the cuff had been cinched too tightly. She fell back onto the leopard-patterned coverlet in defeat.

There was no denying the truth. The Centurion Cohort had found her.

A barb of terror lanced her chest and nausea stormed her anew. With a moan of misery, she closed her eyes thinking she might be sick, but the sound of footsteps outside her door had eyes flying open. The latch turned and the door swung inward, revealing a familiar visage. As Ashton Ravenel, her one-time fiancé and Centurion elite, joined her, shutting the door behind him, McKenzie cringed.

The blood drained from her head as he drew closer, smirking. Dressed in white slacks and a yellow Bermuda shirt, still wearing the signet ring that declared him a Centurion, he looked like he might have been vacationing in the Gulf for the summer tan on his fleshy face.

"I see you're finally awake." He spoke in the same old-money, southern drawl her father had affected his entire life.

She suffered his oily gaze as he leisurely took inventory of her. "Well. Who could have guessed that such a slip of a girl could cause her father and his entire empire so much grief?"

Don't listen to him. Just think about escaping.

Seizing the bars of the headboard, McKenzie managed to pull herself up to a sitting position in order to appear less vulnerable. Ashton seated himself on the mattress next to her, causing it to dip. She tried not to flinch as he stretched out a hand. The moist pads of his fingers grazed her cheek as he slid them down her neck, toward her pounding heart. Repulsed, she held his gaze defiantly. His watery eyes, half-veiled by puffy folds of skin, testified not just to his age but to his decadent lifestyle.

"You were supposed to be my bride, McKenzie. What happened to the ring I gave you?"

She'd left it on her dresser the morning before she vanished from Savannah with Miles, taking her mother with her. "One of the servants has it, I imagine."

Anger glittered in his gray eyes. "You killed your father, you know that? He was my closest friend."

"He was a snake." It pained her to say so of her own father, but he truly was.

Ashton drew his hand back and slapped her hard across the face.

With a surge of outrage, McKenzie delivered a roundhouse kick to his head. "Don't touch me!"

Ashton toppled off the bed, landing on his knees. WITSEC's mandatory course in self-defense had paid off.

With grim satisfaction, she watched him shake his head to recover from her blow. Her victory was short-lived. Ashton's breath became labored. He tried and failed to come to his feet. As she waited for his inevitable recovery, remorse plunged through her. She and Miles had come so close to being reunited. So close. Now she would never again know the joy of feeling his arms around her.

Oh, God, what about Your plans to prosper me?

Making his way through the quiet galley, headed for the cabins on the lower level, Miles froze at the sound of the door he'd just entered opening behind him. He whirled to find his father leaning heavily against it. Drake's left eye was already beginning to blacken, and his upper lip was cut and bleeding.

"Thanks a lot." Pushing off the door, his father joined him. "What'd you do with the kids?"

"Paid 'em off. You okay?"

"Paid 'em with what?" Dad licked his bleeding upper lip.

"Money for my current assignment. What'd you do with the skipper?"

His father jingled a set of small keys. "Locked him in the engine room." He gestured with his head toward the back of the boat. "Let's do this."

Miles wheeled away, intent on getting to McKenzie immediately.

His father caught him by the shoulder for a second time that morning. "Slow down there, hotshot. Your silver tongue might have gotten you this far, but Ashton Ravenel's going to recognize you from the trial. I'm betting he's armed and ready to kill."

At the reminder, Miles retrieved the pistol from under his pant leg. "I hope he tries."

His father flashed him a smile. "That sounds like something I would say. But you're not authorized for a home invasion, so don't get carried away."

"Right."

"Best we can hope for is to charge him with kidnapping. A few years in jail's better than nothing."

Miles nodded. He and his father agreed on that much, at least.

With a lurching of his stomach, he remembered McKenzie was alone with Ashton down in the bowels of his boat. He launched himself down the steep carpeted stairs. He had to get to her before Ashton killed her—or worse.

Ashton recovered faster than McKenzie had hoped he would. As he slowly stood, huffing with the effort it took, she twisted onto her knees to face the headboard. It was bolted to the wall, which meant tugging wasn't going to free her. Still, she had to try.

A glance over her shoulder showed him putting a knee on the bed. One cheek was bright red from where she'd clobbered him. His sunken eyes burned with hatred. *Oh, God, help me.*

"Now you've asked for it." His slate gray eyes burned with loathing. "I was going to kill you quickly and painlessly, but not now. Oh no. I'm going to drag it out for days. You'll be begging for mercy by the time I'm through cutting you to pieces."

The words came as no surprise. She'd known of the Cohort's torturous techniques since she'd read her mother's journals. Her only hope was to lose consciousness early on and never wake up again.

He lunged suddenly, making a grab for her ankles, but a quick heel-strike to his chin caused Ashton to bite his tongue. He howled in rage and lunged again. Manacling both ankles at once, he yanked her knees out from under her.

McKenzie's temple plowed into the brass bar so hard her head rang. She willed oblivion to overtake her, but with a painful tug on her hair, Ashton kept her conscious.

His weight pressed her down into the mattress. He breathed hard, expelling his foul breath into her face. "I'm going start with your ears, and then I'll take off your pretty little nose." He pinched it between his fingers and twisted it.

McKenzie shuddered at the visions in her head. *This cannot be happening. God loves me.*

As if in confirmation of that thought, the door crashed open.

Ashton sprang off the bed, allowing her to see two men surge through the door that now listed on torn hinges. Pointing their guns at Ashton's gaping expression, they shouted, "FBI! Get down on the ground!"

Boneless with relief, McKenzie watched Ashton stumble back to the far wall, blubbering threats. The elder of the two men tackled him to the floor, grappling him into submission in seconds.

Then the first man pivoted toward the bed. "McKenzie."

She blinked to clear her vision as he joined her on the mattress, his hazel eyes skimming her for injuries.

"Miles?" She reached out with her free hand to be certain. His features, faded from memory after three long years, were suddenly, dearly familiar. "Is it really you?"

"It's me, Angel." His expression reflected a tangle of emotions ranging from delight to fury upon finding her chained to the bed.

"Get off me!" Ashton roared on the floor. "You're dead! You're both dead!"

As the man straddling him pushed Ashton's face into the plush carpet, McKenzie banished the two from her thoughts. She and Miles were essentially alone, a circumstance for which she'd longed for three lonely years. God still had plans to prosper her. The evidence was sitting right in front of her, his knee touching hers, their eyes locked. "Tell me I'm not dreaming." After that blow to her head, it was all too possible.

"You're not. See?" He drew her hand to his chest where she could feel his heart thumping through the soft fabric of his shirt. "I'm really here. You're safe. No one's going to hurt you again."

She caught back a sob of joy. *Thank You, Father!*

"Dad," Miles called over his shoulder, snapping her out of her trance. "See if you can find the keys to these cuffs. Then you can put them on him."

McKenzie peered in surprise at the other man. His hair, evidently once as dark as Miles's, was shot with silver. He was a larger man with harder features, but there was no doubt they were blood related. Searching Ashton's pockets, the older agent turned up a set of tiny keys. Within seconds, McKenzie's wrist was free.

"Where else are you hurt?" Miles rubbed her chafed skin as he tossed the cuffs to his father.

She shook her head to signify that she was fine, but sobs of relief got the better of her. Miles pulled her close, crooning words of comfort. Burrowing into his embrace, McKenzie let his never-forgotten scent anchor her in this new reality, even as his father hauled a resisting Ashton Ravenel to his feet. Spittle flew from that man's mouth as he cursed the men for arresting him.

"I swear you'll regret you ever laid a hand on me, Ellis."

"Good, so you know who I am. I must have you worried, Ravenel." The elder Ellis turned toward his son. "Let's go, before any of his friends show up."

"Right." Miles looked down at her with real concern. "Can you walk, Angel? Or do you need me to carry you?"

McKenzie wiped the tears from her face. "I—I can walk." After scooting to the edge of the bed, she pushed shakily to her bare feet, refusing Miles's help.

His encouraging smile faded as he caught sight of the swelling on her forehead. "That's quite a goose egg. You sure you're okay?"

"I'm fine. Could you carry my bag?" She pointed toward her meager possessions, stashed in the corner of the room.

With Miles's steadying hand under her elbow, McKenzie made her way through the maze of sleeping quarters, up a set of stairs, and through a plush galley, none of which she remembered seeing before. Shock caught up to her suddenly, sapping the strength from her legs. As she sank onto the nearest sofa, Miles looked back at his father, who was wrestling Ashton along behind them.

"What's the plan?"

His father shoved Ashton onto the opposite sofa before pointing his gun at his chest. "I thought you were the man with the plan."

"Well, my plan is to take McKenzie and disappear."

Miles and his father stared hard at each other. Only then did McKenzie pick up on the tension between them.

"I hear you, but I'll need McKenzie's testimony so you can't leave the country yet. When it's time for that, I'll help."

Miles frowned as if finding his father's words difficult to believe. "Thanks." The words sounded like they had been dragged out of him.

"Okay then. You drop me and Ravenel off at the nearest police station. Find a quiet hotel and stay put until I reach out to you."

Being stuck with Ashton in a car did not appeal to McKenzie any more than knowing she would have to testify against him.

Miles did not look happy, either. "And then what? I'm not giving her back to WITSEC."

"We'll talk about that later." His father's reply was terse, unquestionable.

Miles's shoulders rose and fell as he processed what his father was telling him. She'd seen that torn look on his face before, back when he pretended to be someone he wasn't.

Without another word, he turned back to McKenzie and helped her to her feet. His father hauled a resisting and sullen Ashton from the couch, and they left the galley to cross a sleek deck toward the pier. Two youths stood on deck watching them with their mouths open.

On their way past the youths, Miles's father dropped a small set of keys into their hands, instructing them to find their skipper. What was that about?

As the decking gave way to gravel, Miles scooped McKenzie into his arms, carrying her past a marina store and restaurant, both closed, past a handful of boats pulled out of the water and sitting on racks, to a blue Ford Taurus. Without releasing her, he managed to unlock the front passenger door, lowered her gently onto the seat, then dropped her bag onto her lap.

His father pushed Ashton into the back and slid in beside him. As she glanced back at the pair, the elder Ellis caught her eyes. "I'm Drake." He stuck out a large hand for McKenzie to shake. "Now that we've met, I can see why my son would risk his career for you."

She turned a questioning gaze on Miles as he slipped behind the steering wheel. "Dad. Keep your comments to yourself, please."

To McKenzie's amusement, his father sat back, unintimidated. With her heart still beating fast, McKenzie donned her seat belt, trying to make sense of where she stood. Was she headed back to WITSEC? Or would Miles risk his career to keep her from going back?

He cranked the engine, reversed onto the road, then pulled them swiftly away from the marina.

A weight sat on McKenzie's chest, stealing her happiness. *I don't want Miles to risk his career for me.* That would condemn him to the same fate as her own, running from Centurion retaliation. Where could they go that neither the U.S. Marshals nor the Cohort could find them?

CHAPTER 5

"We're not going to be here long," Miles informed McKenzie as they stepped into their room at a hotel just blocks from the police station. "Only long enough for you to freshen up and feel better. Then we need to leave." After dropping their bags, he turned to catch her by the shoulders. "I'm going to take you far away from here—so far no Centurion or WITSEC agent will ever find you again."

"Miles." Her auburn head gave a slight shake. "I can't ask you to do that for me."

"You don't have to ask. I'm not letting you go again." His chest hurt as he took in every sweet line of her face. "Do you have any idea how much I've missed you?"

Her moist eyes turned a luminous jade hue. "I do, actually."

"Now that I have you with me, there's no way I can let you go again."

"But your job, Miles."

"My job doesn't bring me joy. You bring me joy." His throat closed suddenly, preventing him from explaining his plans to her.

She looked so battered standing before him with a lump on her forehead, her eyelids weighted. "Are you sure you're okay? Maybe we should get you to a hospital."

"I'm fine. I just…"

"What, Angel? Tell me, what do you need? I'll get it for you."

"I need to shower."

"Of course." He nearly added, "But hurry." They didn't have much time if they were going to stay ahead of his father. While she washed away the memories of her abduction, he would devise a plan for their disappearance.

McKenzie picked up her pack, headed into the bathroom, and quietly shut the door.

Miles turned toward his duffel bag to pull out a worn little book he carried in it. Normally, he accessed his contacts using his cell phone, but on their way to this hotel, he'd lobbed the latter into the truck bed of an out-of-state pickup headed to who-knew-where.

Obviously, the fastest way for anyone to track McKenzie and him was by his cell phone. This little book, on the other hand, couldn't betray them. It listed the private numbers of important contacts at the Bureau. He riffled through the pages. Who in Support could get him a passport for McKenzie on the sly and lightning fast?

Not that guy.

Not him, either.

Nope, not her.

The staff were all straight-laced, by-the-book types. With a hopeless sigh, Miles tossed the little book back into his bag.

Okay, so leaving the country by air probably wasn't going to happen. *Oh, of course.* He nearly slapped himself on the forehead. He would take her out by boat, since his alias as a yacht salesman opened all kinds of doors for them. First he'd switch the plates out on his rental and then drive them down to Florida. From there, they'd hop on a yacht to the Bahamas and then board a freighter bound for Morocco. Boy, would his sister, Maggie, be surprised when he showed up at her place with McKenzie on his arm!

He paced to the window and searched the parking area for any sign of suspicious activity. Several businesspeople were leaving the motel, but otherwise, the parking lot stood quiet.

He heard the shower run. And run. Would it be fair to McKenzie to ask her to hurry?

At long last, the water stopped running. He waited some more and heard her brushing her teeth. *Come on, Angel.*

The bathroom door finally yawned open. McKenzie came out wearing a pair of jeans and a rumpled blouse that matched her light-green eyes. Regarding her bare feet, he realized they would have to stop somewhere to get her shoes.

Before he could collect her bag and escort her to the door, she sat on the nearest bed, then keeled over into a prone position, too tired to even sit.

With his heart in his throat, Miles reconsidered his timeline. His angel clearly needed to sleep before he took her anywhere. As he consulted his watch, a huge yawn overtook him, nearly unhinging his jaw and causing his eyes to water. He'd be a lot sharper himself after a power nap.

"Okay, we'll rest first. And then we'll leave."

Rounding McKenzie's bed to gauge her response, he found her fast asleep. His heart clutched with emotion as he gazed down at her. She'd be a lot more comfortable under the covers, but he didn't want to wake her, either. He contented himself with lifting her dainty feet onto the mattress and sliding a pillow under her head.

Possessive feelings stormed him as he fetched a blanket from the closet and shook it over her. From this day forward, he would stay with her, protect her with his life if he had to. Who cared about what happened with his career? But what about his mother?

Guilt needled him as he pictured his sweet mother living all alone. Then again, that was Dad's fault, not his. And it wasn't like

Miles had a choice. McKenzie needed him even more than his mother did.

A frightening dream jerked McKenzie awake. For an awful second, she thought she was still on Ashton's yacht, trapped in his smothering grip and threatened with being cut into little pieces. But it was Miles's sleeping visage that greeted her as she rolled over and found him sprawled atop the second bed fully dressed, while a midday sun beamed through the window beyond him.

His soft snore muted the swift beat of her heart as she memorized every angle of his face, the way his dark lashes fanned his cheekbones.

It hurt to love him so much. But it would hurt even more to watch him give up everything for her sake. She had to take responsibility for her own actions, not put Miles in a position that forced him to break ties with the FBI, to lose his job. Why should both of their lives be ruined?

Slipping quietly off the bed so as not to wake him, she went to collect her things. With stealth she had learned as a child to avoid her father's notice, she let herself out of the hotel room and closed the heavy door soundlessly behind her. As she coursed the corridor in her bare feet, she passed a housekeeping cart. How was it possible that just yesterday she'd been cleaning rooms for a living? It felt like days had passed.

Down two flights of stairs she hurried, before she emerged into bright sunshine at one end of the hotel. Vulnerability assailed her. *What do I do now?*

Exactly what she ought to have done last night—head straight for the bus station and leave town.

On North King Street, midday traffic whizzed past her. McKenzie sought to orient herself. Where was the Sea Dip in relation to this hotel? All the restaurants, all the souvenir shops along this four-lane road looked the same. But the bus had to stop around here somewhere, so she started up the sidewalk, bare-footed, careful not to step on glass. Did she dare spend the scant money she'd counted in the bathroom to buy herself some sandals?

The sight of a police cruiser halfway up the block broke her stride. A deputy popped out of it, intent on leaving a parking ticket on a car parked near a fire hydrant. As he tucked it underneath the violator's windshield wiper, he caught sight of McKenzie and stared. In Savannah, many young policemen had joined the Cohort. Surely, that wasn't the case here.

All the same, McKenzie backtracked to the crosswalk to avoid walking past the deputy. She had nearly made it to the other side when an approaching car, rather than stop for her, sped up and cut her off.

She checked her indignant outburst as the driver's window came down, revealing a tight-lipped man in a dark suit and sunglasses.

"Where do you think you're going?"

Special Agent Higgins! Dismay froze her in her tracks. How had he found her so quickly?

"Get in the car." He jerked his head toward the door behind him.

A car horn blared in her ear, urging her to do just that. Instead, she darted around the back of Higgins's car and hurried to the curb. *I can't go back to WITSEC. I can't!*

A frightened glance back showed Higgins's passenger door opening. Out climbed Drake Ellis. *Him, too?*

Oh, help. They were going to put her right back into the program, and this nightmare would continue until some Centurion caught up to her and killed her.

Running was stupid, especially in bare feet. But the instinct to flee overpowered McKenzie's reason. She hadn't run half a block before Miles's father caught up to her, hooked her from behind with his powerful arms, carried her kicking and squirming back to

Higgins's car. Passersby gawked at them, clearly uncertain what was going on.

The words Mr. Ellis spoke into her ear finally penetrated, causing McKenzie to cease her struggles.

"Calm down, McKenzie. It's okay, I swear. We're on your side. None of this was supposed to happen. You'll be safe now."

CHAPTER 6

a brisk knock at the door startled Miles awake.

He sat straight up. Seeing an empty room, his skin flashed cold.

"Angel?" He leapt out of bed and peered into the dark bathroom on his way to the door, his panic blooming. This had to be her at the door. In case it wasn't, he withdrew his Glock from under his pant leg, even as he peered through the peephole.

A vision of his father's frowning face made Miles blink. Impossible. How had his father found him here when Miles had no cell phone that could be traced? Unless…He hauled the door open and saw his guess was right. McKenzie stood in the grip of a square-jawed man whose attire screamed U.S. Marshal—black suit, white shirt, black sunglasses.

"What's going on?" The question was for McKenzie.

"I'm so sorry." She spoke with breathless apology.

Miles looked back at the man in the suit. "Let me guess. You're McKenzie's case handler."

His father answered. "Miles, put the gun away and let us in."

His hopes blown away, Miles met McKenzie's pleading gaze. It persuaded him to put his Glock away and admit the trio before shutting the door firmly. Did his father not realize that Higgins's negligence had gotten McKenzie abducted in the first place? Planting himself in the middle of the room, Miles folded his arms across his chest and glared at his father. "Start explaining."

"Let's all take a seat," Higgins suggested.

Really? He needed to be sitting for this? With a sigh of frustration, Miles approached McKenzie, who searched his face with remorse. Taking her hand gently, he let her know none of this was her fault before drawing her down beside him on the end of the nearest bed.

His father occupied the armchair by the window, and Higgins had straddled the desk chair, sitting on it backward, in lieu of turning it around. "Well?" Miles prompted.

His father met his impatient glare and grimaced. "The first thing you should know, Miles, is that Higgins didn't intentionally hang McKenzie out to dry. What happened last night was a sting operation gone bad. We've been setting a trap."

Miles divided an incredulous gaze between them. "You're working together? Trapping who?"

His father pitched his voice lower. "The Architect."

The name sharpened Miles's attention. "Oh. I knew he had something to do with this." More than one broken Centurion had dropped The Architect's name during interrogation, imbuing him with godlike powers to protect the Cohort. "Let me guess. He's infiltrated the U.S. Marshal's Service."

"Worse than that." Dad's tone was grim. "But we know who he is now."

Miles blinked in confusion. "What could be worse, and why didn't you tell me this earlier?"

"Because The Architect's been watching you."

A shiver ran through Miles. "Who is he? And how?"

Dad glanced at Higgins, who gestured for him to go ahead and tell.

"He's the executive assistant director of the Criminal, Cyber, Response and Services Branch. As such, he has oversight of the CID. I'm sure you've heard of Steven Sauers."

Goose bumps ridged Miles's forearms as he pictured a benign-looking, ginger-haired man with spectacles. "Him?"

His father nodded. "Sauers spent three years in Savannah in the late seventies. Learning that was my first break in the case. He joined the Centurion Cohort when Jared Jones's father was its leader. The membership rosters weren't kept on computers back then, and the physical ledger with Sauer's name in it went missing decades ago."

"How do you know he was actually a member, then?"

His father smiled rather smugly. "A diligent bookkeeper backed up all the records onto microfiche."

"You've got to be kidding me." Miles thought for a minute. "If he's been protecting Centurions, how come so many are going to jail?"

"Well, it's not a question of loyalty." Drake shrugged. "It's a question of extortion. For those who could pay—Ashton Ravenel, for instance—Sauers offered his protection and made the evidence vanish on our end. He let the Centurions who couldn't pay burn, safe in the knowledge that they couldn't finger him, as he's hidden his identity for decades."

Miles ran a hand through his hair. "Wow. But there still had to be a leak in WITSEC for him to find McKenzie."

"There was no leak." Higgins smiled apologetically. "McKenzie admitted to us she'd called you twice, once from Omaha and another time from Portland. Both times, Centurions showed up a short time later searching for her. Her calls to *you* were what gave her away."

Miles glanced at McKenzie. "But I use a secure phone. How's that possible?"

"I had the same question," Higgins admitted. "So, I went to your father with my suspicions, and he confirmed the only way to monitor your phone was from inside the Bureau."

His father gestured. "Remember that mandatory software upgrade on your phone a few years back? Every field agent in the Bureau had to have it, allegedly for security purposes. That was Sauers's doing. We think he uploaded software onto your phone that allowed him to bug your calls—in fact, any conversation you have within *range* of your phone, whether it's turned on or not, was probably being monitored."

Those words answered a question that had hitherto puzzled Miles. "That's why you said on the plane that you knew what was going on, and I didn't have to explain it."

"Well, I also knew because Higgins and I set it up." Drake had the grace to look chagrined. "I know you don't trust WITSEC to protect McKenzie, but what happened to her was our doing."

Miles divided a frown between the two men. "Explain."

Higgins answered first. "Over the past month, we called you a couple of times from Myrtle Beach, using McKenzie's number and then hanging up."

And here Miles had thought it was her calling him.

"At the same time, we kept a close eye on her, figuring Centurions might show up looking for her. And sure enough, they did."

Indignant, Miles turned toward his father. "You knew all this when I called you for help last night. That's why you flew me down here. Why didn't you just tell me?"

"Because you had your phone on you the entire time. I didn't want Sauers overhearing that I was on to him."

Good point. Miles closed his mouth.

"Don't blame your father." Higgins took off his sunglasses, revealing bright-blue eyes. "It's my fault our plan took a wrong turn." He nodded at McKenzie. "I should've explained to you what we were up to. That way you would have stayed put in the safe room."

McKenzie curled her small hands into fists. "Why didn't you?"

Miles covered her hands with one of his and squeezed them, resentful that they'd both been played. "Because they used you as bait, McKenzie."

Higgins briefly closed his eyes. "Okay. That's true in a way, but if you'd stayed in your safe room like I told you to, you'd have been fine. I would have explained everything when I came to collect you. My men and I were right outside, putting a tracker on their van." His blue eyes swiveled toward Miles. "The minute the intruders left, we went inside to free McKenzie from the safe room, only she'd somehow slipped right past us."

Miles couldn't believe they'd be so careless. "What if Centurions had grabbed her before she went into the closet? What if they'd shot and killed her on sight?"

Higgins rolled his eyes. "That's what the alarm was for. She had plenty of warning."

With much to think about, Miles rubbed his forehead while stroking McKenzie's knuckles. At least the so-called leak in WITSEC wasn't a real concern. It was his cell phone that had been compromised, betraying McKenzie's location. Now that his phone was gone, she would be safe again.

With a soft whimper, she dropped her head onto Miles's shoulder. "I don't want to go back into protection."

"It won't be for long, McKenzie." Drake's tone softened as he reassured her. "We're this close to nailing Sauers."

Miles searched his father's confident expression. "You sure you have enough evidence to convict him?"

"Probably."

Miles felt his agitation rising. "How do we know Sauers isn't slipping out of the country as we speak? He knows you flew me down here. He's got to be worried at this juncture."

Dad patted his cell phone. "Because his wife hasn't called me yet."

Miles's eyebrows shot up. "His wife is in on this?"

"She's our lead witness." His father's confident smile faded. "But you make a valid point. He's bound to be antsy, so I need to get back. Let's head to the airfield."

In other words, it was time to relinquish McKenzie to the U.S. Marshal. Miles tightened his hold on her, every cell in his body protesting.

Higgins started to stand. "She'll be safe."

Miles sent him a hard stare. "You'll answer to me if anything happens to her."

Higgins inclined his head in acknowledgment.

Dad also pushed to his feet. "Let's give them a minute." He ushered Higgins out of the room ahead of him, leaving the door cracked.

With his heart in a vise, Miles stood, pulling McKenzie up next to him so he could gaze into her eyes one last time. "This isn't what I wanted, Angel." He could barely speak through his constricted throat.

"I know." She raised both hands to frame his face. "And it's better for you this way."

It was hard to convince himself of that. His vision blurred.

She sent him an encouraging smile. "Seeing you has given me the strength to wait until Sauers is arrested. We can do this, Miles."

He sure hoped so. "Whatever happens, I'll wait for you. As long as it takes, I'll wait."

She threw her arms around him. "I love you."

His heart seemed to fold over on itself. Crushing her to him, he savored the way it felt to hold her. "I love you more, McKenzie."

Drake leaned into the door. "Son, it's time."

As McKenzie pulled back, Miles pressed a final, heartfelt kiss to her lips. "See you soon."

Releasing her regretfully, he grabbed up his duffel bag and headed for the door to fly back to northern Virginia with his father. A final glance back showed McKenzie looking sad but not utterly bereft.

Surely once The Architect was apprehended, she would be free to live her life with him. Miles didn't want to guess how long that would take.

CHAPTER 7

*S*teven Sauers snatched his suitcase out of the taxi driver's hand, waved off the porter heading toward him, and stalked into Ronald Reagan Washington National Airport. Both the idiocy of those he protected and the savvy of those he supervised had jeopardized his footing.

Even with a pacemaker, or perhaps because of it, his heart pounded unnaturally fast as he rolled his carry-on straight toward the international travel wing. On this Wednesday morning, the airport was crammed with holiday travelers. *How I detest public transportation.*

Owning his own jet, Steven normally avoided milling with ordinary people. But flying out of the country on his private jet was what Drake Ellis expected him to do, so here he was.

Oh yes, with a little probing, Steven had discovered that a mere public corruptions section chief in CID was on a mission to expose the Centurion mole. Ellis's involvement with the McKenzie Jones fiasco down in Myrtle Beach last month had told Steven who his nemesis was. He might have just killed off the man, but who else knew what Ellis knew?

He'd told his wife he was leaving on a business trip. Armed with a passport identifying him as a German American and wearing a convincing disguise, which he had donned in the bathroom of the cinema near his home, Steven was confident he could escape to Iceland. He hadn't become executive assistant director of the CCRSB by being stupid.

Arriving at the queue for international travel, Steven double-checked his false mustache. He had left his cell phone behind so no one could have followed him here. He was nearly in the clear.

The line kept him shuffling continuously closer to baggage check. Soon it was time to unlace his shoes. As he did so, Steven spared a thought for the life he was leaving behind. One thing was certain: He wouldn't miss his frigid wife. His dog, his fishing boat, and the power he'd enjoyed as The Architect—those he was loath to leave behind. Not to worry. He had enough money in his Swiss bank account to buy himself a pack of dogs and a fleet of boats, so why waste time being sentimental?

At last, it was his turn. Just one more hurdle and then he'd be home free. Iceland offered asylum to just about anyone willing to pay for it. Steven laid his carry-on atop the conveyor belt, slipped off his shoes, hauled off his belt, and laid the latter next to his suitcase. His favorite watch went inside a plastic bowl.

Following the plump woman in front of him, he shuffled forward toward the metal detector in his socks.

Perhaps he was leaving the country prematurely. None of the Centurion elite could name him, after all, not even Ashton Ravenel, who'd sent him a ridiculous sum via the dark web to avoid going down the drain with Jones. What an idiot that man was thinking The Architect would protect him indefinitely. In fact, Steven had used Ravenel to discover who in CID suspected him. How much could Drake Ellis really have by way of evidence against him?

Even so, it was best to vanish while he could.

Nudging the woman in front of him, Steven impelled her

toward the metal detector before the TSA agent even waved her over.

Then he'd be next. In just seconds, he'd be on his way to Reykjavík.

A whispered conversation between the TSA agents ahead of him kept his pulse erratic. The larger of the two men studied the line of passengers while consulting a printout in his hand. Steven's skin tightened. *They won't recognize me.*

Sensing a commotion behind him, he looked back and gasped. It couldn't be!

But it was. Drake Ellis, in the company of five FBI agents, all in their signature blue windbreakers with the gold lettering were casing the line of passengers, moving ever nearer. Impossible! How could anyone have known he was leaving town? His wife was the only one he'd told.

Oh, that witch!

Averting his gaze, he assumed a placid expression while counting on his disguise to avoid detection.

"Next."

Steven stepped eagerly toward the metal detector. With a cold sweat beading his brow, he ducked through it. As the machine beeped, the large, dark-skinned TSA agent barred his escape. "Sir, do you have metal in your body?"

Steven cursed him silently. "Pacemaker." *Just hurry. Let me out of here.*

Ellis whipped his head toward the sound of Steven's voice. He gulped. *Oh, no.*

The TSA agent was pulling him aside. "I'll have to pat you down."

Ellis barked across the scant distance between them. "FBI. Seize that man!"

A meaty hand closed around Steven's elbow.

People screamed and ducked as the blue jackets elbowed their way through the crowd toward him.

Ellis was the first to confront him, his green eyes mocking. "Steven Sauers, you're under arrest for the deliberate concealment of evidence pertaining to the crimes of the Centurion Cohort, for conspiracy to commit murder, and for extortion."

Steven feigned bafflement along with a German accent. "You have me confused with someone else." He caught the eye of the TSA agent. "My name is Hans Steuben. May I take out my passport now?"

The TSA agent shrugged. "Go ahead."

Before he could reach for his passport, Ellis seized the corner of Steven's fake moustache and yanked. It came off, along with a patch of artificial skin. Witnesses gasped in one accord. Denial kept Steven numb.

"Like I said." Wresting him from the TSA agent, Ellis whipped him around. "You're under arrest."

Steven resisted only to find himself bent over the luggage scanner, his feet kicked apart, his arms twisted painfully behind him. His own carry-on suitcase whacked him in the back of the head before Ellis hauled him upright.

Indignation exploded in him. "I'll have you fired for this, Ellis! You'll be sleeping on the streets, living on food stamps by the time I'm done with you!"

To his chagrin, those who heard his vociferations only chuckled. He was prodded away from the crowd, surrounded by a phalanx of FBI and TSA agents.

"We'll read you your rights on the way to jail."

Meeting Ellis's confident smirk, Steven tasted dread for the first time.

Well, this might really be the end.

Miles turned into his mother's driveway after three weeks away. As he neared the garage, the beams of his Acura slid over a familiar

Volvo XC90 parked in the driveway, nearly bringing him to a halt. What was *he* doing here? Dad hadn't stepped foot in the old family home since storming out two years earlier.

Miles parked in the garage next to his mother's reliable Honda. As the large door rumbled shut behind him, he wondered if his father had picked up Maggie from the airport and brought her over. That would only make sense if his sister flew in for Thanksgiving a day early.

Maybe his father was here for *him*. Maybe he had an update on the Centurion roundup. Steven Sauers, hoping for perks at his cushy federal prison, was throwing every Centurion elite he'd ever protected under the bus. Maybe McKenzie could leave Witness Protection sooner rather than later.

Reenergized by that prospect, Miles hastened into the house with his suitcase. His assignment in Freeport was finally over, thank God. Every time he saw a yacht, he thought of McKenzie's close call with Ravenel and ached for her company.

The aroma of pecan pie wafted toward him as he emerged from the mudroom into the kitchen, coming face-to-face with his parents who stood in awkward silence.

His mother, wearing an orange apron dusted in flour, lit up to see him. Petite, with short chestnut hair and brown eyes, she looked nowhere near her fifty-four years.

"Miles, I'm so glad you're back." She approached him to kiss his cheek. "How was the trip?"

All Miles heard was the forced levity in her voice. He focused on his father. "Why are you here?"

His father blinked at the rather confrontational question, then leaned back against the counter, making himself at home. "Good to see you, too, Son. Congrats on your Freeport assignment."

"Thanks." Miles glanced at his mother to gauge whether she needed him to eject his father out of the house by force—not that he could. She looked flustered but not necessarily in need of rescue. In fact, all kinds of emotions were showing in her flushed face.

He looked back at his father. "So what's the latest with the Centurion shakedown?"

Dad sent him a satisfied smile. "I'm glad you asked. Given Sauers's testimony, we've built cases against twelve former Centurions, and we've already won six of them."

Only half? "What about Ravenel?" The last Miles had heard, McKenzie's kidnapper had never gone to trial, his charges having been dismissed by the local judge who, Dad found out later, was an old fraternity brother of Ravenel's.

"His time is coming." Dad seemed to have shaken off his disappointment. "Lucky for us, his original trial never aired. With Sauers's cooperation, we've recovered the evidence he deleted in the first place, and a new trial's set to take place just before Christmas."

That was the good news? Defeat knuckled Miles, draining his energy. Abandoning his suitcase, he dropped into a chair at the kitchen table. Maybe Ravenel would go to jail by Christmas, but what about the other six Centurion elite? How long would it take to put *them* away?

To his surprise, his father stepped up to him. "I hate to see you like this, especially around Thanksgiving." He dropped a heavy hand on his shoulder.

Miles didn't know what to say to that.

His mother made an exasperated sound. "Oh, just tell him already!"

Miles looked up. "Tell me what?" Possibilities jumped into his mind. "Is McKenzie okay? Did something happen to her?"

Dad shook his head. "No, Son." Then he raised his voice. "Karima, come on in here, dear."

Who the heck?

Furtive footfalls approached the kitchen from the living room. Miles took in the petite woman wearing a hijab over her black hair and holding a measuring tape. His heart skipped a beat. The outfit, the black hair, and the heavy eye makeup couldn't disguise the familiar contours of the woman's pretty face. "McKenzie!" As she grinned at him, he shot out of his chair, crossed the room in two strides, and engulfed her in a hug.

"Miles." She buried her face against his neck, unable to say more.

Glancing back at his father, Miles was surprised to see a sentimental smile on his face.

"It's Thanksgiving tomorrow." Dad shrugged. "I wanted to give you something to be thankful for."

"Oh, so…" The hope that McKenzie had left WITSEC for good shriveled and died. "This is temporary."

"That depends."

"On what?"

As his hope winged upward, McKenzie released him to wipe the tears from her face. "Just listen, Miles."

"Listen to what?" He eyed his father in earnest.

"A case crossed my desk a week ago that didn't exactly fit our criteria for investigation. An American national is smuggling exotic pets out of Africa, using a port in Morocco and his own boats."

"Morocco?" That was where Maggie worked.

"I decided CID would take the case, and I talked Higgins into going with my plan."

Miles held his breath. "And your plan is?"

"You're going to Morocco to investigate this smuggler, and McKenzie's going with you. That way you can be together while we tie up loose ends. What do you think?"

"Hah!" With an incredulous laugh, Miles met McKenzie's shining eyes before sweeping her off her feet and turning full circle with her. How ironic that he'd considered hiding with her in Morocco in the first place. And building a case against some scumbag trafficking in exotic pets was right up his alley, but…He stopped and met his mother's damp gaze. "But I'd have to leave Mom all alone here."

"Pfft." Karen Ellis gestured grandly. "Are you kidding? I'll be just fine. I couldn't be happier for you both."

Her overly bright response didn't fool him. She would be lost without him.

His father spoke up. "I'll look in on your mother, Son. You don't need to worry about her."

As Mom shot Dad a startled look, Miles scoffed at the offer. "Um...you've ignored her for two years."

His mother turned a warning glance in his direction. "Don't go there, Miles. I do *not* need looking after by either of you. But there is something you should do before taking off to Morocco, honey." She eyed McKenzie fondly. "You should marry McKenzie first, this weekend while Maggie's here."

Miles's head spun. Marry? This weekend?

Noting McKenzie's tentative smile, this plan had been suggested to her already. Miles's incredulity gave way to excitement. Well, why not? He'd wanted to marry her since first laying eyes on her.

But he wasn't about to let his parents deprive him of a proper proposal. Dropping to one knee, he gazed up at McKenzie's expectant expression. "What do you think, Angel? Will you marry me and not just because you want to escape to Morocco?"

Tears of joy sparkled in her light-green eyes. "Yes, Miles. I would go to Antarctica if it meant staying with you."

He grinned. "Then we'll do it."

A stifled sound wrested his attention to his mother, who'd covered her lips with her fingertips. "Sorry. I'm just overjoyed," she smiled through her tears, "and a little overwhelmed. I'd better call Reverend Miller to see if he's available this weekend. Now, where'd I put my phone?" She whirled away in search of it.

Miles pushed to his feet. "Sorry I don't have a ring for you."

Holding up her hand, he noted the tape measure she still clutched. "What's that for?"

"Oh." She laughed at herself. "I'm going to paint a mural in the living room for your mother before we take off."

"You paint murals?" Gosh, there was so much about her he had yet to learn.

"I do. I studied visual arts in college."

"Well, that part I know."

"And I hope to paint murals for a living."

The determined lift of her chin made him love her even more. "You can do anything you want to, McKenzie. The world is your oyster."

"Especially after Ravenel goes to jail."

Miles frowned at his father for reminding them. But then he realized McKenzie wouldn't be here at this moment if it weren't for his section chief. Nor would Miles be marrying her and spending the next few months in Morocco with her. He would have been alone and miserable. So…

Releasing McKenzie for the moment, he stepped toward his father and offered his hand. "Thanks, Dad. Really." *You're not the heartless jerk I thought you were.*

Given the wry twist of his father's lips, Dad could tell what Miles was thinking. He shook his hand firmly. "Just do me a favor, Son."

"Okay." Miles braced himself.

"Don't let your work ruin your marriage. Your wife comes first. Remember that."

Out of the corner of his eye, Miles saw his mother appear at the door holding her cell phone. Her wide brown eyes were fastened on Dad. "Um, Reverend Miller says he can marry you two on Saturday evening. Does that sound good? Maggie will still be here, which is perfect. Can we invite anyone else, Drake? Close friends? Neighbors?"

"Mmm." Dad didn't seem too keen on the idea. "Let's limit it to ten people we trust implicitly."

Karen nodded. "Okay. And you'll be there, too, right?"

"Of course." He seemed offended she would even ask.

Stunned by his changing circumstances, Miles met McKenzie's expectant gaze. "You sure you want to marry me in three days? That doesn't feel rushed?"

The dimples in her cheeks flashed. "I've wanted to marry you for the past three *years*, Miles."

"Well, when you put it that way, it doesn't seem so spontaneous." A thought occurred to him. "Wait, do you even have a current passport?"

She flicked a glance at his father. "Yes, under my alias, Karima Anderson. Supposedly, my mother was Moroccan."

Huh. Miles glanced back at his father. He had obviously planned their exodus a while ago. "So...am I marrying Karima or McKenzie?"

"McKenzie, of course. The passport is just a safety measure. Once you're in Morocco, you can call her by her real name." Dad's gaze rested warmly on the pair of them. "Well," he seemed to recollect himself, "I'd better get going. You're safe with Miles, McKenzie."

She abandoned Miles to intercept Drake's path. "Thank you so much for everything, Mr. Ellis."

"Drake, please. Or even, Dad." He hugged her like he meant it.

Miles thought for a second McKenzie might cry. As she fought for composure, he viewed his father through her eyes. Compared to Jared Jones, Drake Ellis was a superhero. Maybe Miles had misjudged him.

"Hey, uh, Dad," he heard himself offer, "why don't you join us all for Thanksgiving tomorrow?"

In his peripheral vision, he saw his mother swing around with the phone to her ear. Her gaze locked with his, and Miles could tell his offer had freaked her out, but he wasn't about to recall it.

His father shrugged. "Sure. What time?"

"Well, I'm picking up Maggie at the airport at eleven, so let's say one o'clock? Maggie will be glad to see you." His mother had turned away to talk on her cell phone.

Dad glanced her way. "All right. If you're sure I'm not imposing."

"No, no. It's the least we can do, after all you've done for McKenzie and me. Thank you."

McKenzie echoed his words. "Yes, thank you, Dad."

His father's visage softened at the appellation. "Well. See you tomorrow, then. I'll bring a centerpiece." As he stepped out of the home's front door, Dad sent one more glance at his estranged wife before closing the door behind him.

Was that yearning in his father's eyes? Miles turned thoughtfully toward McKenzie. By the grace of God, they were finally together and would stay that way. If God could do that for them, perhaps He could heal the rift between Miles's parents.

EPILOGUE

Am I dreaming?

McKenzie tried to wrap her head around it. Here she was her wedding reception, dancing with Miles for the first time ever, not the least bit surprised to find that he danced as skillfully as he did everything else. A dozen people, including Miles's family members, looked on with indulgent expressions as the couple completed their obligatory dance together, weaving through the patches of sunlight that shone through the tall windows of his church's reception hall.

The wedding itself—hastily planned and modestly attended—had been perfect. With only three days' notice, Karen had pulled together flower bouquets, a wedding soundtrack, a gorgeous three-tier cake, and even a beautiful white dress for McKenzie to wear.

During the ceremony Miles gave her a ring once belonging to his maternal grandmother; she'd loved it on sight, just as she was loving this intimate reception taking place a mere twenty steps from the sanctuary where they'd pledged to have and to hold each other, until death parted them.

Speaking of death, Mr. Ellis—Dad—had assured McKenzie that in the extreme unlikelihood some vengeful Centurion caught wind of her wedding, the entire church was surrounded by people who worked for him. She caught Drake's eye as he stood at the edge of the parquet floor, watching them dance. He sent her a crooked smile. What a blessing to have a father she could respect!

As his gaze wandered toward Miles's mother, McKenzie knew beyond a shadow of a doubt that he longed to reconnect with Karen.

Sudden movement wrested her attention from Dad back to Miles, who dipped her without warning. She swallowed a gasp and clung to him, delighted when he planted a stirring kiss on her lips. Everyone watching them cheered.

When he pulled her upright again, she tottered, both hot in the face and light-headed. *Oh, my.*

In her peripheral vision, she saw Maggie, Miles's tall, raven-haired half-sister conversing with her father. One look at Maggie, and McKenzie had realized Karen wasn't her biological mother, a circumstance that puzzled her as they behaved just as mother and daughter would.

And now Maggie was crossing the room toward Karen. Her purposeful expression told McKenzie she had an agenda.

"Hello, I'm right here."

Miles's words snatched McKenzie's attention back to him. "Sorry, but I think your dad sent Maggie to ask your mom to dance."

Her words startled Miles into glancing toward his mother. Sure enough, her wide eyes went from Maggie to Drake as she took in what Maggie had to say. With the firming of her lips, Mom shook her head and turned pointedly away to look at Miles and McKenzie.

Miles sighed. "Pretty sure that's a no."

"But he's so lonely, Miles. Why won't she give him a chance?"

"She gave him twenty-seven years, Angel. He was off working that whole time."

Hearing resentment in his voice, McKenzie finally gleaned the reason for the tension between father and son. She glanced briefly at the elder Ellis. "Maybe he wants to make up for that."

"Well, I think it's too late for Mom. She's moved on, if you know what I mean."

"She's seeing someone?"

Miles's shoulders rose and fell. "I don't know. Some guy from work, I think."

"Well, what about you, Miles? Will you give him a second chance?"

"Me?" He met her earnest gaze, clearly startled. "You know, you're not just beautiful, you're insightful also."

"Well," she grimaced, "I had to learn to read my father from a young age."

"I get that." He glanced toward his father, caught his eye, and sent him a nod of acknowledgment. "Yeah, I'm open to starting over."

His words warmed her heart. Lifting a hand from his shoulder, McKenzie stroked her new husband's face, marveling that she'd ever believed he was just eighteen, amazed they were married now. "You're a good man, Miles. Believe me, there were times I thought God had forgotten me, and I would be isolated and in WITSEC for the rest of my life. But I kept praying that He'd give me hope and a future, like He promised in Scripture."

Miles grinned rather smugly. "So, I'm your future now. I like the sound of that."

"You're my present, my past, *and* my future."

Her words made him swallow. "I love you so much."

Wrapping both arms around his neck, she kissed him as boldly as he'd kissed her earlier. "Same," she murmured against his lips while friends and family cheered them on.

FEAR NO EVIL

THE LOST ARE FOUND, BOOK ONE

Am I dead? Pain seared Maggie's side as she tried to draw a breath. Lying flat on her back in a narrow, bricked alley just a few steps from her apartment in Casablanca, she assessed her injuries, took stock of her situation, and groaned.

The bit of violet sky visible between the overhanging roofs informed her it was nightfall. Raising her arm to check the time, Maggie launched a cloud of flies that had been crawling on her. According to her watch which glowed 8:37 P.M., she'd been lying here for at least an hour. Summer was peak tourist season in Casablanca. People must have skirted the comatose and bleeding woman, ignoring her plight. Even now, she could hear somebody edging around her—a woman with a baby. Maggie murmured reassurances and the young mother hurried past.

The jig was up. Her cover was blown. As Jake would have said in the Irish Gaelic of his paternal grandfather, *"Nách mór an diabhal thú,"* which loosely translated meant, *Well, aren't you the devil?*

The gut-lurching realization that her identity had been discovered had hit her on her walk home from work when Kamal's bodyguard materialized in front of her—no sign of Kamal anywhere. One look at the dark intent in Farid's dark eyes and she'd realized both he and Kamal knew exactly who she was. She'd been handily played, all the while thinking herself in control of the game.

But that was hours ago.

By some incredible stroke of luck, she still wore her watch, not yet stolen by one of Casablanca's many thieves and pickpockets. The watch contained a GPS chip, broadcasting her location. So long as she could get to her apartment to place the necessary call, an extraction team would be deployed to recover her. But what if Kamal and his bodyguard suspected as much and followed her? The whole extraction team could be targeted.

She held her breath and listened. Her neighbor's dog wasn't barking, which it always did when strangers were in the building. So maybe the path was clear.

Summoning her strength, Maggie rolled from her back to her front. A moan escaped her clenched teeth. Oh, man. Kemal's bodyguard had broken at least one of her ribs. Pushing to her hands and knees, she waited for the tsunami of agony to subside.

The CIA had assigned her here just fifteen months ago. Her objective was simple: verify the rumors that the weapons arriving in a warehouse on the waterfront were earmarked for the Russian Wagner Group, a circumstance with frightening implications for Morocco, not to mention Europe in general.

Born in Venezuela, Magdalena Montoya Ellis had been a shoo-in for the CIA. Not only was she fluent in Spanish and French but her father was a public corruption section chief for the FBI. The Ellises were patriots. She'd been assigned first to Bogotá, Colombia then to Caracas, Venezuela. Morocco was next. She pretended to be a French fashionista, selling clothing at a boutique not far from the warehouse in question. Befriending the warehouse's foreman, Kamal, had been laughably easy.

With very little coaxing on her part, Kamal had taken her out to dinner and for walks along the waterfront. To her relief, he hadn't pressured her for intimacies. In fact, he'd spilled everything there was to know about the shipments bound for Russia—their point of origin and how they would get there.

Now it was plainly apparent Kamal had been testing her. No doubt he had fed her a string of lies, and a mole in the CIA had reported them all back to him, proving Maggie was a spook, as he obviously suspected.

I'm sorry, Kamal. Despite his radical political convictions, she had genuinely liked the man, though he didn't hold a candle to Jake. And he must have liked her, too, because his bodyguard, Farid, whose fists were the size of hams, could have easily killed her. Instead, he'd roughed her up and walked away.

I have to get out of here.

With the help of the rough earthen wall next to her, she managed to get vertical. Blood slid from her split lip to her chin before dripping onto her Christian Dior blouse.

Gritting her teeth, she shuffled toward her apartment building, a two-story structure of dried clay, entirely whitewashed. Through her one good eye, she plumbed the shadows, terrified Farid would return to finish the job.

The neighbor's dog began to bark as she reached the building. She froze, looked, listened.

Was the dog just barking at her...or was Farid following her? The courtyard, with its burbling central fountain and decorative blue tiles, stood quiet. Everyone was having dinner, as evidenced by the aroma of roasting lamb and mint tea.

One step at a time, Maggie dragged herself up the stairs to her second-story flat. The fine hairs at her nape prickled as she spotted her door ajar. Someone had come this way before her—or were they still here?

She approached the door trying not to breathe, only to listen. The dog stopped barking, a circumstance that assured her whoever had been here was long gone. Thank goodness she lived alone, her brother Miles and his bride having returned to the States two months earlier.

Shards of broken porcelain crackled under her soles as she waded inside. So much for her collection of ornamental plates, torn off the wall, shattered and scattered like confetti. They were supposed to be souvenirs of her Moroccan tour.

I'll be lucky to have myself as a souvenir at this point.

In her semi-dark living room, Maggie could tell her furniture had been flipped over, cushions strewn across the Persian rug for which she had haggled at the outset of her tour. She headed for her kitchen, where every dish had been pulled from the cupboards and smashed. Glass and ceramic crunched and squealed under her soles as she limped toward the counter. God forbid they'd found her Company phone.

The spray bottle of liquid cleaner was still beneath her sink. With a groan, she retrieved it, removed the false bottom, and breathed a sigh of relief. The phone was still here.

She cast a wary glance behind her before entering the passcode, followed by the letters *E-X-I-T* on the alphanumeric keypad. That would bring an extraction team to the escape-and-evasion point within one hour. Maggie swallowed hard and ended the call.

If she could make it there in time, she'd be whisked away. Not exactly a triumphant withdrawal, as had been the case in Venezuela two years earlier, when she'd been rescued with a thumb drive full of priceless intel. Not to mention the most astonishing thing of all: Jake Carrigan, her nerdy college boyfriend, had been the SEAL in charge of the extraction team.

What an exhilarating moment that was! He had tucked her under his protective wing and delivered her to a U.S. aircraft carrier in the Gulf only to vanish on her, as suddenly as he'd vanished from Paris.

She'd made inquiries and discovered that not only was Jake Navy SEAL but he'd been trained by the CIA's Special Operations Group to protect case officers like herself. Crazy, because the time she'd checked on him before that, he'd been working for The Peace Corps. Never in a million years would she have guessed he'd become a SEAL, let alone a SOG.

As Maggie bent to stow the phone in the secret pocket by her calf, searing pain made the room turn black. She caught herself on the counter to keep from passing out.

How am I going to make it to the exfil site?

With pure Ellis determination, that was how. She slowly straightened then limped out of the kitchen. As she crossed her living room, she took one last look at the apartment she'd called home. It had never occurred to her, not once, that she would be leaving with her tail tucked between her legs.

At least I'm alive.

She stepped resolutely onto her balcony. Her Escape and Evasion plan involved going over the balcony, dropping to the flat rooftop of the building below, crossing the roof, then descending a fire-escape ladder to a different alley that zigzagged toward the coast. Easy, right?

In a nondescript mosque about a klick away, an asset would be waiting for her. Supposedly there was a tunnel under the city that led from the mosque to the ocean, where the extraction team would pick her up.

If she made it that far.

Standing on her balcony, Maggie inhaled the warm Moroccan air, forever infused with the sweet and savory scents of couscous, *ras el hanout*, and fresh-baked *khubz* bread. Her thoughts flitted to the local baker, who always knew whose son fancied whose daughter and was always glad to see her. *I'll miss this place.* Probably because the French-influenced culture here reminded her of Paris and time spent with Jake.

A glance at her watch told her she had better get a move on.

Only how was she supposed to climb when she could barely even stand?

Lifting her gaze to the stars obscured by a layer of dusty desert haze, Maggie recollected the words Jake had spoken to her more than once. *One day, Lena, you're going to figure out that you can't save the world by yourself. If you ever need help, just reach up. God's right there, waiting for you.*

His faith had always inspired her. She gripped the railing on her balcony and swayed.

"So…I think I might need help right now."

She had some gall even talking to God. Not since she was a child and used to go to mass with her Venezuelan mother had she acknowledged her Creator's existence.

With no other choice, Maggie lifted a long leg over the railing, sat a moment, then heaved her other leg over. As she lowered herself to the outer ledge, she pivoted to face the building. Remarkably, only mild discomfort accompanied her movements.

One at a time, she moved her hands from the railing to the vertical balusters. Next, she put her weight to one foot and lowered the other to the flat roof of the bakery a meter beneath her. Her ribs barely protested. *Huh.* It was like God was helping her already, which wasn't likely.

Encouraged, Maggie crossed the roof to the fire escape on the other side. The last time she'd looked at the rickety ladder, some of the bars were starting to rust.

Climbing down the ladder backwards, she waited for the crushing pain to return, but it didn't. Maybe adrenaline was finally kicking in. She dropped down into a quiet alley, then made her way toward the mosque about a klick away.

The unlit street kept her wary. She'd never ventured out at night without a *djellaba*, the hooded robe most local women wore, and for good reason.

Wait, what was that? The sound of furtive footfalls reached her ears as an old man walked up on her. He gasped in alarm at her disfigured face and gave her wide berth.

She had to look awful with one eye swollen shut, her lip oozing blood. Thank goodness the odds of Jake being the SOG to rescue her were low. She didn't want him seeing her like this.

In Venezuela, she'd been confident and still in one piece, just seven years older than the previous time she'd seen him in the hospital in Paris. His parents had come to collect him there, whisking him away before she'd gotten a chance to say good-bye. After snatching her from the Venezuelan warehouse, she'd expected to reconnect, but Jake had vanished with his team just as suddenly as he had left Paris.

Dragging her thoughts to the present, Maggie glanced at her watch. Only thirty minutes remaining, and she was just now reaching the mosque.

Arriving at a door painted gold, she knocked on it firmly. Her lower lip throbbed as she waited. At last, the door popped open, and a dark-skinned man dressed in the blinding white robes of an imam swept her inside.

"I've been expecting you." He ran a worried gaze over her, his English perfect. "Can you walk?"

She swayed on her feet, clutching her side. "Sure."

"Good. The team is nearly here. We have to move quickly."

He pulled her into the mosque's dim antechamber, through a side door, and down a hall to an alcove. A push against the wall sent it rumbling backward, revealing the hidden tunnel into which he ushered her inside, leaving it open and clicking on penlight. A curve in the tunnel beckoned them, its floor of hardpacked dirt angling downward, taking them beneath the adjacent buildings toward the pier where the team would be waiting.

They seemed to walk for forever, though Maggie knew it wasn't even one klick to the extraction point. Her pain was returning with a vengeance, shortening her steps.

"Just a little farther."

The man's encouragement was all that kept her going.

Moisture now hung in the air, dampening her cheeks. The tang of sea salt was unmistakable. When they came upon a door that marked the tunnel's end, she thought she might weep with relief. A glance at her watch showed her ten minutes late for the rendezvous. What if the team had left already? She'd be stuck here.

The door opened, and Maggie startled back, but the silhouette ducking through the opening was identical to the one that had come bursting into the office in Venezuela.

"Lena!"

When he tacked on a phrase in Gaelic, she knew she wasn't just imagining Jake. With a whimper of relief, she stumbled into him, letting him take her weight.

Just like the last time he'd appeared, she asked herself how this was possible.

"What hurts?" He held her firmly but gently.

"Everything."

She felt him turn toward a teammate. "Decker, pass me an autoinjector of morphine."

His dense chest pillowed her head. She could hear his heart thumping sure, steady strokes that proved he was really with her. She closed her one good eye. She'd made it to the exfil site. Jake could take it from here.

A click and light sting sent morphine swirling into her bloodstream. It spread sweetly through her, smoothing the razor edge of agony, turning the world fuzzy.

She was only vaguely aware of Jake scooping her off her feet to carry her across his arms.

The *rat-tat-tat-tat* of a semiautomatic weapon shattered her relief.

Jake moved so fast, she didn't know what was happening, only that someone had fired at them from farther up the tunnel. *Oh no.* Had she led Farid to the extraction site?

She squirmed as the cacophony of the firefight spiked her adrenaline.

"Hold still!" Jake subdued her struggles while bounding up a run of steps. "We got this."

By the time they reached the top of the stairs, the burst of gunfire was over. Farid, or whoever had followed her, was probably dead. Jake was bearing her through an open door, out onto an unlit pier. Starlight winked through the haze overhead. The warm breeze smelled of freedom.

Jake started passing her off to someone else. "Careful. She's injured."

"No." She clung to him, protesting the handoff.

"I'm just getting us in the boat."

Sure enough, she was lowered directly down to him, into a rigid-inflatable boat that rocked against the pier. He sat with her across his lap.

The boat pitched abruptly as several more SOGs jumped in. The stealth motor thrummed to life, practically silent over the slapping water. Warm air streamed over her as they pulled away.

Up and over waves they went, kicking up sea spray that dampened every inch of her, though Jake did his best to shield her. The glow of Casablanca faded, leaving nothing but a star-studded sky above and waves below that had subsided into swells.

She was conscious of Jake asking his men to report in. One of them indicated he'd been nicked by a bullet, nothing too serious. Another stated that the target was dead.

Jake scowled down at her. "Did you know you were followed?"

She had trouble getting her tongue to cooperate. "Possibly."

"Who did this to you?"

There was no mistaking his fury. Regardless, she wasn't authorized to tell him. "My fault. I was played."

He adjusted his hold, cradling her like he never meant to let her go. The thighs she sat upon were as solid as tree trunks. The gangly young man she'd loved in Paris had morphed into someone else.

She had so many questions to put to him. Like why had he vanished on from the hospital in Paris, then again after plucking her from Venezuela? But she was too drugged to speak.

At last, their motor cut off, and a massive shape emerged from the dark, scarcely visible against the night sky. They coasted silently into an enclosure—the port of a Navy vessel, given the smell of motor oil and steel and the sound of sloshing water. With a low hum, the jaws of the port closed behind them, and the lights blinked on.

Half a dozen sailors stood around what resembled an indoor swimming pool. They helped to moor and stabilize their boat.

Jake managed to clamber off the RIB without handing her off to anyone. Maggie's head lolled on his shoulder, too heavy to lift. Her clothing was damp. The urge to fall asleep nearly over-whelmed her. *Stay awake!* But the morphine he'd given her was dosed for a man half again her size.

His boots rang along a metal corridor before he ducked into a room that smelled of antiseptic. When he laid her gently on what had to be a gurney, she clung to the sleeve of his night ops uniform.

"Stay wi' me."

The words made him hold her gaze. He didn't wear glasses anymore. She wanted to ask if he'd had laser surgery.

"You need a doctor, Lena. And I can't stay."

The terse words betrayed a certain level of frustration. Was he mad at her? Sensing him about to leave, some desperate emotion pushed tears into her eyes. "Don't go."

With a firming of his lips that was all too familiar, he tugged her left hand from his sleeve, regarded her bare fingers for a split second, then brushed his lips across her knuckles.

The sweet gesture made the pressure in her chest expand. *Oh, Jake, I miss you!*

"Be well." Releasing her, he swiveled on his boots, ducked out the door, and disappeared.

Again? Her heart unraveled like she was a spool, and he was walking off with the end of the thread. How dare he blow in and out of her life like this without any explanation? This was crazy.

Available in Paperback and eBook from Your Favorite Bookstore or Online Retailer

ABOUT THE AUTHOR

Rebecca Hartt is the nom de plume for an award-winning, best-selling author of a different name who, compelled by faith, decided to spin suspenseful military romance where God plays a vital role in character motivation and plot.

Living near the military community of Virginia Beach, Rebecca is constantly reminded of the peril and uncertainty faced by U.S. Navy SEALs, many of whom testify to a personal and profound connection with their Creator.

Their loved ones, too, rely on God for strength and comfort. These men of courage and women of faith are the subjects of Rebecca Hartt's enthusiastically received Acts of Valor romantic suspense series.

Please follow Rebecca Hartt Romance on Facebook, Instagram, and TikTok.

www.RebeccaHartt.com

Want to read Karen and Drake Ellis's story? Get *Be Strong, A Christmas Short Story,* **for FREE when you sign up for my newsletter at https://rebeccahartt.com/contact/ Or send me a short note telling me you're already a subscriber.**

f facebook.com/rebecca.hartt.102
instagram.com/rebeccaharttromance
tiktok.com/@rebecca.hartt